THE LAST SALE

Also by Raegan Teller

Murder in Madden

THE LAST SALE

Raegan Teller

Raegan Teller

Pondhawk Press LLC

Columbia, South Carolina

Pondhawk Press LLC
PO Box 290033
Columbia, SC 29229-9998
www.PondhawkPress.com

THE LAST SALE/Raegan Teller. 1st ed.
ISBN 978-0-9979205-2-9

Dedicated to my father, a man who didn't talk much
but said a lot.

Ezra Franklin Bryant
(1895-1965)

You must do the things you think you cannot do.
—Eleanor Roosevelt

CHAPTER 1

Just as he did every morning, Theo Linard arrived at the church's soup kitchen early to begin overseeing the day's preparations. The steadfast routine kept his mind focused on the tasks at hand, although inevitably his thoughts returned to his missing daughter.

As a young man, he had attended Johnson and Wales University, College of Culinary Arts, and helped pay his tuition by working as a personal chef to some of the elite faculty and administrators, stocking their kitchens with prepared meals, for which they often took credit. There was a waiting list for his fish and seafood bisques and stews. After classes, Theo would cook for his clients, deliver the meals, and then return to his room to study. It was a hard life and long hours for the young man, but he felt blessed. Later, he studied in France at the finest schools and earned recognition as a master potager chef, responsible for all the kitchen's soups.

Today, the big pot held mostly vegetables. Contributions to the soup kitchen had been low lately, so meat was scarce. The local grocery stores donated their wilted and soon-to-expire vegetables, and volunteers collected them every morning and brought them to the kitchen to be cleaned and chopped. The donated bounty was added to a stock simmered for hours under Theo's supervision. If they couldn't have prime ingredients, at least the stock would be superb. He took pleasure in seeing the homeless men and women sop up the last bit of broth in their bowls with a piece of bread or sandwich.

He was deep in thought about the one topic that consumed him when a redheaded woman walked up to introduce herself. "Hi, I'm Enid Blackwell from the *Palmetto Weekly*. I have an appointment to talk with you about the soup kitchen and the work you do here."

Theo forced himself back to the present. "Oh, yes. I'm sorry." He put out his hand. "I'm Theo." He motioned for her to sit at one of the tables in the dining area. "We can sit over here and talk."

"I hope you were expecting me."

"Yes, the church office told me you wanted to do a story on our soup ministry. We appreciate your agreeing to do this article. Hopefully, it will spur some additional donations. Things have been a little slow lately."

For the next fifteen minutes, Theo shared information about the church and its mission, the number of soup meals served, and why donations were critical to its continuation. After checking her notes, Enid said, "Is there anything else I haven't asked about that you think I should include?"

Theo paused before replying. "I think you've got what you need for the article, but if you have a minute, I'd like to talk to you about something else."

Enid set her pen down and closed the notepad. "Sure. What do you want to talk about?"

Theo opened a folder that was on the table in front of him. Inside were copies of *The State* newspaper articles Enid had written more than a year ago about the murder of Rose Marie Garrett in Madden, South Carolina.

"When the church told me you were doing an article on the soup kitchen, I did a search on you, you know, just to prepare myself. And I found these articles. That's you, isn't it?"

• • •

Theo tapped the articles with his finger. "This was good investigative work, and damn good writing. I'm not a journalist, but I know solid work when I see it."

Enid managed to smile wanly. "Thank you." How could she tell him how much she had sacrificed to write those articles? She was trying to figure out a polite way to excuse herself and leave when Theo put his hands together, as if in prayer.

"I need your help. Please." His face showed the etchings of prolonged suffering. Enid had seen that look on her mother's face as she battled cancer, on her friend's face as she grieved for her lost son, and on her own during the past year as she battled the demons of grief and guilt.

"I don't understand. What do you need from me?" Even as she asked, a sense of dread crept over her.

Theo pulled a photo from his wallet. "That's Hari, my daughter. She's missing." Theo dropped his head, as though the burden of just saying those words was too much to bear.

"I'm so sorry. What happened to her? When did she go missing?" Enid's journalistic instincts forced her to push aside her own pain momentarily.

"Hari, that's what I called her, short for Harriet. She moved here about six months ago to attend the University of South Carolina. She wanted to study visual arts and become a photographer, an artist who painted with light, she used to say. One day, after she'd been here a couple months, I got a call from Kat, her roommate. She told me Hari hadn't been in her room in two days. We both knew that just wasn't like Hari." He shook his head slowly. "She was very responsible for her age."

"Why did Kat wait so long to call you?"

"Kat is an interesting young woman. She doesn't like authority and told me she didn't want to 'rat,' that was her word, on Hari when she might just be out having fun."

"I recall seeing something about it in the newspaper. They asked for anyone with information on the missing girl to call the police. Surely, they are investigating. And what about the campus police?"

Theo nodded. "The campus police talked to some students, as I understand it, but found nothing suspicious about her not returning to classes. The Columbia Police Department is in charge of the investigation."

"What else do you know about Hari's disappearance?"

"I was living in Boston, but I called the Columbia police immediately after Kat notified me. They questioned Kat and other friends, but they didn't find anything. Hari's credit cards haven't been used and her cell phone was never found. It's almost like the earth just opened up and swallowed her."

Theo pulled out a handkerchief and wiped his eyes. "I call the detective every week. He's a good guy, but he's run out of leads. Besides, I don't think he ever thought a crime had been committed. He kept telling me about all these teenage girls that leave school without telling anyone but then show up later." Theo looked directly into Enid's eyes. "But that's not my Hari. She wouldn't do that."

"Have you hired a private investigator?"

Theo nodded. "Yes, I hired a guy, an investigator, who did little or nothing, other than to wipe out the last of my savings. I have nothing left. I quit a potager chef's position at a Michelin-rated restaurant to come here in February. I get free meals and a room from one of the church's generous parishioners."

"How did you end up here, at the soup kitchen?"

"Hari volunteered here a few times. She had a generous heart. Being here makes me feel close to her."

"They are lucky to have you here. But I can't imagine how upset you must be. The not-knowing must be agonizing. But what is it you need from me? Do you want me to do a story about her?"

Theo shook his head and made direct eye contact with Enid. "No, I want you to find her."

CHAPTER 2

Enid fought to catch her breath but struggled to keep from passing out. The overhead light in the soup kitchen was now a glowing pinprick and getting smaller. *Take deep breaths. Stay calm.* This wasn't the first time she had experienced a panic attack, but it had been almost three months and she hoped the last one was it.

At the end of the long tunnel with the tiny light, she heard Theo. "Here. Sip some water." He handed her a glass as someone put a cool, damp rag on her forehead. It smelled like dishwashing detergent.

After a few moments, the tunnel transformed back into the soup kitchen and the glaring overhead light was burning her eyes. "I'm fine."

A plump woman in an apron stood over Enid holding the wet rag. "You scared the piss out of us." Her face softened. "You alright?"

Enid pushed a strand of damp hair from her face. "It's just a panic attack. I didn't mean to scare you."

Theo took her hand. "Shall we call a doctor? You look pale."

The last time Enid had gone snooping around for information on a girl, a dear friend had been killed. The past year was filled with "what if" conversations with herself. What if she had not gone to Madden to research Rosie's death?

What if she had returned to Charlotte and resumed her life with Cade? The list went on endlessly in Enid's head. Working with her therapist, she had managed to bury much of her guilt and sadness, but the pain was always there, just beneath the surface.

The woman put her hands on her hips. "A panic attack? Do you think you're in danger here? What are you panicking about?"

Enid stood up, holding onto the edge of the table to steady herself. "No, it's nothing like that. Please, don't worry. I'm fine." She turned to Theo. "I'm sorry, I can't help you find . . ." Enid stopped as she wasn't sure what the woman knew about Theo's daughter. "I'm just a community reporter, not an investigator any longer."

"That's bullshit!" the woman blurted out. "Sorry, but I mean, Mr. Theo told me you found that girl's killer when no one else could. If that ain't investigatin' then what is it?"

Enid looked back to Theo. "I'll be in touch in a few days so we can finalize the soup kitchen article."

• • •

"Tragedy can ruin lives, and not just the immediate family's. But we can't let it overcome us." Dr. Wright smiled at Enid. "It's been almost a year since your friend was killed, but the after-effects may continue for a while. We've talked about that. Your panic attack was simply your body reacting to those memories when you saw the articles. Can you accept that by letting go of your guilt and going on with your life you're actually honoring your friend?" Without waiting for a reply, she continued, “And from what you’ve told me about Cade, he would want you to move on with your life."

Enid nodded. "I think so. I mean, yes. I'm ready to get my life back in order." She glanced at the clutter-free desk and neatly arranged bookshelves in Dr. Wright’s office, a glaring contrast to her own disorder.

"You made the decision to stop reporting on crime and to start fresh by reporting community news. We talked about the regrets you might have later. Remember that you are in control of your life. Just because this man asked you to help him doesn't mean you have to."

“I know, but I feel guilty. He has no one else to turn to.”

Dr. Wright patted Enid’s arm. “I trust that you’ll make the right decision, and you need to trust your instincts. We can argue with ourselves and the decisions we make, but in the end, we each have to take the journey before us. Only you can define what it will be.” She paused to glance at the time. "When will your divorce be final?"

"Yesterday. After we sold the house and furniture, there wasn't much left to divide.”

"How do you feel about life without Cade?" Dr. Wright smoothed her black silk slacks and waited while Enid thought about her reply.

"I had hoped we could work things out, but we had both changed a lot. It's for the better."

Dr. Wright smiled. "That's not what I asked you. Are you ready to resume your life without Cade?"

Enid looked up and met her psychologist’s gaze. "Yes, I'm ready. But we'll always be friends. At least I hope so."

The alarm on Dr. Wright's iPhone chimed softly, and she tapped the screen to silence it. "Well, then I'm here if you need me." The two women stood and embraced. "Good luck, Enid. I'm sure you'll be fine. You're a strong woman, stronger than you know."

• • •

Enid walked down Main Street to her car. The meter was red, but she didn't see a parking ticket on the windshield. Feeding the meter was illegal, but Enid glanced around and didn't see anyone, so she added enough quarters to give her another hour and a half in the parking spot. She was just a few blocks from the restaurant where she was supposed to meet her friend, and also her landlord, Madelyn. The two women had become close friends, despite Enid's once suspecting Cade of having an affair with the attractive attorney.

When Enid walked into the restaurant, Madelyn had already claimed a table and ordered two unsweetened iced teas. Although it was just March, the weather was already unseasonably warm. Madelyn hugged Enid. "Are you feeling better now? I was concerned when you texted me that you might have to cancel our lunch."

"Yes, I feel better."

Madelyn tossed her brunette mane and settled back into her seat. "Jack called again this morning. He really wants to talk to you."

Enid winced at the mention of the former newspaper reporter who had helped her find Rosie's killer. "I know I need to call him. Dr. Wright thinks it's time for me to face him."

Madelyn put her hand on Enid's. "He doesn't blame you for anything that happened, you know."

Enid pulled her hand away and studied the menu. "I'll call him, I promise."

As they were finishing lunch, Enid glanced at the time on her cell phone. "I've got to write this article on the soup kitchen." She decided not to mention Theo's missing daughter.

Madelyn shook her head slightly. "You're serious about reporting community news for the *Palmetto Weekly*? Really? I know you're in the healing process, but come on." Madelyn leaned in toward Enid and spoke softly. "You've got to get back in the game."

"It's a living, and at least I'm writing. For now, I'm content to do this column and other local stories. And if this article encourages more donations for the soup kitchen, then I've done something good. Right?"

Madelyn nodded. "Ah, yes. Atonement is a powerful driver." She placed the napkin from her lap onto the table. "Speaking of drivers, I've got to get one out of a DUI charge this afternoon-one of our state's finest legislators. Talk about under-utilizing your skills. What a waste of time."

CHAPTER 3

As Enid walked down the narrow, shrub-lined gravel path to her garage apartment behind Madelyn's house, Enid tried to forget her conversation with Theo. But since Madelyn's house was near the University of South Carolina campus, her conversation with Theo played in her head. His pain was etched in her memory. She couldn't imagine the raw anguish a parent must feel when a child just disappeared.

Enid walked into the spacious apartment, measuring almost 800 square feet on two levels. This place had become a safe haven during the past year—her sanctuary. She had learned to leave the world and its problems outside, but today it was harder than usual.

Madelyn had done a great job remodeling the space. The three-car garage portion had been converted to an open living area with a dining room and kitchen on the ground floor. A spiral stairway led to a large bedroom with a balcony overlooking a wooded area. The view reminded her of the house she and Cade had once shared in Charlotte. While sipping a cup of chamomile tea, she thought of Madelyn's admonishment about calling Jack. A few minutes later, she scrolled through the contacts on her phone until she found the familiar name: Jack Johnson.

After two rings, she was about to end the call when he answered. "Enid, is that you?"

A flood of emotion washed over Enid and her voice choked. "Hi. It's been a while."

"My, God. I can't believe you actually called. It's been ... what, a year or more? At least I knew you were okay, thanks to Madelyn's updates."

"I didn't mean to disappear. It's just that I had to work through some things."

"I know you did. That's why I haven't driven to Columbia to track you down." He sighed heavily. "So, how are you?"

"I'm okay." It was the automatic reply she gave people. "I thought I might come down and visit. That is, if it wouldn't be an inconvenience."

"An inconvenience? Are you serious? I can't wait to see you. You know my sister from Chicago is running Glitter Lake Inn now. Marriage number four ended after a couple months, and she came down to Madden to stay with me. She's always been a great hostess and cook, so I talked her into managing the inn, after . . .." He cleared his throat. "Anyway, you're welcome to stay there any time. I know she's got a vacancy, so pack your bags and get on over here."

Enid was beginning to have second thoughts about returning to Madden, especially to the Glitter Lake Inn, considering the events a year ago. Could she see Jack without feeling overwhelming guilt? But she had to face the memories and Jack, sooner or later. "I'll come in the morning. I'm a little tired, so I'm going to bed early."

"I expect you to get here in time for lunch tomorrow. I'll tell Ruth to get your room ready and fix a special meal. Can't wait to see you."

After ending her call with Jack, Enid called her editor and filled her in on the soup kitchen story, promising to turn in the draft in time for next week's edition. A hot shower made her sleepy, so she curled up on the bed and drifted off.

When she woke up, it was nearly dark. She turned on the lights and pulled her laptop from the worn leather tote that Cade had given her many years ago. She started doing some research on the church as background information for her soup kitchen story but instead found herself searching for information on Theo's daughter. Flipping through her notes, she found Theo's last name and typed in "Harriet Linard + missing girl + Columbia." Several articles appeared immediately. She printed them out and put them in a folder to take with her to Madden, stuffing it in her tote. There was no way she was going to allow herself to get involved in looking for Hari. If she had learned anything, it was to stay out of open police cases. And besides, she was in no emotional shape to help anyone. The trip to Madden would be a good change of scenery for her. And she really had missed Jack. They had quickly become close friends, until tragedy made Enid withdraw from their relationship.

She texted Madelyn and told her she was going to be in Madden for a few days. Madelyn replied quickly, "Good! So glad you called Jack. He misses you."

Enid crawled into bed and fell asleep almost instantly. *She was all alone in the middle of a field as a dark tornado cloud approached. There was no place to hide, and she was terrified.* She bolted upright in bed, drenched in a cold sweat. While she had experienced many nightmares during the past year, this one was different. It felt more like a warning rather than a view of the past.

Turning on the light beside her bed, Enid looked at the clock. Two o'clock in the morning. She tried to go back to sleep but couldn't shake the dream from her mind.

CHAPTER 4

Jack jumped out of bed earlier than usual to make sure all the chores were done and out of the way before Enid's visit. He had missed Enid's companionship. She was a good friend and the only person who understood his grief. He had learned after his wife, Mattie, died years ago that the only way he could deal with grief was to stay busy, and getting up early was part of his routine. But today, he felt an unusual excitement.

Jack shook off the memories and went to the barn. Only a few horses were boarded at the ranch now. If it were up to him, there would be none. But Rachel loved the horses, so he agreed to keep them.

Rachel was the daughter he and Mattie never had. As a twenty-something young woman, she was capable of living on her own, but she needed family and so did Jack. They were emotionally bound by tragedy, but neither of them allowed it to define their relationship.

She had eagerly accepted Jack's offer to take care of the horses he boarded on his ranch in return for paying her college tuition. However, she was at Clemson University during the week, working on a veterinary degree, while staying at the ranch on weekends and holidays, as well as the coming summer. In hindsight, he wished he had just given her the money and stopped boarding horses. Then he wouldn't have hungry animals waiting for him. But tending them made her happy, and Jack would do most anything to make Rachel smile.

After feeding the horses, he made himself a big mug of coffee and toasted some stale raisin bread. He slathered it with the homemade cinnamon apple butter his sister Ruth had given him and checked the news headlines on his iPad. After reading a few articles, he slammed the worn leather cover shut in disgust. "Same garbage," he muttered aloud.

He glanced at his watch. Ruth would be in the kitchen at the Glitter Lake Inn, preparing breakfast for the guests. Everyone loved her jolly laugh and the way she made them feel welcome. With four failed marriages, she had little to laugh about when it came to relationships, but nothing seemed to bother her. Lately, however, she had mentioned to Jack that running an inn was hard, confining work and not her "cup of tea."

Jack glanced at his watch. Enid would be arriving in several hours. He glanced at his reflection in the mirror. He needed a haircut. By the time he got to Madden, the barbershop would be open. If not, he'd stop in for coffee at Sarah's diner.

• • •

Jack peered in the glass door of the barbershop. Lester, the old man who had cut hair in Madden for more than forty years, was moving around slowly inside. After finding the door was still locked, Jack knocked on the glass and watched Lester shuffle toward him. "Hey, Jack. Go get a cup of coffee. I ain't ready to open yet."

Jack threw up his hand in acknowledgment and nodded. "See you in a while then."

Lester's expression didn't change. "Yep." He shut the door as Jack walked away.

Sarah's place was the only diner in town. It was actually Sarah's Tea Shoppe, but the locals called it Sarah's diner. In the mornings, a waitress and cook opened the place and served mostly retired men who were either widowers or just wanted to get away from their wives and talk "man stuff," mostly hunting, farming, the weather, and politics. After lunch, Sarah herself came in and served afternoon tea to the town's ladies. She prided herself on the best scones outside of London, and the best tea selection in South Carolina. She hosted birthday parties, bridal showers, and other events with an elegance that matched the Savoy Hotel. Truth be told, Jack preferred to come in the afternoons. The world needed a little more civility.

Jack was polite but usually avoided the old farts' social club, as he called them. When he walked in, four of them were in a booth near the back arguing about whether raising taxes to repair the state's crumbling roads was unconstitutional. "They can't do that!" one of them shouted. When they saw Jack, they stopped talking. He waved at them and then sat at the counter as the social club resumed its discussion.

Jack was stirring his coffee to cool it down a bit when the Madden police chief, Joshua Hart, sat at the stool next to him. "Morning, Jack. You're in town early."

The waitress quickly swooped in to take Josh's order. The chief was Native American, tall and handsome, like a romance novel cliché. He worked out in his home gym and had the physique of a model. The men in Madden regarded Josh as they would any non-white man. They were respectful but let Josh know he wasn't one of them. On the other hand, the women practically swooned when Josh walked in. He exuded an air of masculine brawn, balanced with feminine sensitivity. His humble nature made him even more irresistible to the town's ladies.

"Waiting on the barber shop to open." Jack tugged at the hair on his neck. "Getting a bit shaggy."

Josh nodded in agreement. "I was out at Ruth's yesterday. She told me your friend was coming in today for a visit."

Jack mostly liked small-town life, but sometimes he felt like he was living in a fishbowl. "Yes, Enid Blackwell, the journalist."

Josh laughed. "Considering she got my predecessor fired, should I be concerned that she's coming back to Madden?"

"No, I think you'll be fine. She's had a rough year. You know what happened."

One of the social club members came over to Josh and asked him why the town hadn't fixed the stop sign someone had knocked over. Josh assured them it was scheduled to be fixed but he'd check on it again. Josh turned back to Jack. "She must be one tough lady."

"She's stronger than she thinks. She's going to stay at the inn, but I'll make sure you get to meet her while she's here."

The door to the diner opened and Lester walked in. "You coming?" He then turned and walked out before Jack could reply.

Jack threw a couple dollars on the counter. "I guess I'd better get going."

CHAPTER 5

When Glitter Lake came into view, Enid was as moved by its beauty as she was the first time she had seen it more than a year ago. The sun danced across the gentle ripples and produced radiant jewels of light. Knowing her friend's ashes had been scattered onto the lake made seeing it again all the more emotional.

She parked her car in one of the guest spaces beside the inn and walked up the steps and across the porch to the massive oak door. While repaired now, the right side had been splintered by a shotgun blast as Enid had run from the house. She shook her head slightly as if to brush away the unpleasant memories. Before she could ring the doorbell, the door opened.

Ruth had a dish towel in one hand and reached out the other one to Enid. "You must be Enid. Jack said you're a redhead." She winked. "He also said you're pretty. Come on in," she said, stepping aside.

Enid took Ruth's hand. "I'm pleased to finally meet you. Jack has spoken about you so often that I feel I know you."

"Jack's a sweetheart, and that's the God's truth." She winked, "But don't tell him I said so. A little sibling rivalry keeps us honest."

Enid could see why the guests loved her. She was attractive in her own way, with short, dark hair and eyes that twinkled when she smiled.

Once again, Enid was struck by the beauty of the old inn. The floors were gleaming with a fresh coat of wax, and the smell of lemon oil hung in the air. "I had almost forgotten how beautiful this place is."

"I've put you in a different room upstairs. You know, not the same one, as when . . .."

Enid put her hand on Ruth's arm. "It's okay. Really."

"Whew. I'm glad. Jack said you might be a little weirded out, you know, coming back here."

Enid followed Ruth upstairs to a bedroom at the back of the house. She was glad of the window overlooking the lake. The room appeared to be freshly painted. "Everything looks great."

"Well, the inn's only been reopened a few months. Jack wasn't sure if he wanted to sell it or what. I first told him no when he asked me to come here. I'm not a gracious Southern hostess, and I had never even been to South Carolina. But when my marriage went kaput, I figured why not. At least I wouldn't be running into my ex down here. Bless his heart." She laughed. "Oh, my God. I'm starting to talk Southern!"

Enid already liked Ruth. "It doesn't take long to rub off on you."

"I'll leave you to freshen up. Jack asked me to let him know when you arrived. Do you want to me to wait awhile? You know, so you can get adjusted?"

"You can call him. I'll just freshen up a bit."

"I've made lunch for you. It's a bit chilly to sit outside, so I set it up in the dining room."

"Wait. Before you go ... how is Jack doing?" Enid asked.

"Oh, you know Jack. He tries to put on a brave front, but I can tell some days he's heartbroken. He needs a friend, so I'm real glad you're here."

After Ruth left, Enid touched up her makeup and combed her hair, fussing over each strand until she approved of her image in the mirror.

It wasn't long before she heard his voice, so she went downstairs to join him and Ruth. Her hands were shaking as she held onto the polished wooden handrail.

• • •

When Enid walked into the dining room, Jack was talking to Ruth. Hearing her footsteps, he turned around and threw open his arms. "Oh, my. How I've missed you."

Tears sprang to Enid's eyes as they hugged, but she was determined not to get emotional. "Hello, Jack. It's good to see you, too."

Ruth finished putting the food on the table and headed out of the room, calling over her shoulder, "Just yell for me if you need anything."

"You look great, but how have you been?" Jack asked Enid.

"I've been, well, I'm doing alright now." She paused. "I admit it hasn't been easy this past year. What about you?" The loss of their mutual friend more than a year ago hung in the air like a dense fog, enveloping them. Being in the inn only intensified the memories.

Jack reached out to put his hand on hers but then pulled back. "I'm staying busy. That's my remedy, you know."

"I'm sorry I didn't return your calls. I know it was selfish of me, but I had to sort through everything. And I had to find a place to live. Madelyn was gracious enough to rent her garage studio to me for a ridiculously low rate. It's a beautiful place, but I know I can't stay there forever."

"She likes having you around." His voice lowered. "How's Cade? Do you stay in touch with him?"

Enid nodded. "We talk periodically. He has an apartment in Charlotte, but he travels a lot. You know he's working with the AP again as a reporter."

"That's where he belongs." Jack sat back in his chair. "What about you? You still working for that weekly paper?"

"I know it's not much of a reporting job, but I couldn't handle the pressures of daily deadlines any more. I was out of it too long, and then after all that happened here, I couldn't do crime stories any longer. It's a family-owned paper, and they treat me well. I'm fine for now." Enid felt her cell phone vibrating in her pocket but ignored it. If it was work, they'd leave a message and she would call them after lunch. She hoped it wasn't another bill collector. After the divorce, she was shocked to learn how poorly Cade had managed their finances. They had sold everything and paid off what they could. The remaining debts were an embarrassment, and she and Cade had set up payment plans to repay everything, but new creditors seem to pop up frequently. "What about you? What have you been up to this past year?"

"Every Sunday I throw a bunch of flowers on the lake and sit at the memorial bench. Strangely, it doesn't make me sad. We have some good chats."

"As much as I wanted to see you, I dreaded my first visit back to Madden. I didn't know if I could face you."

"You've got to stop blaming yourself." He sipped his tea before changing the subject. "By the way, you're looking at the proud new owner of the *Madden Gazette*."

"You mean you bought the local newspaper?"

"Finished the paperwork this morning after I got my haircut." He rubbed his chin. "Not sure what I was thinking, to be honest. I really don't have much interest in working a lot these days, but now I've got a horse ranch, an inn, and a weekly newspaper. I just didn't want to see it shut down or be sold to a conglomerate that would let it die a slow death like most of the weeklies."

"What happened? Why was it sold?"

"Well, after Dick Jensen resigned as police chief, thanks to your reporting," he said raising his glass to Enid, "the Jensen dynasty began to crumble. The paper was owned by the family, and people began canceling their subscriptions after the paper published an article claiming the police chief had been unfairly treated. People just got fed up with all that happened." He smiled. "I guess it's your fault I got the dang paper now."

"What happened to Helen, the managing editor? She had been at the paper a long time, as I recall."

"She's going to stay on as editor until I decide how much I want to get involved again. If she had the money, I know she would have bought the paper. It's in her blood."

Enid felt the phone vibrating again. "I'm sorry. but someone is trying to reach me. Do you mind?"

Jack shook his head. "No, go ahead."

Enid pulled the phone from her pocket. The image of her editor in Columbia smiled at her from the screen. Enid listened and then replied. "Yes, I'm in Madden, and, yes, I talked to Theo Linard about the soup kitchen." Enid felt the blood draining from her face. "Yes, he told me about his daughter being missing."

Enid listened to her editor's request. "Isn't there some one else that would like to do a story on his daughter?" Her editor's next few words clanged around in her head like someone beating a pot with a spoon. "Oh, my God. They found a body? Have they identified it as Hari?" Enid felt like someone had punched her in the stomach. "Please keep me posted."

"Are you alright?" asked Jack after Enid ended the call. "You're as white as a sheet. Has something happened?"

"While I was talking to a source yesterday about a piece I'm doing on a soup kitchen, he told me his daughter was missing. Now they've found a body of a young girl."

"That's terrible. Poor guy."

"I'll tell you about it later. Do you mind if I excuse myself? I need to answer a few emails.

"No, of course. Go on. I'll call you later."

As Enid turned to leave, she caught her foot on the chair leg and almost fell. Jack grabbed her arm. Seeing him had conjured too many memories. And now this. But as she walked up the stairs, all she could think about was Theo and how he must be feeling.

CHAPTER 6

Enid woke up, lying on her bed at the inn. She looked at her iPhone and realized she had been asleep almost an hour. At least she had avoided a full-blown panic attack last night.

Sitting on the side of the bed, phone in hand, she debated with herself about whether she should follow up on her editor's call. Her survival instincts were telling her to ignore it—there was nothing she could do. But instead, her reporter's instincts kicked in.

"Hi, it's Enid. Just wanted to check on the body they found. Has it been identified yet?"

Her editor replied, "Not yet. The *State* will be all over it for tomorrow's edition, but I thought we could do a piece on Theo. You know, a piece on how he's handling all this. Would you be up to it?"

Enid heard herself say, "Do you want me to wait until they confirm the identity?"

"I'll leave that to you. Just keep focusing on the human interest angle. That's where your strength is." She hung up before Enid could rescind her agreement to write the article.

Enid pulled her notes from her meeting with Theo and called his number. After several rings, she hung up, as she didn't want to leave an awkward message. *Have you heard yet if the girl's body was your daughter? And if so, how are you feeling right now?*

Since Enid had asked not to work the crime beat any longer, she had few reliable contacts in the police department. She called one of them, but he said he couldn't give her any information. He did, however, hint that the identity had not been confirmed. Frustrated, she called Jack.

"Jack, it's me."

"Are you feeling better?"

"Yes, I'm fine. Do you have any solid contacts with detectives in the Columbia Police Department?"

"No, my guy retired. But Josh may know of someone."

"Who is Josh?"

"Oh, sorry, I guess you wouldn't know him. He took Dick Jensen's place as the Madden Police Chief. I wanted you to meet him anyway. If you'd like, we can drive into town and see if he'll help."

Doctor Wright had told her that at some point, she had to step back into her life, rather than just being a spectator. Was this that point? Her attention now was on Hari and the unidentified body.

• • •

Walking into the Madden police station with Jack brought a flood of memories. Enid tried to focus on being in the present, as Dr. Wright had shown her. *Deep breaths. Stay focused. To be at peace, you must stay in the present, not the past or the future.*

A young man in uniform was sitting at the reception desk and looked up when they walked in. "Hello, may I help you?"

"We'd like to talk with Josh, I mean Chief Hart, if he's in," Jack said.

"I'll see if he's available. Please have a seat," the officer said, motioning to the metal chairs against the wall.

Enid sat while Jack stood. In last than a minute, the young man returned, followed by another man in uniform.

"Jack, what's up?" he asked.

"Hey, Josh, sorry to barge in like this," Jack said as he motioned for Enid to join them. "I'd like to introduce my friend, Enid Blackwell. She's a journalist."

Josh extended his hand. "Honored to meet you."

"And this is our new police chief, Joshua Hart," Jack said.

"Nice to meet you," Enid said. Trying not to be too obvious, she studied Josh's features. It was his eyes that held her attention. They were dark and mesmerizing.

"Come on, let's go in my office where we can talk." Josh turned to the young man at the desk. "Pete, hold my calls unless it's an emergency."

Enid was surprised, and a bit amused, when Josh pulled his chair from behind the desk and sat close to Jack. *Nice move.*

"Chief Hart, I'm here to ask a favor of you," Enid said.

"I'll gladly help you if you call me Josh."

Those eyes!

"You may have heard that a young girl's body was just discovered in Columbia. It may be the daughter of a source I interviewed on an unrelated topic. My editor wants me to follow up on it. Since I don't do the crime beat any longer, I can't get any information. I was hoping you might be able to find out if she has been identified."

Josh looked at Enid for what seemed like an eternity before he responded. "I see. I don't mind making a couple phone calls, but that's all I can do unless there is an official reason for me to get involved."

"Of course, I wouldn't expect you to."

"Just a call, that's all," Jack said to Josh.

Josh pushed his chair back behind the metal desk that looked like it had been rescued from Goodwill. The former police chief must have taken the nice desk with him when he left. Josh looked through the contacts on his cell phone and called one of them. "Hey, buddy, what you doing, man? Look here, I need a little favor. A friend of mine is worried that the young woman that was found might be someone she knows. Can you tell me if she's been identified yet?" Josh listened and made a few scribbles in a notebook. "I see. Yes, that would be great. Thanks. I owe you one. Take care, buddy." He hung up and turned to Enid. "Nothing yet, but he promised to call me. Why don't you leave your number, and I'll let you know when I hear back from him."

Enid reached into the worn leather tote and pulled out a business card. "That would be great. Thanks. My cell number is on there."

"We appreciate the help," Jack said. "We'll get out of here now and quit taking up your time."

Josh was still studying Enid's business card. "May I ask you a question?" He locked eyes with Enid.

Enid shifted in her seat. "Of course."

"You know I've read all the stories you did on Rose Marie Garrett. They were good. Not the usual investigative reporting, but more like, uh . . ." Josh seemed to be searching for words.

"Human interest," Enid said. "That's my style. You know, the people behind the story."

"Anyway, they were good articles."

"Thanks."

"So why are you writing about community events now for a weekly paper?" Josh put her business card on his desk, as he waited for an answer.

"I just needed a break from crime reporting. You've done your research, so you know what happened."

"I also know you solved a ten-year-old cold case. I think my predecessor described you as bull-headed but smart as a whip."

Enid could see Dick Jensen's face with the wide-brimmed hat, just as though he were standing in front of her. "I'm sure he did."

Jack opened the door to Josh's office and motioned for Enid. "Thanks again, Josh."

As they were leaving, Josh called out, "Damn good articles, Ms. Blackwell. You should be proud of your work. I'll be in touch."

CHAPTER 7

Theo was peeling potatoes for tomorrow's soup. He cut the pieces small, so they would cook quickly. He liked it when the stores donated the little red or white potatoes that didn't have to be peeled, but all food donations were appreciated. He was absorbed in his work when he heard his name called.

"Are you Theo Linard?" A woman in a navy blazer and tan slacks flashed a badge. "I'm Detective Pointer. Your daughter's case was recently assigned to me. The prior detective was transferred to another area."

He laid the razor-sharp knife, a prized possession, on the counter. "I am. Do you have news for me?"

"I wanted to follow up with you on your daughter's case." She glanced at the small spiral-bound notebook in her hand and added, "Harriet Linard."

Several times during the few months, Theo had been approached by the previous detective in charge of Hari's case. Each time, Theo had allowed himself a brief moment of hope that she had been found alive. Not today, though. He sensed that Detective Pointer wasn't here to deliver good news. "What's happened?"

"Can we sit down and talk?" she asked.

Theo wiped his hands on his apron and motioned toward the dining area. It was late afternoon and the room was empty. He pulled out a chair for her. "Please, have a seat." He sat across the table.

"There's no easy way for me to say this, Mr. Linard, but a girl's body has been found. The body's description matches your daughter's."

Suddenly, the air had been sucked from the room, and Theo was having trouble catching his breath. "Where was she found?"

"There's a public park not far from here. The body, the girl, was found buried when they were laying new drain pipes near the creek. From what they can tell, she's been dead a while, at least several months. There's significant decomposition."

"Then what makes you think it's Hari?" Then he remembered the small, tasteful dragonfly on her left shoulder. "Oh, God. Is it the tattoo?"

"There is body art on her back, but it has not yet been identified as matching your daughter's. It's just that there are no other blonde girls reported missing in this area recently. We have your DNA on file, so we'll run the tests and let you know as soon as possible."

"How did she die?"

"We don't know yet."

"May I see her?" Theo clasped his hands to keep them from shaking.

Detective Pointer shifted in her seat. "We rarely take relatives to the morgue. It's not like you see on TV. Besides, I don't think that's a good idea."

Theo interrupted. "I demand to see her. I will know if it's Hari, no matter how . . ." He paused and collected himself. "No matter how decomposed she is." Theo stood up and began taking off his apron. He looked back at Pointer. "I will see her now."

• • •

The smell in the county morgue was unforgettable. “Wait here,” Pointer said. “I had to pull some strings to get you in here, and I need to make sure the tech on duty is in the loop.”

Theo sat in one of the metal chairs in the hallway until Detective Pointer returned and motioned for him to follow her.

They walked into a sterile room that smelled of strong antiseptics. The morgue tech directed them to a stainless steel table on castors sitting near the back of the room. A white cover was draped over the body.

“Are you sure you want to do this?" Pointer asked.

Theo nodded and took a deep breath.

"Ready,” Pointer said to the tech, who then pulled back the cover to reveal the corpse’s head and shoulders.

Theo gasped. What was left of the deceased girl was a mangle of blackened and missing flesh. Her hair was streaked with dirt but undeniably blonde. Theo forced his eyes to study every square inch of the girl's face, or what was left of it. "Can I see the tattoo?"

"The body is too fragile to handle without further damage." Pointer pulled a photo from the folder in her hand. "Here's a photograph of her back. There's not much to see, I'm afraid."

Theo studied the image of decayed flesh. Suddenly, his lunch churned in his stomach, and he reached out to put his hand on the wall beside the window to steady himself.

"Are you okay? Do you need to sit down?" Pointer asked.

Theo could no longer hold back and began sobbing. Detective Pointed nodded to the technician and he pulled the cover over the body. She took Theo's arm and guided him out into the hallway. "Mr. Linard, let's go out and get some fresh air or at least go out and sit in the hallway."

He put his face in his hands and wailed uncontrollably. "I don't know if it's her. I thought I would know, but I don't."

CHAPTER 8

"Do you want to grab a bite to eat at Sarah's?" asked Jack. "Or do you want me to take you back to the inn?"

Enid had been staring out the car window but refocused her attention on Jack. "Sorry. Just lost in thought. What did you say?"

"I said, let's go for a bite to eat. I'm buying." He made a three-point turn in the road and headed back toward downtown Madden. Parking was never a problem in the small town, so he pulled into a space right in front of the diner.

The after-work crowd hadn't arrived yet, so the only other person in Sarah's was an elderly man. He was apparently hard of hearing because he was yelling at the waitperson, although she didn't seem to have any trouble hearing him. Enid remembered how her mother had started talking loudly when she lost her own hearing, as though everyone else was having a problem hearing, too.

Jack motioned for Enid to take a seat at a table near the back of the restaurant. After they ordered, he pushed his chair back from the table slightly. "So, what are you going to do about the missing girl?"

"You mean Hari? Nothing, other than to write about Theo and how her disappearance has affected him."

Jack pulled his chair back up to the table. "Now look here. I won't let you shut off that great mind of yours. Not out of fear. You've got to get back in the saddle before you become paralyzed."

"Gee, Jack. How do you really feel? Has it occurred to you that maybe this is the life I want? You know how much I enjoy writing human interest stories. I'll write Theo's story because I don't have much choice, not if I want to keep my job. And I do want to help him. But I'm going to keep a distance." She paused. "I have to."

Jack reached out and put his hand on Enid's. "Whoa. Hold on. I'm not picking a fight." He paused. "And I also have a professional interest."

"How's that?"

"I told you I bought the *Madden Gazette*."

Enid nodded.

"Well, I'd like for you to work for me," he said.

"You mean move to Madden? I don't think so." Enid withdrew her hand from Jack's. "As they say, it's a nice place to visit, but . . ."

"What if you only reported on special topics, you know something like a series on hot issues, rather than the usual women's club activities and such. You wouldn't have to be here all the time."

"I'm not sure my editor would appreciate me working for the competition. Besides, I've already got a full work load."

"Our papers report on different geographic areas with different readers, so we're not really in competition."

The waitperson brought their food, and they switched to small talk while they ate. Jack wiped his mouth with the linen napkin, a luxury for a small diner in a small town. "Will you consider it? I mean, if I get a good enough story, will you think about it?"

"How does Helen feel about your proposal? Or have you even discussed it with her?"

"She'll be fine. She appreciates good reporting, so what's not to like about the idea?" Jack motioned to the waitress for a refill, and waited for her to leave their table before continuing. "I know your editor well. And I think she would be fine with sharing you, perhaps even collaborating with us on some joint ventures."

Enid slapped her palms on the table. "You've already talked to her, haven't you?"

Jack shrugged. "Well, it might have come up when we chatted. But it's your decision. Just think about it, okay? And don't be mad at me. You should be flattered that I'm doing anything I can to get you to write for my paper."

Before Enid could reply, the police chief walked in and sat next to Jack. "Sorry to intrude, but I saw your car and figured you were in here grabbing a bite." He took a fried potato from Jack's plate and popped it in his mouth. "Best fries in town."

Jack laughed. "The only fries in town, you mean. But, yes, they are good. To what do we owe the pleasure of your dropping by?"

Josh looked at Enid. "I just wanted you to know that they're going to run the DNA on the girl's body. The father insisted on viewing her remains, but she was too far gone for him to know if it was her." He shook his head. "Poor guy. I can't imagine what he must be going through."

"How long before they'll get the DNA results?" Enid asked.

"Unlike "CSI" on TV, it will take a couple weeks. Maybe a little sooner, depending on the backlog." Josh ate another of Jack's fries.

"Can we order you something?" Jack asked.

Josh stood up. "No, I've got to run. Just wanted to update you," he said to Enid.

"Thanks. I appreciate it."

As he walked away, Enid said to Jack, "I'm guessing that Theo's search for his daughter is one of the stories you'd like to 'collaborate' on."

Jack rubbed his chin with the familiar gesture Enid had missed the past year. Realizing how much she had missed Jack eased her annoyance a bit. "Well, now. That's an excellent idea. Wish I had thought of it."

Enid made a face at Jack and threw her napkin at him. "You're such a bad liar. But I'm curious. Why would the folks in Madden be interested in Theo's story? I mean, I realize a missing girl, especially if she's found murdered, would be big news. But the *State* will carry it, and many of the people here read Columbia's daily newspaper. What could the *Madden Gazette* and the *Palmetto Weekly* add to the story?"

Jack pointed a finger at Enid. "You. That's what. The *State* is a great paper, and they'll do a wonderful job with the news part of the story. But if something else comes up in the next news cycle, they'll move on. I, that is, your editor and I, would like for you to stay on it and follow Theo's reactions and how it impacts his life."

"What makes you think Theo will want to share his feelings with the world?"

Jack waited briefly before replying. "He'll open up to you." He put his hand on her arm. "Just talk with him. Then make the decision. I promise I'll accept whatever you decide." Jack rubbed his chin again. "If the body is his daughter's, then you can do a couple stories on the disappearance, his search, and the tragic ending. If it's not her, then sadly he's got no one to turn to other than you," he said, pointing at Enid again. "Just you. You can help him *and* write a great story."

"I'm hardly in a position to offer strength and comfort to anyone." Enid rubbed her temples. "Can you drop me off at the inn?"

When they returned to the car, Enid tried to visualize the waterfall that she had been using as her mental "safe place" during the past year. Whenever she felt stressed, she imagined herself in a beautiful paradise, watching a waterfall gently flow into the lake. As she imagined herself looking into the clear blue water, the pale face from Harriet Linard's photo floated to the surface. Her beautiful blue eyes were open and staring right into Enid's.

CHAPTER 9

After tossing and turning most of the night, Enid woke up tired and irritable. When she and Cade were together, they used to talk about those nights when the snakes slithered through your head. Thoughts became entangled in your brain and you couldn't rid yourself of them. Part of her wanted to help Theo, if only to write an article that would bring attention to Hari's disappearance, and perhaps her death, if the body was identified as hers. Maybe someone would come forward with new information. If nothing else, it would serve as a cautionary tale about the predators that stalked college campuses.

The other part of Enid wanted to run or hide—or both. She didn't need to take on another open police case. Doing research last year on Rosie's murder had brought closure for Cade's family, but not without a cost. Was she willing to take those risks again? Enid stepped out of the shower and shook her wet hair vigorously, as if trying to rid herself of the snakes.

The tea and muffin Ruth had left on the hall table was tasty, but Enid didn't have much of an appetite. Ruth seemed to be doing a good job running the inn. At least she was trying to carry on the traditions.

A spring storm had blown through the area last night, causing the lights to flicker off and on several times and dropping the temperature down to 43 degrees by early morning. She tiptoed across the cold wooden floor trying to find her shoes.

The time on her phone showed it was still early, but Theo would be busy preparing for the day's meal—that is, if he was working today. She decided to stop guessing and call him. Taking a long, deep breath, she called his number. After three rings, she was preparing what to say in her message when he answered. "Hello." His voice sounded deeper than she had remembered.

"Theo, it's Enid Blackwell. I'm sorry to bother you but I wonder if we could talk today. If you're up to it, of course."

"I'm pretty busy until after lunch. Can we talk then?" His voice was weak, and he sounded tired, as if he, too, had battled with snakes all night.

"That's fine. I'll meet you at the church."

That left Enid almost six hours to kill before their meeting, and the drive from Madden to Columbia was less than an hour. She finished dressing and packed her tote with notepad, pen, and a small bag of peanuts.

In the car, she called Jack, but there was no answer. She left him a message that she was going to see the Madden police chief, Josh Hart.

CHAPTER 10

When Enid walked into the small concrete block police station, Chief Hart was making coffee in the back. "Dang it!" He rushed to the men's room to blot the water he spilled on his shirt. "Be with you in a minute," he said without looking at her.

Enid sat in the front area in one of the old metal chairs and waited.

"Ah, it's you," Josh said as he walked toward Enid.

Enid stood to greet him. "Don't sound so excited."

"Sorry, we're short on help this morning, so I'm doing kitchen duty as well. May I offer you a cup? I promise not to spill it on you."

"No, thanks. I'm a tea drinker, but I've had my fill already. Do you have a minute?"

Josh motioned for Enid to follow him into his office. "Of course." He was intrigued with Enid, but when she showed up like this unexpected, it made him wary. He pulled up a chair for her and then sat behind his desk. "I guess you want an update on the girl's body that was found."

"I had hoped you might have heard something. I'm meeting with Theo, the father, this afternoon."

Josh pushed his chair back slightly. "I got a call back from my friend. He told me Detective Jan Pointer is handling the case. She took the father to the morgue after he insisted on seeing the body."

"Poor Theo. That must have been horrible for him."

Josh recalled his visit years ago to identify his wife's remains. She wasn't decomposed like this young woman, but it was still hard to look at her. The person lying on the table had not been his vibrant wife of more than ten years. Instead, the pale, stiff woman was something he didn't recognize. "Yes, it's hard on the family, so matter what the circumstances."

Enid nodded.

"I worked another case with Detective Pointer. She's good people, so I know she'll do whatever she can. Although, when I talked with her late yesterday, she said they were just waiting on the DNA results. Otherwise, they have no other leads to pursue."

Enid stood up. "Well, thanks for checking. Will she let you know when the body is identified?"

"Yes, she promised to keep me in the loop. But she also asked why I was involved." Josh had asked himself the same question.

"What did you tell her?"

"Just that a friend of mine was also a friend of the father." Josh smiled. "She didn't seem to happy to know you were also a reporter. Unfortunately, Jan, Detective Pointer, has had some bad experiences with the press."

"Look, Chief Hart—"

"It's Josh, please."

"All I'm going to do is write about how Theo is dealing with the disappearance, or perhaps the murder, of his daughter. I won't get in Detective Pointer's way if I can help it. On the other hand, I will do my job."

Josh found himself watching Enid with interest. She had a way of squaring her shoulders when she wanted to stand firm. But she also seemed vulnerable in a way that made him want to protect her. It was his nature to protect people, especially women, which made some people mistakenly assume he was chauvinistic. Actually, he thought women were far more capable than most men. In fact, he was in awe of their strength and spirit. Raised in the Native American culture, his mother told him from a young age that his assignment while on this earth was to protect others from evil and harm. Josh took her words to heart and had never questioned his duty.

"Good luck with your meeting this afternoon. I'll call when I know anything further." His voice sounded more formal than he had intended.

CHAPTER 11

When Enid walked into the church soup kitchen, Theo was sitting alone at one of the tables, his shoulders slumped. "Good afternoon, Ms. Blackwell. Thank you for coming." The dark circles under his eyes made him look older than his years.

Enid sat down across from him. "I heard about your trip to the morgue. I know that must have been hard on you."

Tears filled his eyes. "I thought I would recognize her. You know, that no matter what, I could *feel* if it was her." He wiped his eyes with the only clean spot at bottom of his apron.

"I've been told that Detective Pointer is good, so I'm sure she'll do whatever she can to find out what happened to your daughter."

Theo leaned in toward her so suddenly that Enid was startled. "I want *you* to help me. If that's not her, then I want to find her." His eyes were pleading to the point that it made Enid uncomfortable.

"All I can do is keep Hari's name in the news. Maybe someone knows something but just hasn't come forward. I've got the go-ahead from my editor to write about her story."

Theo reached over to the seat of the chair next to him and picked up a worn manila folder crammed with papers. "Here, this will tell you who you need to talk to."

Enid started to protest, but his eyes silenced her. "I'll get this back to you after I've gone through it." She took the folder and put it in her tote.

"Wait here." He walked to the kitchen and returned with a plastic container. "We had some leftovers today. This is my Greek minestrone. It's good. Take it." He handed the container to Enid.

"Thanks, I'll have it tonight."

"Remember the magic of soup."

"Magic? I don't follow what you're saying."

"Soup is always better the next day. That way the flavors and ingredients blend and become one."

Enid thanked him for the soup. As she was leaving, he called to her, "You will feel differently tomorrow. You'll see."

In the car, Enid called Ruth at the Glitter Lake Inn and told her she was staying in Columbia but would return tomorrow. Despite her reservations about getting involved, Enid was anxious to review the contents of Theo's folder.

• • •

When Enid pulled into the driveway, Madelyn was just getting out of her car. "Hey, how was Madden? I bet Jack was happy to see you." She pulled a bulging briefcase from the backseat of the BMW Enid had once owned. During the divorce settlement discussions about asset allocation, Madelyn had offered to buy the car when both Cade and Enid said they couldn't afford to keep it. "Wait, I thought you weren't coming back for another day or so. Everything okay?"

"Yes, Jack and I had a chance to talk some. I'll head back to Madden tomorrow morning. I got some notes from a source and wanted to go through them." Enid held up the container of soup. "I'm making dinner if you want to come up."

"Wow. This is a treat. Let me change into jeans, and I'll be up in a few." Madelyn shook her head, laughing as she walked to the house. "Enid making dinner."

Enid climbed the steep stairs to her garage apartment, and put the soup and her tote on the kitchen counter. Her phone vibrated in her pocket. Jack's image was on the screen. "Hey, Jack. Where have you been all day?"

"One of the horses we board took sick. Been with the vet mostly. She's better now. The horse, I mean, not the vet. What you been up to? Want to have a bite to eat with your favorite newspaper owner?"

"I'm staying in Columbia tonight, but I'll be back tomorrow and will catch up with you."

"Any news on the body they found?"

Enid had learned that Jack's matter-of-fact attitude had nothing to do with the depth of his feelings. He usually hid his emotions, especially when he was thinking like a reporter.

"Not yet. I've got to run, but we'll talk tomorrow."

Enid hung up and looked in the small kitchen for a pot big enough for Theo's soup. She found one lurking in the back of the cabinet. She rinsed out the pot and poured the contents of the plastic container into it. Even cold, the soup smelled good. She put Theo's folder on the small table by the window that served as dressing table and desk.

A knock on the door announced Madelyn's arrival. "Yoo-hoo, it's me," she said as she walked in. "Damn, I did a good job decorating this place, if I do say so myself."

Enid stirred the soup as it began to bubble around the edges. "Yes, it's a great place." She turned toward Madelyn. "And it comes with a great landlady."

Madelyn put her arms around Enid's shoulders and laughed. "Aw, you're just saying that because it's true." She watched as Enid put the soup into two bowls. "That from your soup kitchen guy?"

"Yes, it's from Theo." Enid wiped some spilled soup from the side of one of the bowls. "I found out his daughter is missing."

"Missing? Like a runaway? Wait, I remember reading something about that months ago."

"Yes, I don't think the police have anything to indicate she was abducted or there was any crime committed. Teenage girls sometimes leave with a boyfriend or just decide to drop out of school."

"Is that what you think happened?" Madelyn asked.

"I don't think Hari's the type to leave voluntarily. She's an honor student, loves her dad." Enid put the bowls on the placemats at the small dining table where she had laid out a sliced loaf of French bread and Irish butter. Pointing to the file Theo had given her, she said, "I promised I'd look at his notes. And I promised my editor I'd do a story on his search for her. But that's it. I'm *not* getting involved in looking for his daughter."

Madelyn blew on her spoon to cool the soup. "This smells heavenly." They engaged in small talk while eating. When they finished, Madelyn took the two bowls to the sink. "I'll clean up. If you're going to read that file tonight, you'd better get started."

As Madelyn started out the door, she turned back to Enid. "Look, I know you're tired of hearing this from me, but you've got to let go of the past and get back in the game. You're a damn good reporter, and you're wasting yourself on these little community event articles."

"Surely you realize the irony of this conversation."

Madelyn stepped back inside the apartment and pulled the door shut. "What do you mean?"

"You and everyone else tried to stop me when I was writing about Rosie. Now, suddenly, all of you are urging me to jump back into researching an open case."

Madelyn walked back to Enid and hugged her. "Oh, 'hon, I know. Last time, we were worried you'd get yourself killed. And you nearly did. But now we're worried that you're giving up on life and putting your head in the sand." She stepped back and held Enid by the shoulders. "Look, that girl they found is probably Hari. Just get back in the game and do what you do best. Write a great article about her that Theo can frame and have the rest of his life."

"But what if it's not her?"

"Then write about how happy Theo is when he gets to hang onto hope for a while longer." Madelyn blew her an air kiss. "Bye. Thanks for the soup."

• • •

Before reading Theo's file, Enid went to the NamUS missing persons database and quickly found Harriet Linard's information, although it was sparse—nothing new. Enid then spread the contents of the file across her bed. Theo had collected newspaper clippings, photos, and a stack of handwritten notes. For the next two hours, she read the *State* newspaper articles, handwritten notes that Theo had made after every conversation he had with anyone related to his daughter's disappearance, and some photos. One in particular caught her eye: a coffee shop she recognized as being near the campus. Enid made a note on the yellow legal pad to ask Theo if Hari went there often, since there was no other reference to it in the file.

One of the newspaper articles stated a search had been organized on and around the campus when Hari's disappearance was reported, but nothing materialized. Everyone seemed to be going through the motions of looking for Hari, but beneath the search there seemed to be a question about whether she had disappeared voluntarily. Theo had insisted Hari wouldn't do that, but parents don't always know what's going on in their children's lives.

As Enid thought about Theo and Hari's relationship, her own father came to mind. She did not remember him, as he died when Enid was a toddler. To compensate, Enid's mother had tried to make Enid's life as complete as possible. Her mother filled in the best that she could, but Enid longed for memories of a loving father who read her stories and took her to the zoo.

But for now, her priority was Theo and Hari. Enid put her notes away and went to bed, drifting into an uneasy sleep as she thought about the missing girl and her father's broken heart.

CHAPTER 12

Enid woke with a headache and tired from tossing all night. She decided to copy Theo's notes before returning them. But she would have to get to the copy shop early to see Theo before the soup kitchen got too busy.

The chime on her phone dinged. It was a message from Jack wanting to know if she would be coming to Madden for the weekend. Rachel was going to be at Jack's ranch and wanted to see Enid. Despite the circumstances that brought the two women together, Enid and Rachel had formed a bond more than a year ago. Rachel had been the best friend of Rosie, the young woman who had been murdered. Enid looked forward to reconnecting with Rachel, so she replied that she would be back Saturday by noon. She would have to finish her story on the soup kitchen tomorrow in order to meet her deadline.

By the time Enid got to the church, Theo was busy directing deliveries. They had received boxes of donated produce that would have to be prepared and used or frozen before it spoiled. Theo got someone to help with the deliveries so that he could talk with Enid.

Enid handed him the file. "I hope you don't mind, but I made a copy of your notes. My editor would like for me to do a story on you, as the father of a missing girl. How would you feel about that?"

"So you'll help me find Hari?"

Enid could hardly bear the pain in Theo's eyes. "The DNA results should be in any day now. I know it's hard, but you need to prepare yourself that it may be Hari. If I do a story it may generate some new interest, maybe produce some new information."

Theo dropped his head slightly and nodded. "I don't want to believe it's her, but I know it could be. I appreciate you doing an article. That's a start."

Enid got the additional information she needed to finish the soup kitchen article. "Do you have time for me to ask you some questions about your notes? If not, we can talk later."

"They can finish without me. They don't think so, but they can."

Enid pulled out the photo of the coffee shop. "There are no notes on this photo, and you didn't mention it anywhere. Is it significant?"

Theo took the photo and looked at it. "Hari's roommate, Katlyn, gave it to me. She said Hari was doing a photojournalism story on some girls." He paused. "That's all I remember," he said shaking his head. "Lots of questions, but no answers."

Enid pointed to one of Theo's notes. "This phone number under 'Kat,' is that Katlyn's number?"

"Yes, that's Kat's cell phone number."

"Was she able to help the police?"

"Kat has been very kind to me, but the previous detective rubbed her the wrong way, and she wasn't very cooperative with him." A young woman came over to Theo and asked him where he wanted the green beans. He excused himself and went to the kitchen for a few minutes before returning.

Theo wiped his hands on his apron. "Perhaps you could talk to her."

"Do you think Kat would tell me anything she hasn't already told you or the police?"

"When she looks at me, I can see the pity in her eyes. She is afraid of hurting me more, but I want to know everything." His eyes filled with tears, and he tapped Enid's notepad again. "All that matters is getting Hari back. You tell Kat that for me. Please."

"Alright, I'll talk to her, and if she tells me anything useful, I'll let you know."

"Thank you, Ms. Blackwell. I know you will help me."

As Enid left the soup kitchen, her heart ached for this father who longed to see his daughter again.

• • •

When Enid called Kat and heard her voice mail message, she knew it was pointless to ask her to call back: "Hi, this is Kat. I'm either busy studying or partying. Whatever. I don't have time to call you back." After several more tries, a female voice answered. "Why do you keep calling me? What do you want?"

"Kat, I'm sorry to bother you, but I need to talk with you. I'm Enid Blackwell, a reporter and a friend of Theo Linard. He asked me to talk with you."

The silence was so long that Enid thought she had been cut off. "Kat, are you there?"

This time Kat's voice was much softer. "Is he okay?"

"He's doing as well as can be expected under the circumstances. I'm doing a story for the *Palmetto Weekly* on Hari's disappearance. Theo suggested I talk with you."

Kat's tone sharpened again. "I'm not talking to any more reporters. The last one was a jerk."

"Wait, don't hang up. Please. I won't take much of your time, and I can keep your name out of it. I know you'd like to help Theo. Just fifteen minutes. That's all I ask."

Kat hesitated. "I'll meet you at the Java Cult in a few. It's a coffee shop near campus. But it's for Theo, not you." She hung up.

Enid grabbed her tote and rushed out to meet Kat. This was the same place in the photo Theo had, and it was only a short distance away. Parking was notoriously bad near the campus. She found a place a few blocks away and practically ran to the coffee shop, hoping Kat wouldn't leave before she got there.

CHAPTER 13

The Java Cult was one of those places you wouldn't go in unless someone reputable recommended it. It was upstairs in a small building that looked like it might collapse from years of neglect. Enid climbed the creaking wooden stairs, following the small neon arrow on the wall. An aroma hung in the air, which Enid recognized from her own years at college. Her first attempt at smoking pot left her dizzy and nauseous, so she never tried it again.

Sitting in the corner was a girl with dark hair and green streaks in it. Enid approached her cautiously. "Kat?" To Enid's surprise, Kat was reading the *NY Times* business and financial section.

"You the reporter?"

Enid nodded. "May I sit down?"

Kat folded the newspaper without responding.

Enid decided small talk and niceties would be wasted on the young woman. "Thanks for seeing me. I won't keep you long." Enid pulled a photo from her folder filled with information on Hari. "Why did you give this photo of the coffee shop to Theo?"

Kat looked at it but remained silent.

"What was the significance of him knowing about this place? Does it have anything to do with Hari's disappearance?"

"I didn't say it did."

"There must be a reason you gave it to Theo."

"How much of what I tell you are you going to put in the story?"

"My story is about Theo and his trying to find his daughter. Is there anything you can tell me that you haven't already told Theo or the police?"

"I guess Theo told you I didn't like that prick cop."

Enid smiled. "He might have mentioned it." She closed her notepad. "Look, I won't take notes. Just tell me anything you can about Hari. If there's something I get from you that I can't get anywhere else, I'll ask before I use it. Deal?"

Kat's shrugged her shoulders. "Whatever." She glanced around the room, as if looking for someone. "Me and Hari got to be close friends real quick. She really got me, know what I mean? She was like the sister I wish I had. Anyway, she was always good about telling me where she was going and when she'd be back." She paused as if reflecting. "I wasn't so good at telling her, though."

"What about the day she disappeared?"

"She said she was going to the library to study and would be back later. But I got worried about ten o'clock and texted her."

"Did she text back?"

"She texted me not to worry." Kat shrugged her shoulders. "But it just didn't sound right."

"Why is that?"

"If she didn't want me to worry, she'd have said 'DW' instead of writing it out."

Enid resisted the urge to open her notepad again. "Is that the last time you had contact with her?"

"I tried to text and call her the next day, to be sure she was okay. But she never responded."

"Didn't you think that's unusual?"

Kat shrugged. "I do it all the time."

"But did Hari?"

Another shrug. "Not really."

"Did you tell all of this to the police or to the campus police?"

Kat nodded. "When Hari moved in our room at the beginning of the semester, I met Theo. He put his number in my phone and asked me to call if we ever needed him. I called him after a couple days and asked if Hari was with him. When I told him what happened, he called the police and flew to Columbia. The cops interviewed me like a dozen times. Treated me like a criminal. I guess they thought I had killed Hari and dumped her body somewhere."

"Why didn't you report Hari missing earlier instead of waiting several days?"

"I guess because I wouldn't want her to do that to me."

Enid glanced around the coffee shop. A few guys were vaping in a corner. A girl with blonde dreadlocks was squeezing a joint between two fingers while she talked to one of the baristas. "I have to be honest. This place is a little creepy. Do you come here often?"

"Oh, it's not bad."

"Did Hari ever come here?"

Kat leaned in slightly. "Hari wanted to talk to some people, so I set it up for her."

"Who did she want to meet with?"

"She was doing a paper on human trafficking for one of her classes. She asked me if I knew anyone who could get her on the dark web."

"You mean the deep web?"

Kat frowned at Enid. "No. I mean the dark web. The deep web is for amateurs. But the dark web is a small portion of the deep web that you can't get to with regular browsers. I thought you were a reporter. Don't you know anything?"

Enid's knowledge of the dark web, the shadow world behind the deep web often used for illegal activities, was limited to what she had read in a few articles. "Thanks for the instruction. So, why would Hari want to go on the dark web? Was she trying to find someone who was trafficking?"

"She said she just wanted to see what some of the websites looked like, so I set up a meeting with Tommy Two."

"Who is he?"

"He knows a lot about the dark web because he's a hacker. But he says he's a programmer." Kat pointed her finger at Enid. "Don't you say that in your article. Tommy Two, he's like a straight-up guy."

"Except for the hacking, you mean."

"He doesn't hurt anybody, like stealing their money or anything. He just gets information for his clients."

"I hope you told the police about this."

Kat played with a green strand of hair. "Kinda. I mean, I told them she was meeting a friend here to do some research."

"You didn't tell the detective about Hari's research into human trafficking?"

Kat looked indignant. "Like, yeah, kinda." She twirled her hair again. "I just, like, failed to mention the dark web stuff or Tommy Two."

"How long was this before she disappeared?"

Kat shrugged. "Like a week or so."

"How can I get in touch with Tommy Two?"

Kat nodded toward a back corner of the dimly lit coffee shop. A lanky man who appeared to be in his early twenties was hunched over a computer staring at the screen. "I've got to go." Kat's expression softened once again. "Is that girl they found, is it Hari?"

"We don't know yet."

"I hope not. Tell Theo 'hi' for me." Kat picked up a shopping bag from Loose Lucy's shop and left abruptly.

Enid drank the last of the now-cold green tea in her cup before walking to the back of the coffee shop. Not wanting to interrupt his work, Enid waited briefly but the young man at the computer never acknowledged her presence. "Excuse me. Are you Tommy Two?"

His fingers flew across the keyboard a few times before he looked up. "Who are you?"

"I was referred to you by a mutual friend, Kat. I need to find some information on the dark web." Sweat was trickling between Enid's shoulder blades. "I need to you to help me find someone."

CHAPTER 14

Tommy Two's eyes were bloodshot, and his hands trembled slightly as they hovered over the keyboard.

"May I sit down?" Enid asked.

He shrugged, much in the same manner Kat had done. Enid pulled a chair over from the next table and sat across from him. "Kat told me you could help me find someone."

"Maybe. Who are you?"

Enid pulled a business card from her tote. "I'm a reporter for the *Palmetto Weekly*."

Tommy eyed her suspiciously and then threw her card on the table. "I don't talk to reporters."

"As interesting as I'm sure your work is, I'm not here to report on your exceptional computer skills. I'm doing a story on a missing girl you met with."

Tommy Two leaned away from the table. "Whoa. I didn't have anything to do with any missing girl. I'm just a programmer who works for clients with special needs."

"Do you remember talking with Harriet Linard, or Hari? Kat says she set up a meeting between you and her."

"That the girl working on a paper about the sex peddlers, the one that wanted to go dark?" At least Tommy Two seemed to be more interested in the conversation now.

"She was doing a school paper on human trafficking, and she wanted to delve into that world to understand it better."

Tommy sat expressionless.

Pulling information from him was frustrating, but Enid knew the nature of his work made him suspicious of everyone. She reached into her tote and pulled out her wallet. "How about I hire you to find someone, and you can show me how you get on the dark web."

"Who you want to find?"

Enid wasn't sure she was ready to take this step, but it seemed like a good way to get information from Tommy Two. "My mother died of cancer. She was terminally ill, but the circumstances were, let's say, suspicious."

Tommy appeared to be interested again. "You mean somebody offed her?"

Enid took a deep breath. "I think her nurse may have hastened the process along. I don't want to do anything to her. I just want to talk, but I haven't been able to find her. Can you?"

Enid gave Tommy Two all the information she had on the nurse, whom she had hired to sit with her mother while Enid was working. All she had was the nurse's name, if that was even real, and the nurse staffing company she worked for, which had since gone out of business. He didn't write anything down, but his fingers moved nimbly across the keyboard. The tremors were gone once he started typing.

"This her?" Tommy turned his laptop around so that Enid could see the screen.

"Oh, my God! Yes. How did you find her so quickly? Are you on the dark web now?" Enid had searched online endlessly but had found nothing in her previous attempts. "Can you send me a link to that information?" As soon as she said it, Enid realized how ridiculous she sounded. "I guess not."

He reached into his pocket and pulled out a memory stick. "I'll drop it on this. You sure you're not here to burn me?"

"No, I'm just trying to get information, and you had the special skills to help me. I'll go ahead and pay you for this job." She paused. "Can I hire you to find Hari?"

Tommy Two pushed back from the table. "I don't know about that. I don't want the police crawling all in my space."

"This will be between us. I promise."

Tommy hesitated briefly and then ran his fingers across the keyboard again. "Here is what I showed that girl." He turned the screen for Enid to see.

"May I make some notes quickly?"

Tommy shrugged. "Suit yourself. It's your dime."

Enid wrote down the information, including an email address for a talent search agency that would "fulfill all requests." Trying to stay in reporter mode, she didn't want to think about the unsuspecting girls that were lured into the sex business with promises of riches and fame.

Enid pulled out three twenty dollar bills she kept in her wallet for emergency money. She didn't want to insult Tommy. "I know this isn't much, but can you take it as a down payment? I'll try to get you more later." She handed the bills to Tommy and was surprised he pushed her hand away.

"Buy me some coffee." He looked at his cup and shoved it across the table. "Triple espresso. Straight." At least Enid knew where the tremors came from.

Enid went to the counter and ordered Tommy's coffee. The barista cut her off before she could finish her sentence. "I got it. Tommy's triple."

Enid walked back to Tommy's table with the espresso. He had returned his focus to the keyboard and everything else in his world was irrelevant. She sat the cup on his table and left.

CHAPTER 15

Enid had planned to stay at the Glitter Lake Inn for the weekend, but Jack had left a message inviting her to stay with him and Rachel at the ranch. Ruth had a big party coming in and needed the room. Enid accepted Jack's invitation at face value, without hesitation. Jack was like family.

Enid had arrived around 8 p.m. last night, and she begged off having dinner with Jack so she could look at the information Tommy Two had given her. Upstairs in her room, Enid opened her laptop and inserted the memory stick from Tommy. A folder named "reporter" contained several digital files. She logged in to the guest WIFI code Jack had given her, printed everything, and then went downstairs to Jack's office to retrieve the copies, before returning to her room.

She spread the papers across the desk by the window and made two stacks. One for information about the sites Hari had visited and the second for anything pertaining to her mother's nurse. The latter stack she put back in her tote. No need to get sidetracked right now. She needed to stay focused on Hari.

Tommy had done screen prints for various online sites selling everything from escort services to hardcore S&M. Kat had said Hari was doing her paper on human trafficking, so Enid focused on anything that might be related. She lived in a bubble when it came to things like this. Who knew you could still get a mail order bride, although now it would be an internet bride. Some of the photos were of naked or scantily clad young women who looked to be in their late teens.

Why would Hari have chosen such a dark topic for her paper? She was studying to be a photojournalist, but there were other, less menacing subjects she could have chosen. Enid made a note to ask Kat why Hari had an interest in human trafficking. Enid then searched online for information about the subject and was shocked to learn that South Carolina was a "target rich" area due to its extensive agricultural and tourism industries. Farm workers were often supplied with girls, and conferences and other large events were ripe with men away from home, looking for something exciting and forbidden. She cringed when she read that most of the victims were between twelve and fourteen years old and lived for only seven years while enslaved. Most were sold ten or more times a day and suffered broken bones and abuse from their captors.

Enid picked up the screen prints again. One in particular caught her eye. It said, "Southern belles make good wives." Enid assumed "wives" was code for slaves in this context. She made a note to ask Tommy how she could find the people running this site. She also made a mental note to run this information past Jack. He was good at seeing things she might have missed.

After putting the information away in her tote, she tried to go to sleep, but she had a hard time relaxing. What she needed was a good night's sleep and a clear head to think about just how far she was willing to get involved in looking for Hari. Or looking for her mother's mercy killer.

• • •

The next morning, Enid awoke with a dull headache from tossing most of the night. She showered and tried to shake off the feeling of doom that hung over her. She had promised herself to stick with community articles. Weddings, showers, and garden parties were plentiful this time of year, so she would soon be too busy to chase people on the dark web. Yet, describing a bridal gown seemed frivolous in comparison to helping Theo. Besides, she had to face the fact sooner or later that she was drawn to stories like Rosie's—and now Hari's.

She went downstairs to join Jack for breakfast, following the aroma of fresh coffee and bacon. She was surprised to see the Madden Police chief sitting at the table with Jack. "Chief Hart, what a surprise." Enid pushed an errant lock of hair from her face and wished she had taken more time getting ready.

"What will it take to get you to call me Josh? Anyway, I'm a regular here on Fridays. I heard you were here for the weekend."

Once again, Enid was reminded of the efficient small-town communication network. News travels fast. "Ruth has a full inn this weekend, and Jack was gracious enough to let me stay here."

"That was gracious of him, although I'm sure he's happy you're here." Josh looked at Enid until she became self-conscious.

"True enough," Jack said.

Enid turned to Jack. "When will Rachel arrive?"

"Not soon enough. I've got two more horses to board, and I'm ready to turn that job over to her."

Enid headed to the stove. "I'll put some water on for tea."

Jack pointed to a teapot on the counter. "Earl Gray. Is that okay?"

"Perfect." Enid brought the pot to the table and sat across from Josh.

After they finished breakfast, Josh turned to Enid. "My contact says they still don't have the DNA results. They're trying to rush it because of the father." Josh stood up. "Well, I've got to go protect Madden's finest." He nodded toward Jack. "Thanks for breakfast. And, Enid, I look forward to seeing you again soon."

Enid despised herself for blushing. What was it about Josh that had this effect on her? "Yes, likewise."

After Josh left, Jack waved Enid off when she tried to help with the dishes. "Oh, no. You're a guest. Just think of the ranch as another inn, where you can relax and enjoy yourself."

"I'm glad that the Glitter Lake Inn is doing so well. And I'm so glad you didn't sell it."

"Seems I can't get rid of things." He gestured with his arm. "This ranch, the paper." He tapped her on the nose gently. "Some things I don't want to get rid of. Like you. You're always welcome here."

For the second time this morning, Enid was blushing. “You're a dear friend. What would I do without you?"

Jack cleared his throat and wiped his hands on a dish towel. "Rachel will likely be in around seven o'clock tonight. I've got a brisket slow cooking in the oven. For an animal lover, that girl sure likes to eat meat."

"I've got some work to do. I want to finish before Rachel gets here so I can spend time with her. It's been over a year." Enid mentally shook away the bad memories of the tragedy Rachel had endured in her young life, first losing her best friend and then her mother. "I'm so proud of her for going to college. And I appreciate your helping her. She would never have realized her dreams without you."

"She's a good kid."

"Before I get to work, do you have time for me to run some information past you? See what you think about it?"

Jack leaned back in his chair. "Sure. Anything you need."

"It's about the missing girl, Hari. I'm not sure what it means, if anything, but before she disappeared, she researched human trafficking for a school paper. She even visited some of the dark web sites, with help from a hacker named Tommy Two."

"That's pretty heavy," Jack said.

"It's possible she got into something over her head." Enid paused. "Maybe I have too."

"What you're doing is what you do best—digging around and finding answers. But you do need to be careful. Trafficking is serious business with big money involved. And this is still an open case."

"I just don't want to repeat past mistakes."

Jack put his hand on hers. "My dear Enid, what you did was not a mistake. You brought a killer to justice and brought closure to Cade's family. But you do need to tell Josh about this Tommy fella. Maybe he can check him out."

"I'll mention it to Josh."

CHAPTER 16

Enid sat in the Madden Police station, waiting for Josh. She had considered talking to him by phone but decided she had better share the information on Tommy Two in person.

"What a pleasant surprise. How's my favorite reporter doing today?" Josh asked Enid as he walked into the station.

"I'm sorry to bother you, but if you have time, I need to run something past you."

"Of course. Just hold on a minute." He turned to Pete at the front desk. "Any calls for me?"

"No, sir. All clear."

Josh motioned for Enid to go in his office. "Coffee? No, wait. I forgot. I think we have tea as well."

Pete looked up from his computer screen. "We do, sir. You asked me to get some in case Ms. Blackwell came in."

Josh looked sheepish. "Ah, yes, I remember."

"I can get it." Enid walked to the back of the office where the coffee pot sat on a folding table. The acrid smell of strong, stale coffee was overwhelming.

Cup in hand, she went to Josh's office and sat across from his desk. "Thanks for stocking tea. That was thoughtful of you."

Josh met her gaze. “Of course.”

Enid fingered a loose thread on her sleeve. “Before we start, may I ask a personal question?”

Josh grinned. “Not too personal, I hope.”

"Have you always worked in small-town law enforcement?"

Josh clasped his hands and looked down at them before replying. "No, but I've always been in police work, one way or another. I did undercover work in Albuquerque for a while."

"Why did you leave it?"

"Family issues." He cleared his throat. "Now, what was it you wanted to tell me?"

Enid filled him in on her conversations with Kat and Tommy Two, although she withheld his name, simply called him "the hacker."

"This hacker. Do you trust him?"

"Hard to say. He is quite possibly a criminal, although a helpful one. I never felt threatened by him." What would Josh's reaction be if he found out she had hired a hacker to find her mother's nurse?

"Want me to do some checking on him? Better yet, talk to Detective Pointer and bring her in the loop."

"I promised to keep my source confidential. And even beyond that, Kat may shut down if she finds out I've talked to Pointer about her friend."

"Well, then what's your alternative? Surely you don't plan to open your own investigation."

Enid looked down into her teacup and could feel Josh staring at her. She looked up and met his eyes. "Perhaps you could pass this information along to Detective Pointer for me. You know, as an anonymous tip."

Josh leaned back and studied Enid. Then he held up his hand to his face, pretending to be talking on the phone. "Hi,

Detective Pointer. Yes, this is Madden Police Chief Josh Hart. I have received information from an anonymous source about your missing person in Columbia. Yes, it came from someone in Madden, but I can't tell you who. I sorta made a promise."

Enid laughed. "Okay, stop making fun of me."

"Sorry, just couldn't resist."

Enid looked away from his deep gaze and shifted in her seat. "Alright, I'll call her. But can you please just give Detective Pointer a heads-up, let her know who I am? Otherwise, she probably won't take a call from a weekly newspaper reporter."

Josh make a note on his pad and nodded. "Done. I'll call her right away."

As Josh walked Enid to the door, Pete stopped him. "Chief, it's Detective Jan Pointer on the phone. She needs to talk to you."

CHAPTER 17

Detective Pointer waited for Chief Hart to pick up her call. When he answered, she replied. "Chief Hart, I wanted to let you know the body of the young girl found was not the person you were asking about. Similar characteristics, but not her. I'm on my way to see the father now."

"Hello to you, too, Jan."

"Sorry, but you know I'm not into small talk. And I want to get to Mr. Linard before he hears the news from someone else."

"I'll pass that information along to my friend. Her name is Enid Blackwell. In fact, she has some information that might be helpful to the case."

"I'll be back at the station around two o'clock, unless something comes up. Tell her to come in or call me to set up another time."

Pointer drove to the church and asked for Theo. As usual, he was chopping vegetables in the kitchen. "Mr. Linard, I'm sorry to bother you without calling first, but-"

"No, no. It's all right. What have you found out?" Theo wiped his hands on his apron.

Pointer motioned to one of the dining tables. "Let's sit."

Theo quickly pulled out a chair. "Please. Is it Hari? Tell me."

"No, Mr. Linard. The young woman is not your daughter."

"Oh, thank God." Theo put his face in his hands and sobbed.

She wanted to tell him that the odds were still against finding Hari alive, that is, if she was taken involuntarily. Nothing pointed toward Hari's running away, but it was still a possibility. Young girls often got restless or met someone and took off.

"We'll keep looking."

Even as she said it, she knew there were new cases stacking up on her desk. Hari had been gone for close to six months. She was either dead or didn't want to be found, and with no new leads, Pointer had only a limited amount of time to keep looking before her chief assigned Hari's case to the cold case unit. Pointer knew the case would never be "cold" for Theo, but the brass made those decisions, not her.

Theo pulled a handkerchief from his pocket and blew his nose. "I'm sorry. It's just that . . ."

"No need to apologize."

"Do you know who she is, the girl you found?"

"No, we're checking missing persons and dental records."

"Was she murdered?"

"It appears so."

"What will you do now to find Hari?" Theo asked.

"We're doing everything we can to find her. I'll keep you posted."

• • •

Enid waited about twenty minutes at the Columbia Police Department, waiting on Detective Pointer to return to her office.

Before Enid could respond, Pointer walked up. “Sorry I’m late. You must be Chief Hart’s friend.”

Enid shook Pointer's hand. "Nice to meet you, Detective."

Jan motioned for Enid to follow her. She moved stacks of files off the chairs and offered her a seat. "Sorry for the mess. I never seem to have time to straighten up my office.”

Pointer sat behind her desk and clasped her hands. Looking directly at Enid, she said, "Chief Hart said you have some information for me. And he said you’re a reporter.”

"Yes, I'm a community reporter for the *Palmetto Weekly* newspaper. I typically do community events and human interest articles. I was assigned to do a story on the soup kitchen where Theo Linard works, to help raise community awareness—and donations.” Enid paused. "But because of Theo's community work after coming here to look for his daughter, my editor asked me to include a story on her disappearance."

"So you're doing a story on this case." Pointer's face was tense again. “Do you have information that hasn’t already been reported? The previous detective gave numerous interviews to the press after Miss Linard’s disappearance, and it was covered extensively.”

"It’s been six months, and as you can imagine, the uncertainty and fear Mr. Linard lives with would be difficult for any parent to endure. My story will focus primarily on what his life has been like, as well as his search for her.”

“So what information do you have for me?”

“Mr. Linard asked me to interview Hari's roommate to get another perspective of Hari, you know, what she was like."

"The original detective talked to her. As I recall, he noted that she was a bit of a smart ass. Had orange hair one time, green the next, according to his description in his notes. I don’t recall that she provided any useful information. Anyway, go ahead."

"Kat told me about a school paper Hari was working on that might have some relevance to her case. The paper was on human trafficking, and Kat introduced Hari to some people who operate under the radar. One of them is a hacker who gave Hari information from the dark web. I've talked with him."

Pointer flipped through the pages of a loose-leaf notebook. “According to the case notes, the roommate said Miss Linard just didn't come back to the dorm, so she later notified the father." Pointer flipped more pages in the notebook. “There was a mention about a school paper, but nothing that raised any flags, as far as I can tell.” She closed the notebook. “But this hacker guy may be of help. How can I reach him?”

"I'm sorry. I can't give you that information."

Pointer gripped the edge of the desk with her hands. "Why not?”

"I promised to protect his identity as a source. Otherwise, he wouldn't have talked to me. He showed me some of the websites he directed Hari to. They're pretty disturbing."

Pointer stood up abruptly. "I need a Diet Coke. You want one?"

After Enid declined, Pointer left her office briefly and then returned. "I'm sorry, Ms. Blackwell. It's been a long day. This case is one of many." She pointed to the files around her office. "This is new information that could be helpful. I should probably thank you instead."

"I'd like to work with you and help any way I can, while protecting my source. I was reluctant to get involved in this story, but I am in it now and intend to see it through." How could Enid describe the pain in Theo's eyes when he begged for her help? She handed copies of the website screen prints to Pointer. "Here's a couple of the sites my source directed her to."

Pointer looked at the copies. "It makes you wonder how people can find pleasure in this kind of thing. Do you know if Miss Linard actually went on these sites herself?"

"According to Kat, yes, she did."

Pointer leaned back in her chair. "We considered that Linard might have been a victim of trafficking, but only because she was missing. As you've probably learned in your research, South Carolina is a magnet for trafficking activities. And, Hari Linard might have flown too close to the flame if she was snooping around the wrong places. From her photo, she's young, attractive, and petite. That's what these predators like."

Enid felt sick to her stomach. "I'm willing to ask my source anything you need to know. And I'll ask him again if he's willing to talk to the police." Enid held little hope that

Tommy Two would cooperate. He seemed to live in the shadows and wanted to keep it that way.

"Before we get you further involved, let me check some with some of my CIs, my informants. I'll show them Hari's picture and see if she's been making the rounds to these camps." Pointer ran her hands through her hair. "Honestly, I hope Hari, Miss Linard, just needed a break and will show up later. If not . . . well, some things are worse than death." For the first time, Pointer smiled slightly at Enid. "Thanks for sharing this information on the school paper and the hacker. Good work, work we should have done."

Pointer stood to signal Enid the interview was over. "Obviously, I'm going to ask you not to write about any of this yet."

"Don't worry. I won't."

CHAPTER 18

Enid barely recognized the young woman standing on Jack's front porch. "Rachel, is that you? My goodness, you look great." The last time Enid had seen her, more than a year ago, Rachel had bitten her nails down to the quick and her hair was thin and stringy. Now she was a beautiful young woman.

After they embraced, Rachel held onto Enid's hand. "It's so neat to see you again."

Enid decided not to ask about her mother. No need to bring up such an unpleasant subject. "Jack tells me you're doing a great job with the horses on the ranch. How's school going?"

"It's hard, and I don't have much free time. I hate that Jack has to do my work here during the week."

"He'd do anything for you, you know. You're the daughter he never had."

Jack came outside with a tray containing a pitcher, three glasses, and a plate of snacks. "Ruth sent some oatmeal cranberry cookies. Mind if I join you, or is this girl talk?"

"I want to hear all about what you're up to," Enid said to Rachel after taking the tray from Jack and set it on the small painted table between two rockers. "You're welcome to join us if you don't eat all the cookies," she said to Jack.

Enid could not help but think of Hari as she watched Rachel. She planned to talk with her later about the dangers on campus, where predators often targeted vulnerable girls.

"Have you stayed in touch with any of your old friends around Madden?" Enid asked Rachel.

"I tried to find my friend Lucy, but she's at USC now and her mom said Lucy had even stopped calling her."

"Did they have a falling out?" Jack asked.

Rachel shrugged her shoulders. "Dunno. She didn't mention it." Her face lit up. "These cookies are so good!"

"Have you emailed or texted Lucy?"

"Sure, but she must be really busy."

Enid and Jack exchanged glances. "I'll stop by and check on Lucy's mom. She used to deliver the *Madden Gazette* around town."

Enid chatted with Rachel and Jack about school and the ranch, but her mind was on how dangerous the world is for young women these days. "By the way, do you have a photo of Lucy? I'm doing a story about a student there, so I might be able to help find her."

Rachel pulled her cell phone from her jeans pocket. "I just sent you her photo. Here, I'll send you her cell phone number too in case you try to text her."

"If I find her, I'll tell her you're worried about her."

"I'm not exactly worried. Lucy's taken off before. But I would like to see her." Rachel tossed her light brown hair off her shoulder. "She was my best friend for a long time."

Enid tried to ignore the icy chill that was spreading through her body as she looked at Lucy's photo on her phone. Like Hari and the young girl they found in the park, Lucy was a petite blonde.

"I need to tend the horses." As Rachel stood up, she turned to Enid. "I'm glad you're staying with us."

"I'll be out in a while to help," Jack said. He watched Rachel as she walked across the yard toward the stables. "She's really blossomed this past year. I guess none of us knew the hell she was living through all those years." He paused. "You look anxious today. Is everything alright?"

"I never knew human trafficking was such a widespread problem. I guess I assumed it was happening other places but not here. When Rachel mentioned she had lost contact with Lucy, I began to worry about Rachel. Have you warned her about all the dangers on and off campus?"

Jack rubbed his chin as he did when worried. "I've tried to. Never been a father, so this is all new to me. But she's a smart girl and has seen more than her fair share of bad things. I think she's smart enough to take care of herself. Anything else bothering you?"

Enid wiped the condensation from the iced tea glass with her napkin. "I thought I had built a safe little life for myself. I wanted to walk away from this story, but I knew I couldn't abandon Theo. He needs to believe that someone was sent to help him. I hope I can."

"Before my wife Mattie died, she often read Kahlil Gibran. There was one quote she really liked, 'We choose our joys and sorrows long before we experience them.'"

"What are you saying?"

"I believe in a certain amount of destiny. Perhaps Theo is right. Maybe you are the answer to his prayers. Finding the truth is why you, me, and Cade chose journalism careers. The path you're on right now was inevitable." Jack gathered the glasses and put them on the tray. "I'm going in to do some paperwork. Got bills to pay."

The rhythm of the rocker was so relaxing Enid fell asleep. But the faces of Hari, Rachel, and Lucy kept appearing, and she work up gasping for air, the beginning signs of an anxiety attack. Pulling her cell phone from her pocket, she found Kat's number in her recent calls and tapped on the number. Since the odds of Kat answering was slim, Enid was prepared to leave a message when Kat answered.

"What?"

"Kat, this is Enid Blackwell. We spoke about-"

"I know who you are. I don't know anything else about Hari."

"Wait, if I wanted to find someone on campus how can I locate them?"

"What are you, the missing student patrol? Who are you looking for now?"

"It sounds like I've caught you at a bad time, but I'm trying to locate someone named Lucy Randolph. She's a freshman."

"I don't know her. Want me to look up her phone number?"

"No, thanks. I have it. Is there an electronic bulletin board or a way I can find her on campus?"

"Maybe she doesn't want you to find her. I gotta go." The line went dead.

Frustrated, Enid found the text Rachel sent earlier and called Lucy's cell number. Not surprisingly, there was no answer. What was surprising though was the message itself. "Hi, This is Lucy, if you've called for something other than to wish me Happy New Year, leave a message." That message was recorded months earlier. Enid hoped that Lucy had simply forgotten to change it.

She heard the squeak of the screen door as Jack stuck his head out to deliver a message. "Josh called. He's headed over here. Didn't say anything other than he needed to talk to you."

• • •

A few minutes later, Josh's police car came up the driveway in a swirl of dust. He sat down in the rocker beside Enid. "Sorry for the intrusion, but I got some news today you might want to hear."

"It's always a pleasure to see you." She hated she sounded so formal around him.

"The body has been identified."

"Oh, no. Is it Lucy Randolph?"

"Who's that? Oh, wait. I know her family here in Madden. No, it's not her. Why would you think that?"

Enid exhaled deeply. "Never mind." She was uneasy that Josh made a point of coming out to here to tell her about the identification in person.

"She's one of the girls on the website your hacker friend directed you to. When Jan saw the girl's photo from one of the copies you gave her, she recognized the girl and pulled the missing person's report."

"That poor girl." She reached out and grabbed Josh's arm. "We've got to find Hari. It may already be too late."

"I knew you'd say that. Now will you tell me how to find your hacker?"

"No, I can't do that. But I'll talk to him again."

"I can't let you put yourself in danger. Again."

"I'll meet him where we met him before. It's a public place, and I'll be careful. What do you want me to ask him?"

"I assume he knows these are sites located nearby, or he wouldn't have given them to you. I want to know how I can find these perverts hiding in the dark web."

Enid nodded but she also knew the odds were slim that Tommy Two would cooperate with her or anyone else. Anonymity was essential in his work. But they had to find Hari, so she would do or say whatever was needed to convince Tommy to help them.

CHAPTER 19

Theo was smiling as he came out of the church kitchen to greet Enid. "Ms. Blackwell. I am glad you are here."

"You seem happy today."

"I dreamed about Hari last night. She told me she was coming home soon."

"That's nice. I hope you're right." There was no need to discourage him if he had a reason to hope. "I sent the story about the soup kitchen to my editor this morning. I hope it helps drive some donations."

"That's good. Thank you."

"Can we talk a minute?"

"Sure, I'll get you some tea. You like tea, right?"

"Yes, thanks." Enid sat at one of the tables. An elderly man in dirty overalls sat in the corner, eying her suspiciously, as Theo brought the tea and sat across from her.

"I've talked to Kat. Did you know Hari was doing research for a school paper on human trafficking?"

"No. Is that important?"

"I'm not sure, but she met with someone who may be able to help us trace her activities before she disappeared."

Theo sat up straight in his chair. "Oh, that's wonderful. When you walked into my kitchen, I knew God sent you."

Enid shifted uncomfortably in her seat. "I'll be in touch again soon. Take care of yourself."

As she was leaving, Enid noticed a broad-shouldered, middle-aged man walk into the soup kitchen with the air of someone used to being in charge. He was wearing a hat and tipped it as he walked past Enid.

CHAPTER 20

Marcus Xavier James, or "Max" as he was often called, was indeed a man in charge. The African-American patrons of the kitchen often called him Malcom X behind his back, although Max was very white. In fact, his skin was extremely pale, without a hint of sun exposure. Theo always thought that was strange, considering that Max owned a farm. He also had a long scar across his cheek and down his neck. A farm accident, he had explained to Theo.

Max owned a number of businesses and was a very wealthy man. Most importantly to Theo, Max was a generous donor to the church and the soup kitchen's mission.

"Max, how good to see you."

Max glanced toward Enid as she left and then embraced Theo. "Theo, my man. How are you today? You certainly are looking well."

"I'm good, thank you."

"Just wanted to let you know, I'm making a big donation to the church in Hari's name. Maybe it will help bring some recognition to her and help us find her."

Theo wiped his eyes with the back of his hand. "You are too kind to us, Max. You and Ms. Blackwell both."

Max motioned toward the exit. "Was that Ms. Blackwell that just left?"

"Yes, I should have introduced you. She's helping me find Hari."

"Is she a police officer or private detective?"

"Oh, no. She's a reporter. She's good at solving things."

"Be careful what you say to her. Reporters can twist the truth to sell papers."

Theo shook his head vigorously. "Oh, no. She's not like that."

Max patted Theo on the shoulder. "I'm sure you're right, my friend. Well, I need to run on. I'll make sure the donation in honor of Hari gets well publicized."

"Bless you, Max. You're a good man."

Theo walked back into the church kitchen crying, but the tears were in gratitude for his friends who were helping him find Hari. He was sure she would be home soon.

Before leaving, Max spoke to the old man sitting at a table in the corner and handed him some cash.

CHAPTER 21

Enid looked up the dark stairs leading to the coffee shop where she had met Tommy Two. The space was dimly lit and devoid of any other people. The worn wooden staircase creaked under her weight as she walked up. Inside the shop, the aroma of coffee and cannabis, and the smoky haze assaulted her senses.

She glanced around the room and then at the spot where she and Tommy had talked. The table was empty, as if reserved, even though the rest of the coffee shop was nearly full. Being a regular must have its privileges. Enid walked to the counter and asked the barista who had helped her before if he knew when Tommy might be in.

"No idea. Probably pulled an all-nighter and catching some Zs."

Enid handed him a business card. "Would you have him call me when he comes in?"

The barista tossed the card on the counter without looking at it. "Sure," he said as he measured finely ground beans into an espresso machine.

After striking out at the coffee shop, Enid decided to try Kat again. No answer. She had made a note of Kat's address from Theo's notes. Since she was only a short distance away, Enid decided to see if she could find Kat.

The student housing building was fairly new and in good shape. She stopped a young man with Beats earphones on as he was dancing down the sidewalk. She waved her hand in front of his face. "Hi. Excuse me."

He stopped dancing and pulled his headphones off one ear. "Yo. Wassup?"

She showed him the address, and he directed her to Kat's off-campus student housing. Before she could thank him, the student had replaced his earphones and was dancing down the sidewalk again. He reminded Enid of Michael Jackson as the Scarecrow dancing to "Ease on Down the Road" in *The Wiz*. She watched the student grinning as he moved fluidly to the music. When was the last time she had been that happy and carefree?

Since there was no security at the front door, Enid walked in the building and found Kat's room. The door was closed, so she knocked lightly. "Kat, are you there?" No response. Enid was looking in her tote for a sticky note to leave on the door, when it opened.

A young woman with black, retro-style glasses had a textbook in her hand. "Yes?"

"Hi, I'm Enid Blackwell, a friend of Kat's. Is she here?"

"No." The girl chewed on her lower lip and started to close the door.

"Wait, may I ask you a few questions?"

The girl pointed to the books and papers on her desk. "I gotta study."

"I promise to be only a minute."

The girl hesitated briefly, and then opened the door. It was easy to see which half of the room belonged to Kat, as her personality was clearly reflected in the bright green and purple decor. Enid pushed some clothes aside and sat on

Kat's bed. "Did you know Kat's previous roommate, Harriet Linard?"

The girl appeared to be thinking and then her eyes lit up. "You mean the girl on the box? Didn't she go missing or something?" Her face was beaming as though she answered the bonus question on a quiz show.

"Sorry, I'm not sure what you mean about the girl on the box."

The girl reached down beside Enid's leg and pulled a cardboard box out from under Kat's bed. She pointed to Hari's name printed in a black marker across the top. Their dorm number was beneath the name. "Hari, right?"

Enid's heart skipped a beat. "Yes, that's her. Hari. What is this?"

The girl shrugged. "I dunno. Kat said she was going to take it to Hari's father, but I think she keeps forgetting. Kat said it was just school papers, or something like that."

Enid reached for the box. "May I take it to him? I know Theo, that's Hari's dad, and I'll see him later today. You can tell Kat I've taken care of it."

The girl shrugged again. "Sure. Why not." She glanced at her desk again. "I've really got to study."

Enid handed her a business card. "Here. So you can tell Kat who you gave the box to."

The girl took the card and studied it intently. "I like this design. Did you do it?"

Enid laughed. "No, my editor at the paper did." Enid walked to the door, Hari's box in hand.

CHAPTER 22

Enid spread the contents of Hari's box on the tiny desk in her apartment. Momentarily, she felt guilty for not taking it straight to Theo. Kat's roommate had been right. It was mostly assignments, class schedules, and other school-related items. Enid was tempted to throw it all back in the box and call Theo to see if he was at the soup kitchen. But, reporting is paying attention to details, her journalism professor used to tell her repeatedly. "Journalists who take shortcuts are soon unemployed reporters," he would say.

With that thought in mind, she sorted the stack of paper into assignments, schedules, and miscellaneous notes. There was also a folder with more papers in it, along with some photographs. Enid set that aside to look at separately. She looked at the shortest stack first: Hari's class schedule and her first-year adviser's office hours. Hari had been taking a full load. The assignment stack held a few completed assignments. All of them were graded "A." In the miscellaneous stack, there was a summary of a paper Hari had submitted for approval. The proposed paper was entitled, "The Underground Highway." As Enid read the summary further, she discovered it was about human trafficking. Enid's pulse raced. This was the paper that had led Hari to Tommy Two. According to her summary, Hari had planned to include data and a couple of real-life case studies in her paper. Her instructor cautioned Hari with a note: "While I applaud your interest in this topic, take care while doing your research with actual victims."

Enid reached for the folder she had set aside earlier. Inside were photographs of two different girls. In some of the photographs, the girls were typical teenagers, laughing and clowning around with friends. But some of the prints were disturbing. In these photos, both girls were thin and their eyes were empty and ringed by dark shadows. Before and after shots. But after what? Some handwritten notes appeared to be interviews with each of the girls. No names though. Enid took the contents of the folder in her hands and tapped them on the desk to straighten the stack. When she did, a business card fell out. On it was a name, Myra Nicholas, and a local phone number, but nothing more.

Enid reached for her cell phone and called the number. A young woman answered. "Yes?"

"Is this Myra Nicholas?"

"Yes, it is. Do you need help?"

"I'm looking for someone and found your business card in her belongings. Do you know Hari, Harriet Linard?"

After a brief silence, the woman asked, "Has she turned up?"

"No, I'm afraid not. That's why I'm helping her father, Theo Linard. Can I meet with you?"

Quickly, the woman replied. "No, I'm sorry."

Enid was afraid the woman was going to hang up. "Please. Wait. Do you know something about Hari?" No reply, so Enid continued. "I'll meet you in a public place. How about-"

Before she could finish, the woman interrupted and gave her an address. Enid quickly scribbled it down.

She looked at the time on her phone. It was getting late and dark. She recognized the street name. It wasn't far away. Reluctantly, she put her shoes on and grabbed her tote. Regardless of her concerns, she had to find out if this woman could lead them to Hari.

• • •

Before getting out of her car, Enid checked the address again to be sure she was at the right place. She then checked her surroundings. The neighborhood was one of the typical rental areas near the University of South Carolina campus. Most of the aging homes were now student rentals and in need of repair. Plastic lawn chairs were on several of the porches, and a large Gamecock flag hung from one of the houses a few doors down.

At the front door of the address the woman had given her, Enid noticed a surveillance camera overhead. She rang the doorbell, and a thirty-something woman partially opened the door, keeping the chain in place.

"May I help you?" the woman asked.

Enid handed her a business card through the slightly open door. "Myra? I think you are expecting me. We just talked on the phone a little while ago."

The door shut, and Enid heard the chain guard being removed. The door opened again and the woman stepped aside and motioned Enid to come in. The small brick house was practically dark inside. A dim light shone from the one-bulb light fixture overhead. "Come on into my office. It's right here."

Enid walked into what was probably the dining room at one time. An old metal desk and a few chairs were the only furnishings, other than a half dozen metal file cabinets along the wall. The woman sat behind her desk, and Enid sat in the chair nearest her. "Thanks for seeing me. As I said, I'm helping Theo, Hari's father, look for her. Your card was in a box of school papers belonging to Hari."

The woman seemed to relax her shoulders a bit. "I'm sorry if I seemed inhospitable, but we have to be very careful here." She smiled slightly. "I'm Evelyn."

"I'm sorry, I thought you were Myra Nicholas. That's who I talked with."

The woman stood up. "May I get you something to drink? I'm going to have a water."

Enid shook her head. While Evelyn was out of the room, Enid looked for anything that might give her a clue as to what this place was about or what they did here. There were no posters, brochures, or anything to indicate their purpose.

Evelyn returned with a bottle of water with a paper napkin wrapped around it. "I'm sure you're wondering who we are."

"I am a bit confused, to be honest," Enid said.

"First, let me clear up the name. You see, we are all Myra Nicholas. We don't use our real names in our work. So if anyone calls for Myra, whoever answers the call is Myra Nicholas."

Enid had heard of call centers using a common name for a group of customer service representatives, so Evelyn's explanation seemed reasonable. "That makes sense, but if I might ask, what is it you do here?"

"In a nutshell, we do whatever we can to rescue and rehabilitate sex trafficking victims. Hence, the name Myra Nicholas."

Enid waited for Evelyn to explain further, but she said nothing. "Sorry, I don't get the connection with the name."

"Saint Nicholas, also known as Nikolaos of Myra, was the patron saint of prostitutes. Since many human trafficking victims are sold as prostitutes, it seemed a fitting name for our center."

Enid laughed. "Sorry, I know this is a serious matter, but I'm impressed with your play on words."

It was obvious from Evelyn's face that she had explained the name more times than she had cared to. "How is Hari's father doing? My heart just aches for him."

Enid couldn't remember Theo ever mentioning the center. "Have you, or anyone here, talked with Theo? Is he aware of your connection with Hari?"

"No, all we know is what we read in the news."

"Was Hari a victim?"

"Not that we were aware of. She learned about us from a girl in one of her classes who we had helped. Hari asked to do volunteer work."

"So Hari worked here as a volunteer?"

"No, she asked but never completed the volunteer training."

Enid rubbed her temple with her finger. "I'm sorry, I'm just a bit confused. So Hari came here, asked to be a volunteer, and that was it?"

"Well, not exactly. Hari was clearly touched by our work. She came back later and said she was going to do a school paper on trafficking victims, and also a photo exhibit of them for one of her art classes."

Enid reached into her tote and removed the photos she had found in Hari's papers. "Are these girls your clients?"

Evelyn studied the photos. "No, I've never seen them. Hari told me she was only going to use pictures of her subjects' eyes, you know, the window to the soul. Perhaps she was going to crop these images later. She wanted to use the photos to tell their stories and to help us raise money for our work." Evelyn sighed. "Non-profits are always short on cash and long on need."

"Did she do research on any of your clients?"

"We asked our girls if anyone wanted to work with Hari, and a few came forward and showed interest. They said if it would help the center raise money, they would participate, as long as they could remain anonymous."

"Have you talked to the police?"

Evelyn looked surprised. "No. Why would we? We had nothing to tell them." She then put her hand to her mouth. "Oh, no. Do you think Hari's disappearance had something to do with our center?"

"I didn't mean to alarm you. I'm just grasping at straws, looking at anyone who might have information." Enid paused slightly. "Would it be possible for me to talk to the girls Hari interviewed?"

"She went missing before she got to talk with any of them." Evelyn shook her head slightly. "I feel so sorry for her family. Is there anything we can do?"

"If you think of anything that might help the police, please call Detective Jan Pointer." Enid scribbled on her notepad. "Here's her number."

Evelyn put the note in her top desk drawer. "If we think of anything, we'll call. But we only had two brief conversations with her. You see, lots of people want to help us until they realize how extensive the training is, how thankless the work can be, and how limited our resources are."

"I'm sure it's difficult work. May I ask why you started the center?"

Evelyn held out her arm and made a sweeping motion. "Each of us has either been a victim or has a family member or friend who was a victim. Unlike some of the bigger centers, those that get United Way funding and big donors who like to see their faces in the paper, we work underground and often use unorthodox methods."

"Do you work on the dark web looking for victims?"

Evelyn ran her fingers through her hair. "Ah, yes. The portal to hell. Unfortunately, we have to be familiar with the tools of the devil."

"Do you use it yourself?"

Evelyn shook her head vigorously. "Oh, no. I'm a bit superstitious. You know, flirting with evil. We have a couple of volunteers who do that."

"Is one of your volunteers named Tommy?"

"Not that I'm aware."

"Never mind. Just thought I'd ask." Enid put her notepad in her tote and offered her hand to Evelyn. "Thanks for your time. I may be in touch again."

"I hope Hari shows up soon." Evelyn crossed her arms across her waist. "But for some reason I don't have a good feeling about her. Maybe it's just an occupational hazard. Anytime I see a beautiful, vulnerable girl, I worry."

CHAPTER 23

Theo was washing vegetables at the big sink in the soup kitchen when his phone rang. It was in his jacket pocket, hanging on the wall hook by the door, so he didn't hear it.

It was more than an hour later when he saw the missed-call notification on his phone. The caller had whispered something, but the reception was so bad he couldn't understand it. The number showed as "unknown," so he called *69 to find out who it was that called. A recording said no information was available on that number.

A few years ago, he might have dismissed the call as a junk call, but now, with all that had happened, this one gave him a strange feeling.

• • •

At first, Kat thought the caller was either a wrong number or a telemarketer. The "unknown caller" on the screen made her suspicious. "Who is this?" she shouted into the phone.

"Kat, It's Hari. Help me." The caller was whispering, making it hard to recognize the voice. It didn't sound like Hari at all.

"Whoever you are, this is not funny. I'm hanging up." But something kept her from tapping the red circle to end the connection.

"No! Please don't. I don't know where I am, but it's a farm of some kind. There are lots of small buildings here, and horses and pigs. I think it's close to where we went riding on your birthday. I saw a glimpse out the truck window. Help me." The line suddenly went dead.

Kat stared at the phone in her hand, unsure of her own reaction. Was it a joke? But then, how would the caller have known about her and Hari going horseback riding for Kat's birthday last fall? And why would Hari call her instead of contacting her father or the police?

After a few minutes, Kat decided the call was likely a prank. After all, almost everyone in school knew she had been the "missing girl's" roommate. And since she had posted photos on all her social media accounts of their horseback riding adventure, their combined hundreds of friends knew about that, too. Still, what if it really was Hari?

"Who was that?" her roommate asked.

"Probably just some sicko," Kat said as she grabbed her car keys, phone, and backpack. "I'll be back later."

CHAPTER 24

Weekends were special at the Glitter Lake Inn. During the week, many of the guests were trying to escape city life or celebrating some event, like a birthday or anniversary. Some just came to enjoy the relaxing atmosphere. But on weekends, the inn was frequently booked for larger events, and guests were often ready to let their hair down and party a bit. This weekend, there was a wedding at the inn, so Jack called Enid to invite her to stay at the ranch with him and Rachel if she returned to Madden. Enid had decided to decline his offer but had not yet returned his call. She needed to look at all of her notes on Hari before she wrote the first installment of Theo's story. It was scheduled to run in both the *Palmetto Weekly* and the *Madden Gazette* and was due to her editor by Monday morning.

Her cell phone rang. When she answered, she could tell right away that Josh's voice was different. Softer, somehow. He soon got to the point of the call. "Are you free this weekend?"

Caught off guard, Enid stammered, "Well, no. Not really. I need to stay here in Columbia and do some work. Why are you asking?"

Josh laughed. "Always the reporter, asking questions. I was hoping you could go with me to a wedding at the inn. If you don't save me, all the ladies will be trying to set me up with someone."

"Well, I'm sorry, but I don't have time to save you from all the women trying to snare you. You'll have to find another protector."

Josh was silent for a moment. "Sorry, I don't think my invitation came out right. The truth is, well, I'd like to spend some time with you. I was just trying not to be too forward. May I try that again?"

Enid couldn't help but laugh. "Okay, you get one more chance."

"Enid, I'd love to spend time with you this weekend. Would you do me the honor of being my guest at the wedding?"

"Much better." Enid was now torn. "But I still have to get this article done."

"I promise to give you time to work. My wife was a workaholic, so I was used to her setting boundaries. Just tell me to get lost when you need time to yourself. Jack says you'll be staying with him."

"Sounds like you and Jack have my schedule covered."

"Hey, don't be upset. I'll make it up to you when you get here."

After hanging up, Enid looked at the stack of notes and questioned her judgment in accepting Josh's invitation. Still, part of her wanted to go.

Her cell phone rang again. This time it was a local number she didn't recognize. "Hello."

"This is Kat's roommate. I met you in our dorm room."

"Yes, of course I remember you. Is everything okay?"

"Kat left suddenly and hasn't been back. She missed an exam." The girl hesitated. "I didn't know what to do."

"I'm glad you called me, but you need to call the campus police. I'll call the detective handling Hari's case."

The girl sighed. "Okay, thanks. I'll notify campus police now."

"Wait, before you hang up. What's your name?" Enid asked.

"Trudy." She hung up.

Enid found Pointer's number and called. Since this was her private cell number, she got voice mail. "Detective Pointer, this is Enid Blackwell. Please call me as soon as you get this message. Hari's roommate may be missing now, too."

CHAPTER 25

When Enid arrived at Jack's ranch, Rachel had already arrived for the weekend. Since Jack was at the newspaper, Enid and Rachel sat on the porch, enjoying the nearly perfect weather. They watched a small, mixed breed dog Rachel had adopted wrestle with a tennis ball on the ground.

"I know Jack doesn't need something else to take care of while I'm away during the week, but I just couldn't let them euthanize her. No one wanted her." As if the mutt knew she was being talked about, she looked at Rachel and tilted her head. "Hey, you," Rachel cooed. "I haven't named her yet, but she answers to 'Hey You' pretty good."

"She looks like a Sophia to me." The pup ran up to Enid and tried to jump on her lap. "See, I told you that was her name."

"Okay, then. Sophia it is."

"I never had any sisters or brothers, but I had a cousin named Sophia I played with. She was so sweet. Beautiful, in her own funny way."

"Do you still see her?"

"No, she died years ago."

"Oh, I'm so sorry."

Enid reached down and petted the dog. "She had a mischievous grin, just like you," she said to Sophia. "Good girl." Enid turned her attention back to Rachel. "How's school?"

"Good. I'm taking some computer classes I really like. If I weren't going to be a vet, I'd study cyber forensics."

"You mean investigating computer fraud?"

"Yeah, and tracking down people and following money trails."

"That sounds exciting. And complex." She paused. "Maybe you could help me find someone. I don't have much information."

"Sure. That would be fun. Who are you trying to find?"

"My mother was dying of cancer, so she didn't have long to live. One day before I left for work, she called me to her bedside and made me promise to get back into the career I loved and to enjoy my life. She was in good spirits. Looking back, I realize she was saying goodbye."

"I guess some people sense when they're ready to die."

"I hope that's all there is to it. She passed away right after I left. I just want to talk to the day nurse who was with her. My mother left her a significant sum of money in her will. Right after the funeral, the nurse left town and disappeared."

Rachel threw Sophia's tennis ball out into the yard, where the pup pounced on it. "Do you think the nurse had something to do with your mother's death?"

"I don't know. I just want to talk with her."

"Give me what you've got. I'll see what I can find."

A swirl of dust preceded the pickup headed toward the house on the long dirt driveway. "Well, I see Jack's here," Rachel said.

But Enid's thoughts were on that last conversation with her mother. *What happened after I left you?*

• • •

When Jack got out of his pickup truck, Sophia jumped up on his leg repeatedly until he picked her up. "Hey, mutt." He scratched under her chin.

"Her name is Sophia," Enid called out to him from the porch.

Jack held Sophia out at arm's length and looked into her brown eyes. She wiggled and tried to lick his hands. "Just what I need is one more thing to take care of." He put Sophia on the ground, and she began running around in circles, nudging the tennis ball with her nose and chasing it. Jack went inside and left the two women alone.

"Did you ever hear from your friend Lucy?" Enid asked.

"No, but I talked to her mother. The school said Lucy just dropped out of her classes. Her mom says Lucy should have contacted her by now, so she's going to ask Josh to look for her."

"Does her mother think she's in Madden?"

"No, but she thinks Josh can do anything, like some superhero," Rachel said.

Enid could see how the locals would feel that way about their police chief. He exuded an air of competence. And yet, there was something about him that seemed gentle. "I need to talk to Josh myself. We're going to a wedding tomorrow."

"Oh, really?" Rachel raised her eyebrow. "How sweet."

"Stop it. He asked me to go so all the women wouldn't hit on him."

"Like that ever stopped any of those hussies."

"Rachel Anderson. How impertinent you are." Enid and Rachel broke into laughter, and Sophia ran up onto the porch to investigate. "Sophia, don't let Rachel corrupt you," Enid said as she rubbed the pup's head and then looked at Rachel. "I know you're a smart young woman, but I hope you are very cautious on campus."

"Cautious about what?"

"I just read an article about the high number of sexual assaults on college campuses, that's all."

Rachel hugged Enid unexpectedly. "I like that you worry about me, but don't. I'm careful."

"Speaking of being careful, do you ever go on the deep web?"

"Whoa, that was random."

"Sorry, it's just that I met someone who gave me the information on my mother's nurse while he was helping me with some research."

"Did he find the nurse on the deep web? Is that why you asked me about it?"

"My Google search didn't turn up anything on her, so he used his own methods. I'll give you what he found to get you started, but I don't want you to go poking around on the dark web."

"Actually, I have been out there. It's mostly junk, you know, drugs, weapons, and sex for sale."

Enid nodded but the thought of Rachel getting anywhere near those sordid websites made her nervous. "Just promise me you won't get too curious or leave a trail that could come back to you."

CHAPTER 26

When Max walked in, Theo was putting a pile of dirty dishcloths in the washing machine at the back of the kitchen. "Ah, Theo, I'm glad you're still here." Max grabbed him by the shoulders. "I wanted to let you know we're doing everything we can to help you find your lovely Hari." He showed Theo a copy of the upcoming Sunday bulletin. A significant portion of one of the pages was devoted to Hari's disappearance, and to Max's generosity.

"You're very kind." Theo wiped his eyes with the back of his hand. "I can't tell you how much I appreciate all you've done to help me."

"Is your living accommodation suitable? Do you need anything?"

"I'm well taken care of and have all I need." As usual, Theo was tired from lack of sleep. Every night, in the quiet of his room, Theo tried to mentally connect with Hari. He had read somewhere that telepathy worked, especially with people you were close to. There were no two people closer than Theo and Hari, so each night, he talked to her and conjured the vision of her face as he remembered her in happy times. Some nights he felt a connection with her, but lately he had not.

"Did I ever tell you about my Belle?" Max asked.

Theo shook his head. "No, I don't think so."

"My daughter's given name is Juliana, but I called her Belle, because she was the quintessential Southern girl. All frills and giggles." He raised his hand and pointed to the ceiling with his finger as the minister often did when making a serious point. "But she was bright. Very bright."

Theo smiled. "Being your daughter, she would have to be. I'd like to meet her someday."

Max clenched his hand into a fist and hit his chest. "It breaks my heart to tell you that she is gone." He dropped his head.

Max was clearly emotional, and Theo didn't want to upset him further by asking questions about her fate. "I'm sorry to hear of your sorrow."

Max sat down in one of the chairs, as if he could no longer hold his own weight. He wiped the perspiration from his forehead and shook his head. "We have that in common, my friend. Both of us live with uncertainty every day."

Theo was in no mood to guess this afternoon. "So then, she's not deceased?"

Max stared down at the floor. "She might as well be." He then stood up so suddenly it startled Theo. "By the way, we have an abundance of produce, so you'll get a truck delivery tomorrow. Can you be here to accept it?"

"Of course. We appreciate your generosity." Theo decided not to press Max about his daughter. Besides, he had enough to worry about.

CHAPTER 27

Enid put on her earrings, the sterling silver ones Cade had given her on their fifth wedding anniversary. He had joked that wood was the traditional fifth year gift, but he doubted she wanted a rowboat. Her heart ached with regret and longing, not so much for the man he had become, but for the Cade he had been years ago. They had both changed.

"Josh is here," Jack called from downstairs.

Enid dabbed a little perfume behind her ears and took one last glance in the mirror. This was the first time she had been on a date, if you could call it that, since her divorce. "Be there in a minute."

Unlike in larger cities where the dress code for weddings was considerably more casual, weddings in a small town were often more conservative. She might have worn a dressy pants suit in Charlotte, but today she had chosen a simple print dress and heels. Hopefully, she looked good enough to ward off Josh's wannabe suitors.

Josh whistled when Enid descended the stairs. "My, my. You look lovely, Ms. Blackwell," he said in a mock Southern drawl. "I do believe your mamma would be proud."

"Why thank you, Police Chief Hart. That's very kind of you," Enid said, imitating his accent. "You look dashing yourself." Indeed, he did. His suit fit impeccably, accentuating his broad shoulders and toned physique.

Josh turned to Jack. "Sure you don't want to come with us?"

"Oh, hell, no. The widow Thompson has been after me for years. I don't want to tangle with her today. You guys have fun."

• • •

After the wedding, Josh invited Enid for a drink at the restaurant and bar just outside of Madden. "Just one. I've got to finish that article tonight."

It was too early for the late-night, rowdy crowd. The only other person sitting nearby was an old man who kept counting aloud on his fingers. Each time he hit "ten," he'd take a sip of beer and start over again.

Josh took her by the elbow and guided her to a table away from the finger-counter. When they were seated, Josh ordered two glasses of Cabernet Sauvignon. "Jack told me what you like. I hope I ordered correctly."

Enid was flattered and a bit uncomfortable with the fact that Josh had planned this moment in advance. "Yes, that's right. I'm impressed."

"You said you had to work on your article. Do you have any more news on the missing girl?"

Enid filled him in on what she had learned about Myra Nicholas and the center's work on behalf of trafficking victims.

"Do you think Hari's research has something to do with her disappearance?" Josh asked.

"I don't know, but we have nothing else to go on."

"I don't have to remind you to be careful, do I?"

Enid shook her head. "By the way, Rachel said you were going to look for her friend Lucy."

Josh sipped his wine and looked up at the ceiling. "Lordy, yes. That is if I can find time between looking for the Martins' cow when it gets out the fence, or watching the Tindalls' yard for the aliens they allege landed on their grass and plowed it up. Never mind that the tire tracks matched their son's Jeep." Josh shook his head and laughed. "Such is small town life."

"You make it sound funny and ... well, safe." Enid ran her finger around the rim of her glass. "It's not always so innocent."

Josh put his hand on hers. His touch was gentle and warm. "No, it's not. And I'll do what I can to find Lucy. I'll make a few calls. I doubt she's hiding anywhere in Madden. It's too small and too close to home if she's trying to get away for a while."

"When did life get to be so dangerous? Especially for young women?"

"I'm glad I'm not raising a daughter. I'd probably never get a good night's sleep."

Enid eased her hand from beneath Josh's. "I need to go work on that article."

• • •

After Enid finished her work, she allowed herself to recall Josh's touch on her arm. She even let herself fantasize about a life with Josh, living in Madden, even though she knew it was far too early in their relationship. The fantasy was more about her than about Josh. What she really wondered was what it would be like to be married again, not just to Josh, but to anyone other than Cade. Could she ever trust another man? Cade changed after they had been married. But then, so had she. Had she caused Cade to change? Had she driven him away with her insistence to return to journalism and then to find Rosie's killer? Or was Cade ready to move on anyway?

Tired of wrestling with the demons in her head, Enid made herself a cup of tea before uploading the article to her editor.

CHAPTER 28

Enid had dozed off while reading John Grisham's latest novel, when her cell phone rang. Still a little disoriented, she didn't look at the screen before answering. "Hello?"

"It's me, Josh. Did I wake you?"

Enid sat up in bed. It was nearly midnight. "No, I was just reading." Maybe something had happened to Jack. Or Rachel. "Is everything okay?"

"I'm sorry to bother you so late, but I got a call I thought you might want to know about. I'm headed there now."

Enid's senses were on full alert now. "Where are you headed? What's going on?"

"After you reported that Kat was missing, the Columbia police pinged her cell phone, and it's just outside of Madden but in the county. The sheriff is short on deputies this weekend, so I'm helping them since things are pretty slow here."

"That's terrible. Will you call me later and fill me in? It doesn't matter what time. I doubt I'll sleep much until I hear from you anyway."

"I'll call you later." Before Josh hung up, he added, "It was great being with you today. I really like you, Enid Blackwell." He hung up before Enid had a chance to reply, which was probably a good thing. She wasn't sure she was ready to commit to a relationship, but she didn't want to shut the door either.

• • •

Despite the circumstances, Josh couldn't help smiling to himself after talking with Enid. He had to admit, she was getting to him. There was something about her quiet resolve that fascinated him. If nothing else, he wanted to learn more about her. At the same time, he reminded himself to take it easy, especially since she had just finalized her divorce.

He punched in the coordinates the county sheriff had given him and followed the mechanical navigation voice down a county road. He turned off onto a dirt road, as instructed. His headlights provided only minimal illumination, as there were no streetlights or nearby houses. Deep woods lined both sides of the road. Instinctively, he patted his holster for reassurance.

According to the route map on the GPS screen, he was in the area where they had traced the ping. The road turned sharply, and suddenly, a stopped vehicle appeared on the shoulder. He slammed on the brakes to avoid hitting it and parked behind the vehicle, so that his headlights were shining directly on it. There didn't appear to be anyone in the car. The driver's door was slightly ajar, and the seatbelt strap was hanging out, nearly touching the ground. He left his motor running, and got out of the car.

With his flashlight in one hand and his gun in the other, he called out, "Hello. Anybody there?" His voice cut through the pitch darkness. When a rabbit darted across the road, Josh jumped slightly. He aimed the flashlight toward the abandoned car and then slowly opened the door. A cell phone was lying on the front seat, its screen shattered. A quick visual check revealed a backpack in the floorboard behind the driver's seat. He put latex gloves on and checked the glove compartment. No registration or other identifying papers.

Another movement in the woods prompted him to turn around quickly. Josh scanned the area with his tactical flashlight and saw movement in the brush, probably a possum or raccoon. He returned to his car and radioed the county sheriff's office. "You probably need to send a crime scene tech out here. It doesn't look good."

CHAPTER 29

Early mornings at Max's farm were a flurry of activity. The cows had to be milked, the chickens fed, and their eggs gathered. There was only one horse on the farm, a feisty thoroughbred that his daughter, Juliana, had begged him to save from being slaughtered. She had shunned the horse's registered name and instead called him Escape, since he had narrowly avoided a dire fate. A thoroughbred that could no longer race was pretty useless, especially on a produce farm. Perhaps on wealthy spreads in Kentucky, they were put out to pasture to live out their lives, but not here. Max had explained all this to Juliana, but she was adamant that they save the horse. Escape was too spirited for most to ride, but Juliana had somehow won his trust. He remained skittish and sometimes threw her to the ground, but her love for the discarded horse never wavered.

In the years Juliana had been gone, Max's unwavering longing for his daughter was as steadfast as her love had been for her equine best friend. Each day, Max allowed himself to hope that this would be the day when Juliana walked through the door and came running to him, throwing her arms around him and begging his forgiveness for breaking his heart.

As he did each morning, Max reviewed the day's work plan with the handful of Hispanic workers who helped him. None of them stayed on the farm, and in fact, they were given explicit instructions that they must leave by five o'clock each afternoon. Anyone violating this order would be terminated immediately. Oddly, none of them questioned Max's strange rules, like never going into any of the outbuildings except those specifically related to their work. In addition to the big barn, the farm had several smaller buildings. The property spread over nearly three thousand acres, but Max had rebuffed any offers to sell off any of the land to developers.

The workers often joked about Max behind his back, especially about his pale appearance and strange ways. But he paid more than the other farms in the area and always on time. When the crops were plentiful, the workers were allowed to share in the bounty. At Christmas, Max paid them a cash bonus. He was, in the eyes of his workers, a kind man.

Taking care of Escape was solely Max's job. He brushed the thoroughbred until his coat took on the subtle sheen of old wooden floors that had been waxed for decades. He had built a riding arena for Juliana, forbidding her to ride Escape on the trails in and around the farm. After the morning feeding, Max put Escape in the white fenced arena to get exercise. Occasionally, Max allowed one of the workers to put a long tether on the horse and run it around the enclosed area. Max was determined to keep Escape healthy for the day when Juliana returned.

• • •

Enid was wide awake this time when Josh called. "I'll be over in a few minutes, if that's okay, and fill you in on last night. Sorry I didn't get a chance to call earlier."

About thirty minutes later, she heard Jack and Josh talking downstairs. Josh offered to take them both to breakfast at the diner, but Jack insisted on cooking blueberry pancakes for everyone. Rachel had returned to school, and Jack seemed to be missing her already. Josh and Enid settled around the big farm style table, while Jack put the food on the three plates.

"Eat up. This is Ruth's recipe, so you know it'll be good."

"I need to see her while I'm here," Enid said.

Josh poured a generous helping of maple syrup on his pancakes. "When are you headed back to Columbia?" he asked Enid.

"I want to go back today, so I can talk to my editor, and to Theo."

"Tell us what happened last night. I can't wait to hear if you found Kat."

Josh took a large gulp of coffee before answering. "Well, I found her phone."

"What do you mean?" Jack asked.

"Her cell phone was in a car abandoned on a dirt road off one of the county roads. They're still trying to find out how the car is connected to Kat. It's registered to someone in New Jersey, probably where she's from. We're trying to locate her family."

"Was there a sign of struggle, any blood or anything in the car?" asked Jack.

Enid's chest felt tight.

"The screen was shattered, but the phone was still working. There was a backpack in the car with Kat's wallet, student ID, and a few other things."

Enid sipped her tea slowly. The pancakes had lost their appeal. "What do you think happened to her?"

"I don't know, but it doesn't look good." Josh ate the last bite on his plate. "Oh, I almost forgot. Detective Pointer wants to talk to you today."

"I'll see her when I get back home."

Enid could feel Jack watching her and Josh, and it made her uncomfortable. It felt like an odd threesome.

Jack began clearing the table. "I'll leave you two alone. Just leave everything on the counter. I'll get it later." He kissed the top of Enid's head. "Don't be a stranger. Come back soon."

She couldn't help but notice the sadness in his eyes. "I need to talk to you about something later. I'll call you," she said.

Josh got a phone call and had to leave, so Enid straightened up the kitchen. She assumed Jack had gone to the inn. Ruth had told her that he often sat by the lake watching the sun dance on Glitter Lake.

CHAPTER 30

Enid sat across from Detective Pointer, trying not to wither under her glare. "Every time I turn around on this case, you seem to be there. I don't know whether to congratulate you or tell you to stay out of the way. "

Enid recalled similar words from the former Madden police chief more than a year ago.

"I didn't know you had been to see Kat's roommate, Trudy. She gave me your business card."

"Are you handling Kat's disappearance as well?"

Pointer leaned back in her desk chair and stared at the ceiling. "I'm sure neither of us thinks it's a coincidence that Harriett Linard disappears and then her roommate at school also goes missing." She pulled back up to her desk and stared at Enid.

"No, and I also don't think it's a coincidence that Hari was doing research on missing girls and then goes missing herself."

"In spite of the fact that you're a reporter, I like you. And Josh told me about what happened last year. You're lucky to be alive." A slight hint of a smile. "I wish I could forbid you to interfere any further. But I can't, and I doubt it would stop you anyway. Plus, I need to know what you know. Josh says you're good people, and I trust his judgment."

The intimate comment about Josh bothered Enid, although she told herself it was meaningless. "What do you want to know?" Enid pulled a bulging folder from her leather tote. "I've got my notes here."

For the next half hour, Enid shared everything she had learned with Pointer, except for Tommy Two's name. "I'm glad we had a chance to talk. Despite what you think about me, we both want the same thing—to help Theo find his daughter."

"As much as I hate to admit it, you've done a good job unearthing some details we didn't have." Pointer gestured to the files on her desk and on the floor. "There's just not enough time or manpower to check every detail." She raised her palm. "Before you say anything, I realize that's not a decent excuse."

"If there's nothing else, I need to talk to Theo."

"Before you go, I have a proposal. You have an inside track with that hacker guy and that human trafficking support center. You really pulled good information from both sources."

"Perhaps they realized I was there to help."

"Ouch. I'll ignore that for now. Anyway, you can probably persuade the center to talk to me, but I doubt the hacker is going to agree to cooperate. Despite what you may think, I do respect the value of confidential sources and the need to protect them. I have my own sources." She paused. "But if you know of any crimes he's committed, I expect you to tell me."

Enid wasn't sure where this conversation was going, but she was ready to leave. "I'm glad you understand about protecting sources. What is the proposal you mentioned?"

Pointer came from behind her desk and sat on the edge of it, near Enid. "I was hoping you'd help us with the hacker, you know, serve as a line of communication."

When Enid didn't respond immediately, Pointer returned to her desk chair. "It would mean an exclusive when we wrap this up. We can't withhold information from the other papers, but you'd get first crack at it, and I'll make sure you get what you need."

Enid wasn't sure she wanted to be in bed with Detective Pointer, but on the other hand, getting an exclusive on a crime just didn't happen to weekly community reporters. Not in real life. "I'll think about it."

"I need your help, and I'm willing to help you in return."

Enid squared her shoulders. "I'll do what I can, but only because it will help Theo. Despite my initial reluctance to get involved, I want to help him find his daughter. I'm a reporter, and it's my job to uncover the truth. If helping you brings closure to Hari's case, then I'll help you. In return, I'd like for you to give this case the priority it deserves. Now tell me what you need from my sources."

• • •

At the coffee shop, Enid was relieved to find Tommy Two at his usual table. He didn't look too happy when she sat down across from him. "I'm sorry to bother you," she said. "But I need your help again."

Tommy's hands were flying across the keyboard, and he acted like he had not heard her.

"I promise to be brief."

He finally looked up. "Why are you bothering me? I gave you what you needed."

"Here's the thing. Kat introduced you to Hari, and Hari went missing. Now Kat is missing. That puts you squarely in the middle of all this."

For the first time, Tommy looked genuinely concerned. "She was supposed to meet me yesterday. Never showed." His hands were shaking again.

"What did she want? Did she tell you?"

Tommy Two shook his head. "No."

Enid pulled a sheet of paper from her tote. "You gave me this information when we met earlier." She pointed to the girl in the low-resolution screen shot. "She was found dead, presumably murdered. I need to know if this website server is local?"

Tommy closed his laptop and clasped his hands on top of it. "I told you, I mine data. I don't know anything about these sites. Never looked at them until Hari asked me to snoop around."

"This is important. It might even be life and death. Can you find out exactly where this site is?"

"Are you going to give this information to the police?"

"Yes, but I've refused to give up your identity. You can trust me on that."

Tommy held his espresso cup with both hands and took a sip. "I'll see what I can do. Give me a day or so. Like I said, this ain't my playpen, and I got clients waiting."

Enid gave him her business card. "I'll expect a call from you when you have something. Remember, time is critical. People's lives may depend on it."

Tommy nodded and started typing again.

CHAPTER 31

The morning light coming through the small barred window woke Hari, just as it did every day for the past few months. She had always considered herself an optimist and someone who saw the best in others. But her resolve had been tested lately. Would she ever see her father again? What was her captor's purpose in keeping her locked up in this place?

As best she could tell, she was in a small, separate building, since she never heard any noises or voices nearby. Occasionally, she heard what sounded like the farm tractor she had seen on her uncle's farm years ago. Once she heard voices just outside speaking in Spanish.

Her captor had only spoken a few words to her. During his visits, he caressed her hair and gently touched her cheek with the back of his hand. Never once had he tried to hurt or abuse her, but his intimacy made her skin crawl. For the first time in her relatively short life, she was deeply depressed. She couldn't help but wonder what endgame he had planned for her.

Her captor would be in soon to feed her and visit with her. The food was good and plentiful, lots of fresh vegetables with baked chicken or broiled fish for lunch, and an assortment of crackers, cheese, and fruit at night. What she wouldn't give for a Wendy's hamburger and fries.

Within a few minutes, she heard the key turning in the deadbolt. It was a sound she both looked forward to and dreaded. Human interaction, even with her captor, was welcome at this point. On the other hand, she was waiting for his next move. Would he kill her, rape her, sell her? He seemed kind in some ways, but the day he found out she had used his cell phone, which had dropped out of his pocket, he was upset. He raised his hand to hit her, but instead, held her to him so tightly she couldn't breathe. "Why do you want to leave me?" he kept asking. His cologne was cloyingly sweet and almost made her gag. She tried to memorize that smell in case she ever had to identify him. In fact, she had memorized everything about him. He looked familiar, but she couldn't place him. Had she seen him on campus? She had been captured not far from the school after parking her bicycle on the side of a building. When she leaned over to lock her bike to an iron pipe the students used as a bike stand, someone grabbed her from behind. She remembered a needle pricking her arm, and then everything went black. When she woke up, she was right where she was at this very moment.

She had finally stopped racking her brain to figure out why he was holding her prisoner. She had also given up hope of being rescued. Her life was now this one small room.

The closet was filled with frilly dresses. He kept bringing them to her and demanding that she wear them, but she had refused to dress like a little girl. There was a limit, and this was one of her conditions. No frilly dresses.

The door opened, and he came in to put a breakfast tray on the table. He then walked over to her and smiled, caressing her head like she was a prized pet. "You look sad today. Are you not happy here?"

This wasn't the first time he had asked Hari if she was happy. The first time he asked, she screamed at him and demanded that he let her go. After a few episodes like that, she learned all he was going to do was smile at her, as if he couldn't hear her. When she cried, he held her close, so she had conditioned herself not to cry, no matter what.

"I'm fine," she said.

"Then let's eat." He handed her the food tray. "Fresh asparagus and mushroom omelet. You'll like it."

He watched as Hari picked at her food. His expression, that strange smile, never changed.

She put her fork down and pushed the plate away. "I want to see my father."

"I'm your father now, and I'm taking care of you."

Hari knew from experience this conversation wasn't going anywhere, so she tried a different tactic. "I want some new clothes, new jeans and tops. Will you take me shopping?" She pouted as she had done with Theo when she was a small child. "Pretty please?"

He caressed her cheek, and Hari was surprised to see tears in his eyes. "We'll see."

Tired of playing games and being held prisoner, Hari screamed at him, "I want out now. What are you, some kind of pervert? Do what you want to, but I want out of this place. Now!"

"The world isn't safe, and there are some bad men out there. You're better off here, with me. I'll take care of you, my Belle."

CHAPTER 32

The knock on Enid's apartment door startled her. She had few visitors in Columbia. When she looked out the small peephole, she saw Madelyn standing there with a bottle of wine in her hand. Enid turned the deadbolt lock and let her in. "This is a surprise. And you come bearing gifts, too. What's up?"

Madelyn put the wine on the kitchen counter and got two wine glasses from the cabinet. "Hope you don't mind if I make myself at home."

"It *is* your home, after all."

Madelyn joined Enid on the sofa and handed her a glass. "Here's to good friends."

Enid took a sip. "I hate to be a party pooper, but you don't just drop in for chic chats. What's on your mind?"

Madelyn put her glass on the table and leaned back. "How do you feel about Jack?"

"Jack? You mean Jack Johnson from Madden?"

"Yes, Jack."

"He's a dear friend. Why?"

Madelyn took a deep breath. "How would you feel if I asked Jack on a date?"

Enid couldn't stop herself from laughing. "A date?" When she saw Madelyn's expression, she realized Madelyn was serious. "I'm sorry, it's just that you don't date, and I had no idea you were interested in Jack."

Madelyn mocked an indignant look. "I'll have you know I do date. Well, sorta. Occasionally. Anyway, how would you feel about it?"

"You don't need my permission to date Jack. But, just out of curiosity, did you have a specific event in mind?"

Madelyn slapped her forehead with the palm of her hand. "Oh, God, I forgot. I was supposed to tell you about the party at Glitter Lake Inn this weekend. It's just a small gathering. Jack called, and I took the message for you. I totally forgot. Sorry." Madelyn looked sheepish. "Truly, I'm sorry."

"Let me get this straight. Jack called to invite me to a party and you want to ask him to take you as his date?"

"When you say it like that, it makes me sound pretty awful."

Enid stood up and paced to the kitchen area and then back to the sofa. She had hoped to spend more time with Jack, as a friend she sorely needed right now.

"Are you interested in Jack?" Madelyn asked. "I mean, as more than a friend? Because if you are, I'll back off."

In the more than a year's time Enid had known Jack, she had thought of him only as a dear friend. But was he more than that to her? If Jack had Madelyn in his life, where would Enid fit in?

Jack's expression at breakfast yesterday when she and Josh were talking had stayed on her mind. She needed to talk to Jack and let him know that Josh would never take his place. But Jack as a suitor? A confidant, a friend, yes. But more than that?

"If you want to go with Jack, of course, I'm fine with it. I assume I can take a date, too."

Madelyn winked at Enid. "You mean that hunk of a police chief, I assume. Yes, Jack said he was also invited."

Madelyn had been a good friend, even when Enid had accused her of sleeping with Cade, Enid's ex. "Then it's all settled. Should be fun."

After Madelyn left, Enid got ready for bed and tried to sleep, but the snakes were back in her head, slithering through the memories, regrets, and losses of the past few years.

CHAPTER 33

The pounding in Kat's temples was unbearable. Slowly, she opened her eyes to survey her surroundings.

The last thing she remembered was driving toward the place Hari had described in her phone call—the farm where they had gone horseback riding. Then she remembered missing a turn and going down a dirt road. She tried to get back on the main road, but there was no place to turn around in the narrow space.

Suddenly, she remembered the man in a pickup who had forced her to pull over. Was he young, old? The memory was too fuzzy. He was tall and a little on the heavy side, that's all she could recall.

Her mouth was dry, so she looked around the small room for a faucet. A plastic bottle of water sat on the small table. She grabbed it and gulped it down. There was a small skylight on the ceiling—just enough to let in a sliver of daylight. How long had she been here? There was no bathroom, only a metal bucket. She made a face at the thought of squatting on that thing. At least there was a roll of toilet paper on the table.

Her legs were weak, and her heart was pounding. The feeling of a severe hangover was familiar to her, but she had not been drinking. Another memory flooded her brain. The man had pulled her from her car when she rolled down the window to yell at him. Why hadn't she just locked the door and called for help? Then she remembered trying to call 911, but he grabbed her phone and smashed it.

The only door to the room was heavy steel. Not much chance of knocking that down. She banged on it anyway. "Help. Let me out of here." Silence. "Is anybody there?"

Wait. What was that noise? She listened carefully. It was a knocking noise, like someone was beating on metal. What the hell was that SOS code she had learned as a child? Was it three dots, three dashes, and three dots? Or the other way around? She pounded on the door again: three taps, then three further apart, then three more taps.

The response was almost immediate: tap, tap tap, pause, tap, pause, tap, pause, tap, pause, tap, tap, tap.

"Hello. Who's there?" Kat screamed. She sent the SOS code again. This time there was only silence. Then she heard the lock being turned on the door. She backed into the corner, trying to get away from the tall man who had entered.

"I see you're awake." He placed another bottle of water on the table and pulled a candy bar from his pocket. "Here. In case you're hungry."

"Who are you? Why am I here?" Hating that she sounded like a victim, Kat continued in a louder voice. "Let me out of here now. I demand it."

The man laughed. "You demand it? My, my, aren't we feisty." His expression changed quickly as he raised his hand and hit her across the face. "Shut up and show some respect."

The force of the blow knocked Kat to the ground. Warm liquid trickled down the side of her face. "Please, just let me go." Even as she studied the long scar on his face, she knew she would never have an opportunity to identify him.

• • •

Hari held her breath and listened for another SOS code. Nothing. And then she heard a woman scream. It sounded fairly close. Her hands shaking, Hari sat on the floor, waiting for her captor but praying he wouldn't appear.

The door opened and the man pulled her up by her arm. "Look," he said, dragging her out the door. "You disobeyed me and look what happened."

The sunshine felt good on Hari's face, even though she had to shade her eyes. She tried to focus where he was pointing. A young woman was lying on the ground, her neck twisted abnormally to one side. She would recognize those purple sneakers with the sparkles anywhere. *Kat, oh, God, no. I should never have called you.*

Hari tried to pull her arm away from his grip, but he was strong and only tightened his fingers. "You're a monster!" she screamed. "Let me go."

Surprisingly, he did just that. Hari ran over to Kat's body and turned her head slightly so she could see her face. When Hari saw those lifeless eyes, she knew her friend was gone. Hari lifted Kat's body slightly and held her, rocking back and forth. "I'm so sorry. I'm so sorry." Without moving her head, Hari kept rocking but shifted focus to her peripheral vision. As she surveyed the area, she saw several small buildings, and off in the distance to the right, she saw what looked like a house. Probably the man's. To her left, she saw a dirt road. Turning her head just slightly, she could see fields of crops. She saw a large truck parked down the road a short distance away. Two men got out but never looked toward her direction. If she ran to them, would they help her?

The man grabbed her arm again and pulled her to her feet. "That's enough. She got what she deserved."

As soon as she was alone in her prison again, Hari fought back the tears. Even though her heart was breaking, she needed a clear head. Grieving would come later. She began plotting her getaway. There's no way he was going to be careless enough again to lose his cell phone from his pocket. And even if he did, she wasn't going to get anyone else killed. It was up to her to figure out how to escape. Hard as it was under the circumstances, her brain was in full problem-solving mode. Strangely, she was exhilarated. Ever since she had been in captivity, she had tried to reconcile with her own inevitable death and had denied herself the luxury of hoping for any other outcome. Now, she was driven by a new sense of purpose: putting this monster in jail where he belonged.

CHAPTER 34

Nighttime was especially hard on Max, because he was alone with only his memories. During the day, the activities of maintaining the farm kept him busy, although he mostly did paperwork and conducted his business by phone and email. After several skin cancer surgeries, he followed his doctor's orders and avoided the sun as much as possible. Occasionally, he would walk out into the fields, wearing long sleeves and SPF 45 on his face and hands.

Max considered himself a God-fearing man. Every evening, he held his Bible in his lap as he read scripture and prayed. While he asked for forgiveness for any sins against his workers or other acquaintances, he never sought absolution for holding Hari hostage. God had put her in his path as a replacement for Juliana, his Belle. He was sure of it. The minute he had seen her at the church kitchen, he knew that she had been sent to him.

Max was blessed with a comfortable home and plenty to eat. He was relatively healthy and highly intelligent. But the one thing he prayed for each night was Juliana's return. If she would only come back to him, he would let Hari go. Until then, she was God's reward to him for being a good father.

He hated the look of fear in Hari's eyes, because he had seen that same look on his Belle's face. Subconsciously, Max ran his finger down the scar on his face that extended down his neck. Juliana wasn't in her right mind when she slashed him, and if only she would return, he would tell her he wasn't mad at her.

Her smiling six-year-old face in the photograph on his dining table was the only thing that gave him hope. Juliana was so happy then. That's how he wanted to remember her. Not the way she looked at him years later.

How long had she been gone? Two years? Three? More? He had lost track of time, mostly because he didn't want his life to be measured by her absence.

CHAPTER 35

If the sun threw jewels across Glitter Lake during the day, the inn's waterside lights cast an array of shining baubles at twilight. Enid slowed her pace slightly as she and Josh walked from the car, so that she could take it all in. Josh walked slightly ahead to wait for her. Seeing him standing there in front of the elegant old inn, Enid allowed herself to dream once again of a new life. She wasn't the type to jump into any relationship, but she found herself thinking of him often.

She walked toward him and slipped her hand into the crook of his arm. It felt natural. Enid's glow lasted until she walked inside and saw Jack and Madelyn together. As much as she told herself she was happy for both of them, Enid admitted that it made her feel that she had lost the special bond she had with Jack. He was her closest friend, and her logic reminded her that nothing had to change because he was dating Madelyn.

Josh took her hand and jolted her out of her thoughts. "I'll get us some wine while you mingle a bit."

Enid nodded as she spotted Rachel talking with another young woman and walked towards them. "Rachel, so good to see you. You look amazing." The two women hugged.

"Enid, this is Lucy," Rachel said.

"You mean your lost friend?" asked Enid.

Lucy looked embarrassed, and Enid realized there was likely more to her story than a simple explanation.

"I didn't mean to worry everyone. I just needed some time, you know, to myself," Lucy said.

Enid took her hand. "No need to explain. As long as you're safe, that's all that matters."

Josh walked up with two glasses of wine in his hands, holding one out to Enid. "Hello, Lucy and Rachel. Good to see you both."

"Evening, Chief Hart," Lucy said.

Enid noticed that Lucy avoided eye contact with Josh. "I see you two have met," she said to Josh.

"We talked after she came home."

"I'm sorry I caused everybody to worry about me," Lucy said.

"We're just all glad you're safe," Enid said.

Josh took Enid's hand and motioned across the room with his head. "Come on, Jack's been asking me where you are." He turned to Lucy and Rachel. "Excuse us."

Josh and Enid walked over to where Jack was standing alone. Madelyn was talking to two women across the room. Jack grabbed Enid by the shoulders and hugged her. "So glad you came," he whispered in her ear.

"I'm going to talk to some folks," Josh said. "Enid, do you mind?"

"No, of course not."

After Josh left them, Jack said to Enid, "Let's walk down to the lake and have a drink."

Enid walked with Jack down the long center hall and out the back door. When they reached the lake, Enid sat on the memorial bench she and Jack had erected to honor their friend. Beneath her feet, buried deep, was the copper urn that had held the ashes before the remains had been scattered on the lake.

Jack sat beside her, both of them silent for a few moments before he spoke. "I miss her."

"Me, too."

Jack reached out and took Enid's hand in his. "Are you happy again?"

The question caught Enid off-guard. She thought before she answered. "I'm getting there. What about you?" She could feel the warmth of Jack's hand spread throughout her body.

"I'm getting there, too."

Enid gently pulled her hand away. "I must admit, I was a bit surprised when Madelyn said you two were coming together."

"I should have told you myself. In fact, I kicked myself for not personally inviting you." He turned so he could look at Enid's face. "I wanted to ask you to come with me, you know, as a friend. But then upsetting the police chief isn't a good idea."

Enid searched for words, unsure how to respond. Before she could say anything, Jack laughed and added, "Besides you're too young for me."

"That's a pretty lame excuse." She tried to make light of her comment, but the air between them suddenly seemed tense.

"There you are," Josh called out as he walked down the path toward the lake. "Am I interrupting something?"

Enid stood up. "No, we were just reminiscing." She looked at Jack as she took Josh's arm. "Should I tell Madelyn where you are?"

"Nah, I'll be up in a bit, give her a chance to work the room. Sometimes I think she should run for office. You two go have fun," Jack said.

• • •

Hours later, as they were leaving, Enid and Josh thanked Ruth for the wonderful party at the inn.

"That was fun," Josh said, reaching down to take Enid's hand.

Perhaps it was just the wine, or perhaps something else, but holding his hand felt as natural as when she and Cade had been happy together. She squeezed his hand slightly.

"How about coffee at my place?" he asked.

"That would be nice."

Enid had often wondered what Josh's house looked like. Jack told her that Josh had renovated an old cottage at the edge of town and had made it a comfortable home. When they walked inside, Enid stopped to take it all in. Recently, she had read an article in one of the magazines about a masculine makeover. While smaller than the featured house, Josh's home was no less beautiful. Enid had always been drawn to time-worn wood and a lived-in style that was welcoming and yet elegant.

Josh's house had that feeling to it. The interior walls were covered in stained wood, and the floors were wide planks, polished to a soft sheen. An antique rug covered much of the living area, and a cowhide rug covered the floor in front of the fireplace.

Enid sat in one of the leather chairs by the fireplace. "Wow, this place is beautiful. I love it."

"I'm glad you approve. Wait here, and I'll make you some tea." While Josh was in the kitchen, Enid watched the flames licking the fireplace, remembering the times she and Cade used to sit by the fire.

"Sorry it took me so long," Josh said when he returned with a teapot on a tray.

Enid poured the tea, then sipped from her cup. "It's perfect."

"Here's some dark chocolate, too." He handed her an elegant truffle.

"You're amazing. I could get spoiled easily."

Josh put his coffee cup on the table and took her hands in his. "And I would love to spoil you, Enid Blackwell." He leaned in and kissed her, running his fingers through her hair.

Enid wanted to protest, to push back. She wasn't ready for a serious commitment. But she was ready to live again, to feel again, so when Josh took her hand and led her to the bedroom, she followed.

CHAPTER 36

The smell of bacon instantly brought back memories of days spent at the Glitter Lake Inn. The recollection was both comforting and heartbreaking. After being with Josh last night, Enid's survival instinct was to run away, to protect herself from the hurt of losing someone close again. But the heart doesn't always listen to the brain.

"Breakfast is ready. Get up, sleepyhead. I've got to go catch bad guys," Josh called out from downstairs.

Josh's voice reminded Enid that she had not let Jack know she wasn't coming home last night, although he probably figured out where she was. Why did she feel like she was betraying Jack? They were just friends, albeit close friends. Besides, he was probably with Madelyn and appreciated the privacy.

She put her party dress back on, since that was all she had, and joined Josh in the kitchen.

"I know my breakfasts are special, but you didn't have to dress formally," Josh said as he leaned over and kissed her forehead. "Hope you like bacon and eggs."

"Thanks. It's perfect.

Before they finished breakfast, Josh got a phone call. "I need to go in and take care of something. Stay as long as you like. Just lock up." He reached in his pocket and handed her a house key on a key chain. "Keep it."

After Josh left, Enid reached for her phone to call Jack but decided not to. If he was with Madelyn, she didn't want to disturb them. Instead, she'd go to Jack's a little later and then head back to Columbia. If he wasn't home when she got there, she'd just leave him a note. Suddenly, she missed the sanctuary of her own apartment. As good as last night had been, it was too much, too fast.

As she walked out the door of Josh's house, her cell rang. It was an unknown number. "Hello."

A male voice she recognized but couldn't quite place spoke. "I'm sending you some information. I don't want to be connected to any of this, understand?" With that, he hung up.

CHAPTER 37

Before she got to Jack's house, her cell phone rang again. It was Josh. "Hey, just wanted to tell you how much I enjoyed last night. I hope it's the first of many."

"Me, too." Quickly changing the subject, she asked, "Do you have any free time today to help me with something?"

"Sure, anytime. What's up?"

"I got some information from my source. I need to show it to you."

After making arrangements to meet Josh later, Enid shifted her attention to Jack. This feeling of being torn between Josh and Jack was getting to her. By the time she got to Jack's house, she had convinced herself that she had confused Jack's friendship as something else. Jack was not home, but he had taped a note on the door to her room, telling her he was at the newspaper office. Usually, he would have texted her, but his note was a reminder that their relationship was changing, even if only in small ways.

A hot shower and a change of clothes did wonders for her mood. She was much more at home in jeans than a dress these days. She opened her laptop to look again at the information Tommy had sent her. It wasn't much, just a screen shot of a Google map. Had it not been for one landmark on the map, she wouldn't have known where it was. The spot Tommy had pinpointed was not too far from where Kat's car had been found, based on the location Josh had described.

She removed the identifying email address and forwarded the information to Detective Pointer. "From my anonymous source."

• • •

When Enid arrived at the Madden police station, Josh was on the phone, but he saw her and motioned for her to come into his office. Pete was at the front desk and kept his head down.

The sterility of the metal desk and painted concrete walls in Josh's office were in stark contrast to his warm, inviting home. The paint color was a pale beige, or maybe it had been white at one time. While waiting for Josh to get off the phone, she went over to the bookcase in the corner. One of her professors had said you can learn a lot about someone by what they read. Most of Josh's books were on police procedure and criminal psychology. This room was where he focused on work and nothing else. Beside the bookshelf, hanging on the wall, was a framed letter of commendation from the director of the FBI, thanking Josh for his help on a case. She made a mental note to ask him about it later.

"Sorry to keep you waiting," Josh said as he hung up the phone.

"I need to show you something," Enid said. "I'm going to forward this to your computer, so you can look at it." She removed Tommy's email address and forwarded it to Josh.

Josh studied the image on the screen. "That's not too far from here." He pointed to the screen. "In fact, that's where—"

"Where you found Kat's car," Enid interrupted. "That's why I wanted to talk to you."

"Your hacker sent this to you?"

Enid nodded. "I asked him to help me find the physical location of the server for the escort service where the girl worked. You know, the one whose body was found. She was on the website."

"So this is where the escort service is?"

"It's where the server is. I guess my source was able to trace the IP address. I doubt these people are technical geniuses, and they probably aren't capable of masking anything from experts like my source."

"Josh took his gun from the locked desk drawer. "Come on. You up for a ride?"

CHAPTER 38

Enid looked at the Google map from Tommy while Josh drove. Tommy had included the GPS coordinates at the bottom, so it was just a matter of putting them into the Garmin and following the instructions. About twenty minutes later, they made the last turn onto a gravel road. Enid looked around at the empty fields, the tall grasses swaying in the gentle breeze.

"There's nothing around here," said Enid.

"Sometimes the coordinates are not exact, but it's got to be close, assuming this information is correct."

"I'd bet on it," Enid said.

Josh parked his pickup on the wide shoulder of the road. "Come on, let's walk from here. I don't want to startle anyone into doing something stupid." He took his gun from the console as he got out and then walked around to open Enid's door. "You stay behind me."

"There's a 'No Trespassing' sign over there," Enid said, pointing to it.

"I saw it. There's a path over by this driveway. Let's take it. Those trees will give us some cover."

The path was well used, beaten down by countless feet for years. The dirt was as hard as pavement. Ahead, a small snake slithered across a fallen branch. Enid slapped at a bug on her neck, as she kept her eye on the snake.

"I'm glad you've got sensible shoes on," Josh said. He put his finger to his lips, signaling Enid to be quiet. "There's something ahead. You stay here."

Enid looked around to make sure there were no slithering creatures close by. "Don't be long," she whispered.

• • •

Still walking, Josh crouched as low as he could. Ahead was a metal building, with electrical lines running to it and a satellite dish on its roof. He crept a little closer and went off the path and further into the woods so he could get a better angle for viewing.

From Josh's vantage point, he was able to get close enough to view the front of the building. Not too far away, a small, single-engine airplane was parked on a paved runway. A closer look at the building revealed that the front was actually a small airplane hangar, and the back part was an addition with its own entrance.

He glanced back to make sure Enid had not followed him. She was hardheaded at times and a bit unpredictable, but he liked that about her. Comfortable that he was still alone, Josh glanced around and then crouched down before he ran to the back of the building. A sign on the door read, "Private." He put his ear to the door to see if he could hear movement inside.

Without warning, a large tan Belgian Malinois ran around the corner from the front of the building. Josh knew the breed as one often used in law enforcement K9 units. They could run thirty miles per hour and rip human limbs with their fourteen-hundred-pounds-per-square-inch bite strength. Instinctively, Josh reached for the pepper spray canister clipped onto his duty belt and aimed for the dog's face. It stopped barking momentarily but stood its ground, wiping its face with its paws.

Suddenly, Josh heard a man's voice, "Get him, boy." The dog lunged at Josh's leg, teeth bared. Josh sprayed him again. This time, the dog backed up slightly and whimpered, so Josh started running. When he saw Enid standing on the path ahead, he motioned for her to run. She moved like someone who had been a track star in high school. Yet another thing he now admired about her. Josh glanced over his shoulder to make sure no one was behind them, when a shotgun blast pierced the still air. It sounded like a cannon.

"Keep running," Josh yelled to Enid. He could hear the dog barking.

They reached the pickup parked by the road. Josh glanced quickly to be sure no one had slashed the tires. "Get in and stay down," he said.

Enid slouched down in her seat.

It wasn't until they reached the state highway that Josh spoke again. "Well, that was intense."

"What happened back there?"

"I guess we weren't welcome for dinner." Josh glanced in his rearview mirror to be sure they were not being followed. "I think we found the right place."

"Why? Did you see anything?"

"It's a small airplane hangar and runway with a separate building in the back. It's not unusual for folks out here to want to run off intruders, but I've just got a feeling about this place, especially since it matches the coordinates your hacker gave you. I'll check out the tax records when we get back to the station."

"Aren't you going to arrest them for shooting at a police officer?"

"No. I'd rather learn more about their operation first. They likely fired in the air, as a warning. If they are running an internet sex shop there, I want to find out more before we move in. Besides, it's not the first time someone tried to sic their dog on me. Comes with the territory."

Josh put his hand on Enid's leg. "I'm sorry I put you in danger, but you were pretty awesome back there."

Enid smiled slightly but didn't reply.

When they got back to Madden, she said, "I think I'd like to get back to Jack's, if that's okay with you. I've got some bug bites on my leg I need to treat."

"Probably red bugs. Take a shower and wash your clothes in hot water. Let Jack take a look at those bites. He'll know what they are and how to treat them."

Josh watched Enid get into her car and drive off.

CHAPTER 39

As she drove to Jack's ranch, Enid's breathing became shallower, and she began to sweat profusely. Another panic attack coming on. Josh was wrong about her not being afraid. She pulled to the side of the road and practiced the exercises Dr. Wright had taught her. In less than ten minutes, she had her breathing back to normal. At least the attacks were less frequent and less severe now.

Jack's car was not in the driveway, so at least she wouldn't have to face him right away.

Enid found Dr. Wright's number and called for an appointment. Luckily, she was able to get in today, so she sent texts to Jack and Josh letting them know she was returning to Columbia. Almost immediately, Jack replied via text.

Jack: You OK?

Enid: Yes, just need to take care of something.

Jack: Call me later.

• • •

"Dr. Wright will see you now," said the receptionist.

Enid regretted coming in. She was feeling better now, and the scare she and Josh had encountered at the airstrip was behind her. They were safe. If only she could be sure Hari and Kat were safe too.

Dr. Wright motioned for Enid to sit on the small sofa across from her. "I admit, I'm a bit surprised to see you here. How are you?"

"I had another panic attack this morning. I thought they were over."

"You were having them much more often a year ago, so don't diminish your progress."

Enid nodded. "I'm actually doing well, at least most of the time."

Dr. Wright put her pen down on the table beside her chair. "But you need to talk about something. What's on your mind?"

"I think I'm in love," Enid said, surprising herself.

Dr. Wright smiled. "That's great. I'm glad you've moved on with your life. So what's bothering you?"

Enid felt somewhat foolish talking to Dr. Wright about her personal relationships, yet she needed to. "Actually, I love one man, and I'm in love with another." She paused briefly. "Jack is my best friend, and I thought he was just that. That is until another friend told me she was dating him."

"How did that make you feel?"

"I feel like I am losing Jack."

"As a friend? Or as a potential mate?"

Enid had asked herself that question many times. "I'm not sure."

"As I recall, Jack is a bit older than you."

"Yes, he's about fifteen years older, but I never think of our age difference. He's young at heart."

"And what about the other man in your life?" asked Dr. Wright.

"Josh is closer to my age. He's charming and fun to be around."

Dr. Wright leaned forward slightly. "So, if I understand what you're saying, you love Jack, as a friend or maybe even deeper, and you're in love with Josh. Is that right?"

Enid nodded. "I wasn't looking for a serious relationship, especially not with a police chief in a small town."

"What do you think you need to do about this dilemma?" asked Dr. Wright.

As much as her therapist had helped Enid through a rough time in her life, Enid was annoyed with herself. What had she hoped to accomplish by coming today? She had already asked herself all the right questions.

"I can tell from your expression that you're looking for answers from me," said Dr. Wright, "but you know those have to come from you. How are you feeling? Are you depressed or upset, or just confused?"

Enid laughed. "Confused, at least about my relationships. But I guess that's life."

"What confuses you about your relationship with Jack? Can't he be just a good friend?"

"Of course."

"You and Jack were thrown together by a horrible tragedy. Sometimes that makes people unusually, perhaps artificially, close. It's understandable that you're reluctant to let go, or at least redefine that relationship."

Enid nodded. "Yes, I realize that."

"What is it that you love about Jack?"

"He's just such a good person. Everyone loves him, and I like spending time with him."

"But why do *you* love him, either as a friend or something more?"

"We have a lot in common. And, he's kind and generous."

"All good qualities in a friend or a mate. You've just got to decide which you want him to be." Dr. Wright shifted in her seat. "What about your work? Is it fulfilling for you?"

"I'm reporting on crime again."

Dr. Wright's left eyebrow lifted slightly. "That's interesting. How do you feel about returning to that kind of work?"

"At first, I admit I was more focused on protecting myself and my emotions than I was on the victim and her family. But then I realized I couldn't walk away from Theo, that's the father of a missing girl, and ever feel good about myself. I really want to help him."

"It's good that you've shifted your focus to others again. That means you're healing, willing to take emotional risks again. But is this what you want to do, as a career?"

Enid smiled slightly. "I've come to realize, it's who I am and what I do." She leaned down to get her tote off the floor.

"Just go slowly. If Josh feels the same way about you, then there's no rush. But you do need to resolve your feelings about Jack." Dr. Wright followed Enid to the front desk. "There's no need to schedule a follow-up appointment," she said to the receptionist. She turned to Enid and hugged her. "But I'm always here in case you need me."

CHAPTER 40

During the past year, Enid's apartment in Columbia had been her refuge, her sanctuary. Now it felt empty. She ran her hand across the small desk and wiped the dust. Maybe it was time to start a new life. But right now, she needed to focus on the next article for her editor. She had enough information from Theo for this one, but she would need more research to continue the series.

She had been working for almost an hour when her cell phone interrupted. Josh's number appeared on the screen and she answered.

"I got your text. You're in Columbia?" he asked.

"Yes, I need to do some work here."

"I miss you."

Enid thought of Dr. Wright's advice and hesitated on how to answer. "Me too."

"Detective Pointer called me after she got the information from you. I updated her on our little adventure in the woods. She's asked me to help her on Hari's case, since Kat's car was found near Madden. I reminded her that the location of Kat's car and the airstrip are both out of my jurisdiction, but she's talked to the county sheriff, and he's more than happy for me to work on it, since he's down a couple deputies. I promised to keep him in the loop."

The implications of Josh's comments were just sinking in. They would both be working on Hari's case. "That's good, I mean, if it's something you want to do. Has Pointer talked to Theo?"

"No, I don't think so. There's not really anything concrete to tell him at this point. We don't know if or how any of this is connected to Hari's disappearance, although it hardly seems like a coincidence. What I'm happy about is getting to work with you." He paused. "By the way, Jack is worried about you."

Enid chose her next words carefully. "I care a lot about Jack."

Josh sighed softly. "I know. And he cares about you very much. Maybe even something more."

"How does that make you feel?" She was amused at how much she sounded like Dr. Wright.

Josh didn't answer right away. "I'd like to answer that one over dinner when you come back to Madden."

CHAPTER 41

A tap on the door awakened Hari. While knocking was a nice gesture, the man usually didn't wait for her to respond before coming in. So today, when he waited, his changed behavior made her nervous.

"Come in."

The man had several shopping bags in his hands. "I brought you something." He approached her and put the bags by her feet. "You said you wanted new clothes."

Hari looked inside the bags, which contained two pair of designer jeans and three casual tops. "Thanks," she said as she put the bags aside.

"I also got you this." He handed her a tube of red lipstick. "You like it?"

Hari wanted to scream or hit him or something. Did he think a few pieces of clothing and makeup would make up for holding her captive? Besides, the red lipstick was creepy and made her feel even more uneasy. She forced a smile. "Yes. But if you really want to make me happy, let me go or at least call my dad. He's probably worried sick."

The man smiled, looking at Hari with affection. "Now, you know I can't do that. Besides, he is busy taking care of all those homeless people. I'm your daddy now."

Again, Hari resisted her natural instincts to lash out at him. Then his words sank in. "What homeless people?"

"You know, at that soup kitchen where you volunteered for a while."

Hari felt faint. "Do you mean my dad is in Columbia?" The realization that he was nearby comforted her. It also made her extremely sad.

"He thinks you've run away. He's given up looking for you."

Hari knew the man was lying, but his words still stung. "Can you at least let me tell him I'm alright?" She then added, "If you let me send him a message, then I promise to be good." She almost choked on those last words.

"I'm your daddy, Belle," he said again as he walked out, locking the door behind him.

"I'm not Belle," Hari said. "I'm Harriet."

Suddenly, Hari remembered where she had seen her captor. She had been clearing tables at the soup kitchen when he approached her. He asked personal questions about school and family, and when she refused to engage in conversation, he just kept smiling at her. She remembered it felt creepy. The scar. When Hari had mentioned the incident to one of the women who worked there, she told him Max was a guardian angel for the soup kitchen. Max. That was his name. She had only seen him once that she could recall. But why had he taken her?

CHAPTER 42

Tonight was like every other night for Theo. He tossed and turned until he fell asleep, exhausted and afraid. The odds were diminishing that Hari would be found. Need he say it, even to himself? The odds were slim she would be found alive. What if she had just run away? She was old enough to make that decision, although he couldn't imagine why she would. Maybe she would just show up one day and apologize for losing touch. But didn't she know he would be worried sick?

The more those thoughts bounced around in his head, the sadder he became. Hari would never just leave him. They had a special bond. After her mother's death, he and Hari had been in it together from that point forward. If she hadn't run away, then she was likely dead. He couldn't bear that thought, but that was easier for him to imagine than her being hurt or held against her will. She was beautiful. What man could resist taking advantage of her under those circumstances?

As trusting as she was, Hari was also strong-willed and smart. Theo finally went to sleep by envisioning her walking into the soup kitchen and throwing her arms around him. "Hi, Daddy," she would say. "I missed you so much." Theo didn't mind that his pillow was wet with tears every night. As long as he could cry, he could hope. He dreaded the day when there were no tears left.

CHAPTER 43

Josh handed the coordinates of the airstrip to Pete. "Here. I want you to find out everything you can about this place. Who owns it? Is it a legit airstrip or something else?" As Josh was walking to his office, he called over his shoulder. "And I need it yesterday."

On his desk were several phone messages and a few letters to be signed. Pushing them aside, he sipped his coffee and enjoyed the relative quiet. Before long, he would be running around, doing all the little things a small-town police chief did. At ten o'clock, he would speak to high school students about staying out of trouble and being responsible citizens. No doubt, some of them would roll their eyes and pull out their phones. But it was worth his time if only one kid thought about his words and refrained from doing something stupid that would land them in jail, or worse. After that, he had to pay a visit to Mrs. Morton. She invented problems just to talk to Josh; he was sure of it. But she was lonely, and she did make a killer peach cobbler. She told him constantly that he needed a wife and had tried to set him up with several women in Madden. He accepted a few of the invitations, but Mrs. Morton's picks were not who he wanted to spend his life with.

Josh leaned back in his desk chair and surveyed the small police station. This position was a far cry from his days as an undercover detective in New Mexico. In many ways, he missed the excitement, but he had missed too many of life's critical moments. Accepting this gig in Madden as the police chief was redemption for his past life. Here, he vowed to engage in life, not merely observe it, as he had done previously. His wife was dead, and he could never repay her the time he had denied her. While he had thrown himself into this new role, work was not his priority any longer. Happiness was the ultimate goal.

His conversation with Enid had stayed on his mind, especially the part about Jack.

"Hey, boss, I found something." Pete was standing at the door of Josh's office.

Jarred from his thoughts, Josh replied, "Come on in. Tell me."

"The airstrip is owned by Rosanne Hermosa, according to the tax records."

"Beautiful," Josh said.

"I don't know if she is or not."

Josh laughed. "*Hermosa* means beautiful in Spanish. Where does she live?"

"Well, that's where it gets a little interesting. That airstrip is listed as a farm residence. I'm still checking on it."

"Good work, Pete. Just keep me posted. But-"

"I know, you need it yesterday."

Since the airstrip was in the county's jurisdiction, Josh called the county sheriff, Boogie Waters. He was born Bernard Waters but got his nickname from dancing the shag at Myrtle Beach's Society of Stranders Festival every year. He routinely won the local dance contests, and now in his sixties, he could still put the younger ones to shame. Boogie was a fun-loving guy but no-nonsense when it came to police work. You didn't want to get caught driving drunk or stealing in his jurisdiction. Boogie and Josh had formed a father-son kind of relationship almost as soon as Josh had arrived in Madden. Boogie helped Josh acclimate to small town policing, and Josh often helped out when the sheriff's staff was shorthanded.

"Is this the handsome Police Chief Josh Hart calling?" Boogie said when he answered.

"Yeah, it is. And is this South Carolina's dance king?"

"What can I say, man, I like to keep my feet moving, so I might as well dance. What can I do for you?"

"I'm working with the Columbia police on a girl that was pimped out on a website. A computer nerd managed to trace the IP address to a location in your area. Also, there's that abandoned car of another missing girl that was found in your area. I wanted to make sure we're on the same page."

"Well, I appreciate the heads up, and the help. That female detective called me earlier. I told her we needed some additional manpower. Appreciate you pitching in. Where's this place where the server is?" Boogie asked.

Josh gave him the coordinates.

"Hold on a minute." Josh could hear Boogie clicking on his keyboard. "That's the old tobacco farm, used to be owned by . . . wait a minute, and I'll think of the name. Oh well, it'll come to me later."

"It is a working farm?" Josh asked.

"The farm is big. Part of it grows produce. But I think they lease part of the land out. There's some crop dusting and private flights on a little airstrip at one end of the place.

I've been out there a few times, because we got reports of them smuggling drugs and worse out of there."

"Care to elaborate on 'worse'?"

"A few of our county citizens swear they're shipping women out in the small planes. I never found anything to back up those claims. From what you're telling me, though, there might be something to these stories."

"The tax records show the owner of the property as Rosanne Hermosa. You know her?" Josh asked.

"Can't say I've heard that name before. Want me to check it out?"

"I know you're short-handed. If it's alright with you, I'll do some snooping. Matter of fact, I've already seen the place."

"Figured you had, 'cuz you're so damn impatient. Youth!" Boogie said.

"They weren't too happy to see me. In fact, they put the dog on me and fired a warning shot, at least I hope that's all it was. On the other hand, I didn't announce myself as police. Anyway, I doubt they reported a prowler."

"Haven't heard nary a word from 'em. Just be careful, and give me a holler if you need backup."

"Will do, Boogie. Keep those feet moving."

"By the way, is Detective Pointer that good looking brunette?"

Josh knew it was pointless to remind Boogie his remarks were sexist. He was a year from retirement and hadn't shed his outdated viewpoints on women. Although, Josh had never observed him disrespect his female deputies, who would walk through fire for him. "Yes, she is attractive."

"When you talk with her, ask her if she can shag, you know, dance. Might want to marry her if she does," Boogie said, ending the call.

CHAPTER 44

Enid looked forward to weekends in Madden. A year ago, she wanted to run away and never see the place again. But her bad memories were because of bad people, not the little town. Jack was in the kitchen cooking spaghetti when she arrived, which made her think of Theo.

"There she is." Jack hugged Enid, and he held her until she pulled away.

"It's good to be back. That sauce smells delicious."

"It's one of Rachel's favorite meals. She'll be in from school later. Let's go out and sit on the porch. I'll bring some refreshments Ruth sent over. By the way, she says you promised to come see her while you're here."

On the porch, Enid and Jack chatted a few minutes before she put her glass down and turned to Jack. "I need to talk to you about something."

Jack stopped rocking and turned to look at her. "Sure. Is something wrong?"

Enid took his hand in hers. "I love that you worry about me." She kissed his hand gently. "You are the best friend a girl could have." Enid couldn't stop the tears, and Jack wiped them away with the back of his hand.

"What's bothering you?"

"I want you to be happy, and you need to stop trying to protect me."

"But I—"

Enid held up her hand. "Wait, let me finish. Taking care of things and other people is who you are. That's one of the many things that makes you special."

"There's a 'but' coming, isn't there?"

Enid held his hand. "But, it's time for you to take care of you."

"Rachel said the same thing. As I told her, I can't promise not to worry or try to protect both of you. You're my family." He paused. "Can I ask you a question?"

Enid nodded.

"What about you and Josh? Is that serious?"

"I wish I knew. It's moving a little too fast for me right now. But I do enjoy being with him."

"I can't fault you for saying that. He's a good friend, and is probably good for you." Jack stopped rocking and turned back toward Enid. "You do know that Josh is in love with you. Right?"

Enid nodded.

"If you feel the same, then I hope it works out. He might wear a gun and look tough, but he's sensitive." Jack laughed. "Go easy on him."

"Now, turnabout is fair play. What about you and Madelyn?"

"Whew, that one, she's a handful. Smart and sexy is a dangerous combination in a woman. Besides, she's not looking for anything permanent, not in a relationship. We agreed to enjoy each other's company with no strings attached. I'm okay with that. I don't think I'm ready for anything too serious either. It's still a little too soon for me, after . . ." His voice trailed off.

Enid wiped her eyes. "I love you, Jack Johnson. My forever friend."

"I love you too, honey. Always. Now I've got to go check on that sauce. Rachel will be here any minute."

CHAPTER 45

Rachel finished her second bowl of Jack's spaghetti. "That was so yummy. I miss your cooking when I'm at school."

"Well, truth be told, that's Ruth's recipe. But, I do add my own special touch to it." Jack patted Rachel's arm. "I love to cook for you." He turned to Enid. "And for you. I have some special women in my life, for which I'm very grateful."

"How's the inn doing? Is Ruth enjoying running it?" Enid asked.

"Truthfully, I don't think she enjoys being tied down. My sister has always been a bit of a wanderer. Can't stay married to one person very long, or stay put in one place either. I think the wanderlust is taking over her again."

"Running an inn is a lot more work than people realize, and it is very confining. As much as I would hate to see her leave, I can understand how she feels," Enid said.

Jack tossed his napkin onto the table. "Yeah, me too. But I don't know what I'll do with the inn if she moves on. I like having her around, too."

"Something will work out, I'm sure."

"This may be your second chance," Jack said to Enid.

"Me? Are you crazy? As I told you the first time you asked, no thanks. I can't cook and have no desire to run an inn."

"Something will work out," Rachel said. "We can't let the inn close or get sold to a stranger."

Enid asked Rachel, "How did you do on your exam? Didn't you have one this past week?"

Rachel sighed. "Not too good. To be perfectly honest, I'm not sure I can handle all these biology classes. Too many Latin terms to memorize." She looked at Jack. "I've been meaning to talk to you, because I know you would be disappointed in me if I quit school."

Jack reached across the table and took her hand. "I could never be disappointed in you. But are you sure that's what you want to do?"

"You know how much I appreciate you putting me through school. Any kid I know would die for that opportunity. But I don't want you to waste all that tuition money until I'm sure I want to spend the next eight years in school. I love animals, but I don't love biology, organic chemistry, and all those other courses I have to take."

"I think you're a smart young lady to step back and evaluate the situation," Enid said. "Perhaps the school will let you suspend your studies for a year. By then, you'll know if you want to return or change majors."

"Enid's right," Jack said. "I'll help you write a letter, if that's what you really want to do. Besides, I could sure use some help with these horses. We've got eight boarded now. I was going to talk to you about hiring someone."

Rachel grinned. "I was hoping you'd let me stay and work here. At least for a while."

"You're hired. Now let's clean up these dishes. I've got some newspaper work to do. Helen had a death in her family, so I'm getting the next edition out for her."

Enid started gathering the soup bowls. "You go ahead and work," she said to Jack. "Rachel and I will take care of these."

Fifteen minutes later, when they were putting the last dish in the cabinet, Enid asked, "What's the rest of the story?"

"What do you mean?"

"Call it reporter's instincts, but I sense you didn't tell us the real reason you want to drop out, or at least not all of the story." Enid folded the dishrag and laid it on the dish drain in the sink. "Come on. Let's go sit on the porch awhile."

Rachel and Enid settled into their usual rocking chairs. The night air was cool but not uncomfortable. "I didn't realize the difference between loving animals and learning to be a vet. Plus, I really can't stand cutting things up. Ugh."

"In a perfect world, what would you like to do?"

"I don't know right now, but I really do want to work here on Jack's ranch for a while and take care of it. Do you think he's upset with me?"

"Honey, that man loves you like a daughter. It would take a lot for him to get upset with you. But I imagine that he worries about your future, as any father would. I could tell, though, that he's really excited about having you around for now. Plus, he needs the help."

"That's good. He's been so good to me." Rachel sighed. "You know, I've never really had choices before. It's kind of weird, but in a nice way."

"Sometimes having choices makes life even more difficult," Enid said. "But, yes, having the freedom to choose is good."

"Oh, I almost forgot. I found your nurse, you know, the one that took care of your mother."

"Really? You found her that quick?"

"I've got the phone number for the agency she works for now. You can call them."

"That's wonderful. Thanks so much." Enid paused. "You're really good at computer searches. You didn't get on the deep web to find her, did you?"

Rachel laughed. "It's not such an awful place if you know how to take precautions."

"Don't tell me anything else. I don't want to know in case the FBI comes looking for you because you went on one of those sites they monitor for terrorists. Is computer forensics what you're interested in pursuing?"

"It's a lot more fun than biology, but I don't know yet. What about you?"

"Me? What do you mean?"

"Are you going to marry Josh?"

"For Pete's sake, whatever gave you that idea?" Enid asked. "It's too early to ask that question."

"Yeah, right. I see how you two look at each other. I know lust when I see it," Rachel laughed. "But I wish you and Jack were, you know, like a couple. You seem so good together. Like married people."

Before Enid could respond, Jack joined them on the porch. "Am I interrupting something? I heard a lot of giggling, so I wanted in on the action."

"Just girl stuff," Enid said. "Did you get your work done already?"

"No, but I need to talk to you about something." He turned to Rachel. "Can I have a few minutes with Enid? Something has come up I need to talk to her about."

• • •

After Rachel left them alone on the porch, Jack sat down beside Enid. "Is everything alright?" she asked.

"Well, that depends. I'm not sure how you're going to take this news."

Enid leaned forward. "What are you talking about?"

"Your editor at the *Palmetto Weekly* called about your series since we're going to run it in the *Madden Gazette* too."

"I've been trying to reach her, because she hasn't responded to the last article I sent her. Is she going to run it this week?"

"The article was great. She loved it. And, yes, she's going to run it this week."

"Is that why she called? Why didn't she just call me?" Enid asked.

"Here's the part you might not like. She's not your editor any longer. She's going to call you tomorrow, so act surprised."

Enid leaned back in her rocker and rubbed her temples with her fingers. "What are you saying? Am I fired?"

Jack threw his head back and laughed. "No, but you might want to start addressing me as Boss Jack."

Enid sat up and turned toward him. "What on earth are you talking about?"

"Well, you know how we were going to co-publish your articles on Theo and Hari's disappearance? Seems the *Palmetto Weekly* is going through some financial difficulties, as most weeklies are these days, and she's going to have to trim down. You were on the chopping block, but she believes in your work. In fact, she asks why you had stayed with her. She was worried about you, which is why she called me first—to see if I had an opening for you."

"I'm sorry to hear that about the paper." She paused. "Wait, did you buy it?"

"Good God, no. Owning one flailing newspaper is enough. But I am offering you a chief reporter position at the *Madden Gazette*. You wouldn't have to move here, but I'm hoping you will. Either way, if you want to, you can continue the series, I'll edit, and we'll share some of the stories, when it makes sense to do so, with the *Palmetto Weekly*. That way, they will save money, and you get to continue as is until the series is finished, just working for me instead."

"This is just too much tonight. First, you tell me Ruth might leave the inn, then Rachel announces she's dropping out of school. And now this."

"You can think about it if you want to."

"No. I mean, no, I don't need to think about it. But what about Helen, your paper's editor? Shouldn't she approve my hire?"

"To be honest, I'm not sure Helen's going to come back. She's been talking about retirement. Her only living relative is in Charleston, so I imagine she'll move there. Even if she does stay, she'll be delighted to have you."

"Well, in that case, thank you for the job offer."

"I feel pretty good about tonight. First, I hire a new ranch hand and then a star reporter. How lucky can a guy get?"

CHAPTER 46

Before returning to Columbia, Enid stopped by to see Jack's sister Ruth at the Glitter Lake Inn. The place, as always, was immaculate and smelled of baking cookies and lemon oil.

"Ruth, it's Enid. Are you back there?" she called toward the kitchen.

Ruth walked down the hall wiping her hands on a dish towel. "I'm so glad to see you," she said as she hugged Enid. "Come on in the library and sit down."

Enid followed her into the familiar room. "Lots of memories here."

"I know. It must be painful for you at times. But you're making good memories here too, right?" She paused and smiled. "You and Police Chief Hart seemed to be getting along pretty good at the party the other night."

"Yes, we seem to be having a moment."

"Oh, honey, I think it's more than that. But that's your business. How's your work going?"

"I'm doing the series on Theo's missing daughter. Jack probably told you about him."

"Yes, he did. That poor man. The uncertainty would drive me crazy. I'm glad you're trying to help him."

"I don't want to break any confidences," Enid said, "but Jack mentioned last night that you might be leaving the inn. Are you?"

"Poor Jack. I hate like the devil to leave him hanging, but this place ... well, all I can say is that it's a lot of work. Way more than I thought. And me and my ex are going to give it another try, but he doesn't want to leave Chicago."

"When will you be leaving?"

"As soon as possible. But I promised Jack I'd help him find someone." Ruth cocked her head slightly. "I need to get out of here soon, so if you know of anyone who wants to work their ass off 24/7, send them my way." A bell went off in the back of the house. "That's the oven timer. Come on back and we can talk while I get the bread out. I made some of those sunflower loaves that Jack loves."

"Thanks, but I need to get to Columbia to do some research for the next article." Enid hugged Ruth. "I hope you'll change your mind about staying." Even as she said it, she knew Ruth would soon be gone. Enid's heart ached to think the inn might close.

"Alright, hon, see you again soon, I hope."

About halfway to her car, Enid decided to walk down to the lake. Just like the house, the outdoor area was well kept. Jack must be spending a fortune to keep it up, but Enid knew Jack would maintain the inn as long as he could.

Enid sat in the turquoise-painted Adirondack chair, the same one she had sat in more than a year ago as she pondered her deteriorating marriage and a young girl's murder. She ran her hand across the back of the granite memorial bench and then slowly sat down. The cold stone was a stark contrast to her friend's warmth.

Enid looked across the water, where small ripples danced in the breeze. "I will never forget you. If I hadn't come to

Madden to do research, you might still be here, perhaps happily married to Jack by now." Enid fought back the tears. "If only I could change what happened, but I can't, and I have to move on. I have a chance at happiness again, and I know you would want that for me. Josh is a good man, and I need to give us a chance, to see if it's the real thing." Enid blew a kiss toward the lake.

• • •

The traffic was light, so the drive from Madden to Columbia was easy. However, as Enid got closer to the soup kitchen, the traffic became heavy. She circled the block looking for a parking place. "Hail Mary, full of grace, help me find a parking space," she said aloud. A good friend, who was raised Catholic, once recited the rhyme to Enid, swearing that it worked magic. Enid was amused and surprised when a car backed out of a place just ahead of her. "Thanks, Mary."

As she started to put money in the parking meter, she noticed there was an hour left on it. It was another sign this was going to be a good day.

Theo came from the kitchen to greet her. He looked paler and thinner since she had last seen him. "Theo, I'm worried about you. Are you taking care of yourself?"

"I'm fine, don't you worry about me."

"Are you up to an interview for the next article?"

"Of course." He motioned toward a table. "Have they found Kat?"

"Did Detective Pointer tell you about her?"

He shook his head. "One of the students who volunteers here told me. Kat's disappearance has something to do with Hari, doesn't it?"

Enid didn't want to alarm Theo, but she wasn't going to lie either. "It appears so."

"When Hari volunteered here, was there anyone in particular she hung out with?"

"The woman who ran the kitchen left just before I came here, but there's another woman, her name is Precious, or at least that's what they call her. You met her the first time you came here. She might know."

"Is she here today?"

"I'll see if I can find her," Theo said as he walked back to the kitchen.

A few minutes later, he returned with a plump woman, who looked to be about sixty years old. "Hey, reporter lady. What you need?" She sat across from Enid at the table.

"Did you know Hari when she volunteered here?"

"Of course. A beautiful girl, God bless her soul." Precious looked at Theo. "Sorry, I didn't mean to imply that she's, you know, I'm sure she's fine. Somewhere. Fine."

Theo patted her arm. "Don't worry, it's okay."

"Did she hang out with anyone in particular?" Enid asked Precious.

"Like I told the police, she was real friendly to everyone. Our diners loved her and asked about her when she wasn't in."

"But did anyone in particular take an interest in her?"

Precious thought for a moment. "Not that I recall. But, poor Max, he was very upset when she disappeared."

Enid looked at Theo. "Is he the man who gives food to the kitchen?"

Theo nodded. "That's him."

Enid asked Precious, "Is there any reason he was more upset than the others?"

"Well, you know, his own daughter disappeared."

Enid looked at Theo. "Were you aware of this?"

"I thought she had just left," he said. "But we really haven't talked much about it. He doesn't like to discuss her."

"When did she go missing, or leave?" Enid asked Precious.

"Like Theo said, he didn't talk much about her. I overheard him talking to Hari one day."

"About his daughter?" Enid asked.

"I don't eavesdrop on other people's conversations," Precious said, "but I did hear him telling her about a horse he had that she would like. Horse had a funny name, but I can't remember what it was."

"A horse?" Theo asked.

"Was Hari interested in horses?" Enid asked Theo.

"Not that I'm aware of. But she was a great listener, no matter what people were talking about. That's one of the reasons everyone liked her so much."

Precious paused. "It's just that . . ."

"What?" Enid asked.

"Nothing. Just something about him, Max, I mean. He's generous and nice, but he still gives me the creeps."

"Why is that?" Enid asked.

"Maybe it's that scar on his face. I'm sure it's nothing. Lots of people creep me out these days. Precious glanced at

Theo. “Hari was, I mean is, a charming young woman. It’s no wonder everyone wanted to talk to her.”

Theo wiped his eyes again. "She is kind. Like her mother."

“Did you mention Max’s interest in Hari to the police?” Enid asked Precious.

“No. I’m sure it was nothing. I need to get back to the kitchen, if that's okay," Precious said.

"Thanks for your help," Enid said.

"I think I have enough for the next article. I want to focus on the dangers young women face on campus, but I don't want you to be upset or read anything in to it. Let's just keep hoping for the best."

"Yes, of course." Theo shoulders slumped, and he stared at the floor.

"I need to go do some research, so I'm going to let you get back to your work. Take care of yourself."

As she walked down the street to her car, Enid thought about Max's interest in Hari. Like Precious said, it was probably nothing, but her instincts told her it was worth a little poking around.

CHAPTER 47

The next morning, Enid decided to return to Madden. Her Columbia apartment was starting to feel less like home than her room at Jack's house. Now that she was officially working for the *Madden Gazette*, perhaps she should look for a place nearby, something small and affordable. She put her notebook and laptop in her tote and pushed those thoughts out of her mind for now. She left a phone message for Madelyn to tell her she wouldn't be home tonight.

Less than an hour later, she pulled up in front of the Madden Police Department. Josh's pickup was parked beside the small concrete block building. As soon as she walked in the station, Josh came out of his office to greet her. "What a surprise. I wasn't expecting you back today."

This time, Pete looked up. "Hello, Ms. Blackwell. Nice to see you again." Before she could respond, he returned to staring at his computer screen.

"Hi, Pete." Enid then followed Josh back to his office. "I'm sorry I didn't call you. I wasn't sure myself until this morning what my plans were." She looked at the handful of phone messages on his desk. "Have you heard anything about Kat?"

"The sheriff department had the bloodhounds out searching. They picked up her scent for a short distance but lost it. I'm headed back over to Boogie's in a few minutes."

"Have they located Kat's parents?"

"Yes, they're in Europe but have been notified."

"I've got some research to do, but I figured I could do it here as well as in Columbia. Besides, I wanted to run something past you."

"Go ahead. Want tea while we're talking?" Enid nodded, and Josh fixed her a cup of tea and refilled his coffee cup.

"There's probably nothing at all to this, but I was wondering if you could check out a guy for me. You know, just to see if he has a criminal record or if any red flags pop up."

"Can you tell me a little more about why you need this information?"

"This man is a benefactor to the soup kitchen where Theo works. His name is Marcus Xavier James, but everyone calls him Max."

"Ooh, giving away money to help the homeless. That sounds pretty suspicious." Josh displayed his most mischievous grin.

"Go ahead, mock me if you will." Enid tore a page of paper from her notebook and made a ball, throwing it at Josh.

"She's not only beautiful and smart, she's dangerous." Josh started writing in his notebook. "There's more to this story apparently. Let's have it."

"He was upset when Hari disappeared, perhaps more so than the others who casually knew her. And his own daughter either ran away or disappeared several years ago."

"None of this still sounds ominous. What else is bothering you about him?"

"As a lawman, I doubt you believe in reporter's instincts. But there's just something that bothers me about him that I can't put my finger on."

"On the contrary, Madam Reporter, I absolutely believe in instincts ... to a point. Gut feelings can be a police officer's best friend or worst nightmare."

"I'm going to order a check on his arrest record, and I'll ask Detective Pointer if she's talked to Max.

"Where does this guy live?"

"Somewhere not far from here apparently. He has a farm and gives some of the produce to the soup kitchen." Enid noticed Josh smiling at her again. "I know, he sounds like a great guy."

"By the way, you still have that house key I gave you?"

Enid looked in her tote and dug around the bottom until she produced it. "Got it."

"Then why don't you set up camp at my place? You can take the guest room, no strings attached."

Enid shifted herself in the chair. "I don't know that I'm ready for that."

"Is it because you'd rather stay with Jack?" Josh was not smiling.

"No, it's just that . . ."

"I promise you can come and go as you please, and later, if you don't think it's working out, you can leave. I'll understand. You let me know how much freedom you need, and I'll give it to you." Josh came from behind his desk and took Enid's hands. "I promise not to rush you or cramp your style. I'm just offering you a place to stay and work, for as long as you want it."

"How can a girl say no to that offer?"

"Good. Now that we've settled that matter. I've got work to do." He motioned toward the door. "Go on, scoot now. Just let me know if you want to have dinner tonight or you've got other plans. I cook a mean pot of chicken chili."

"Sure, I'd love that."

• • •

On the way to Josh's house, Enid attempted three times to call Jack, but she couldn't make herself hit the green call button. Part of her was brimming with joy, but part of her felt like she had put even more distance between herself and Jack. On the fourth attempt, she found the courage to call him.

"Enid, this is a pleasant surprise. Are you still in Columbia?"

"No, I'm here, in Madden."

"That's great. I'll fix us some lunch when you get here."

Enid took a deep breath. "I'm staying in Josh's guest room, just for a while. But I'll come over to visit later this afternoon."

Jack cleared his throat. "Moving in is a big step. Are you ready for that?"

"I'm not moving in. It's no different than staying with you temporarily. Besides, it'll give the Madden ladies something new to gossip about."

Jack laughed softly. "That it will. Look, I think I'll head on over to the newspaper. While you're in town, we need to do some paperwork to make you official."

"I'll drop by later." Enid paused briefly. "Jack, thanks for your concern, really."

"You just be happy. That's all that matters."

Enid pulled into Josh's driveway and got her suitcase out of the trunk. Before going inside, she surveyed the house, since it had been dark on her last visit. Most of the yard was a natural area, with a few neatly manicured plant beds.

A noise startled her and she turned around quickly to see what it was. A beautiful doe stared at her from a short distance away before darting off into the woods.

As Enid put her house key in the lock, she hesitated before opening the door. She glanced back at her car, tempted to run back to her apartment in Columbia. She heard the same noise again and turned around. The doe was at the edge of the steps leading up to the porch. "Are you welcoming me?" The doe continued to watch Enid as she went into Josh's house.

Remembering Jack's earlier comment, she asked herself aloud as she pushed the oak door open, "What am I doing?"

CHAPTER 48

In Josh's guest room, Enid dropped her suitcase and surveyed the room. The bed faced a large stone fireplace. French doors opened to a screened porch that was furnished as comfortably as the rest of the house. Two chairs with fat cushions flanked a low table, and a patterned rug covered the stained wood floor. "Oh, my. I could live out here," she said as she looked out at the woods surrounding the house.

Enid walked back into the bedroom. A large desk sat on one side of the room. A handwritten note had the router code on it with instructions on how to connect to the internet.

She unpacked her clothes and hung them in the large closet, which was totally bare. She had never kept her guest closets this neat.

Her cell phone rang and Rachel's face appeared on the screen. "What are you doing?" Rachel asked. "Why aren't you staying here with us?"

Enid dreaded this conversation and had hoped to delay it a while longer. "I'm just staying in Josh's guest room a few nights. Don't make it more than it is." She regretted the defensive tone of her voice. "I'll be over to visit later."

"Can I come see you? I want to ask a favor."

"Sure, I'll text you Josh's address and some directions. It's a little out of the way."

"I know where it is," Rachel said as she hung up.

Enid tried to push Jack and Rachel out of her mind. She had work to do, so she set up her laptop at the desk and searched for "Marcus Xavier James." Numerous hits appeared immediately; most were articles about his charity work. One that caught her eye was a plea from Max for the public to keep an eye out for Hari. He described her as "an angel."

Enid found only one article that mentioned Max's daughter. The county sheriff had been interviewed and said they had found no evidence of a crime in her case and it was being closed. Enid made some notes so she could do some additional research.

Enid then focused her attention on gathering information for the next article. The statistics on human trafficking were alarming, with its $32 billion annual sales surpassing the illegal sale of guns. One figure that caught her eye was that seventy-six percent of sex trade transactions were done on the internet. She hadn't known Hari other than through Theo, but the thought of the beautiful girl being sold as a sex slave made Enid sick to her stomach. If she had been taken, she was likely in another state by now, or even out of the country. If she had simply been abducted, then she was likely dead. There were no good scenarios she could imagine.

The sound of a car driving up announced that Rachel had arrived. Enid closed her laptop and put her notes away. She opened the door before Rachel could knock. "I'm glad to see you," Enid said, hugging Rachel.

"Hey, sorry to barge in on you, but I have a favor to ask."

"Sure, what's up?"

"I want to meet your hacker guy."

"Tommy Two?"

"Yeah."

"I guess that was a silly question since he's the only one I know. But why would you want to meet him? No, wait, you're not going to start hacking, are you?"

Rachel made a face. "No, but I told you I was interested in computer forensics, and looking for your mother's nurse was so much fun."

"I haven't done anything with the information yet, but I appreciate your help. But I don't know about introducing you to Tommy. We don't know much about him. He could be a criminal. Although, I admit he's been pretty helpful."

"Pleeeze," Rachel said, batting her eyes at Enid.

"Oh, so that's how you've learned to get your way with Jack. But it won't work with me."

Rachel pretended to pout.

"Oh, alright. But you're not to contact him again on your own. Understand? This is a one-time deal."

Rachel threw her arms around Enid. "Thank you, thank you. When can we do it?"

"It's not like I can call and make an appointment. We'll just have to show up and see if he's there. Maybe in the next couple of days. I've got an article to write."

"Okay, that works. Jack told me you're working for him now. That's neat."

"Yeah, neat," Enid said. "Are you upset with me for being here at Josh's house?"

Rachel seemed to be thinking. "No, not if that's what you want. But I'll miss having you at the ranch."

"Hey, you're not going to get rid of me that easily. I'll be around so often you'll get tired of me."

"Does that mean you're moving here permanently?"

"Whoa, no decisions yet. I'm just taking it a day at a time. Besides Jack is seeing Madelyn."

“I know, but she’s not right for him.”

You, young lady, need to stay out of it and let Jack make that decision. Come on in the kitchen and I'll fix us a sandwich. Josh keeps his fridge and pantry well stocked."

"No, thanks. I've got the vet coming to check on one of our boarded horses, so I've got to get back. Let me know when we can go see Tommy."

As Enid stood on the porch and watched Rachel drive away, she wished it were possible to live in simultaneous, alternate universes so she wouldn't have to choose which life she wanted. In her peripheral vision, she saw movement beside the driveway. The doe was bouncing toward the woods again. She would have to ask Josh if he had been feeding her and causing her to hang around the house.

• • •

From the thicket of trees that surrounded Josh's house, the man watched a young girl get in her car and drive away. The woman on the porch kept watching the girl, and then turned suddenly when she saw a deer that bounded through the woods near him. He stepped back behind a large pine tree so she wouldn't see him. As he watched her looking in his direction, he admired her copper hair and ivory complexion. She was younger than he anticipated. She would be easy.

CHAPTER 49

Enid made the last changes to her article just as Josh walked in. "How was your day?" she asked.

"It's much better now." He kissed her nose. "Did you finish your work?"

Enid nodded. "It's ready to send to Jack, even though I've had a lot of company today."

Josh went to the kitchen and poured them a glass of wine. "What company?"

"Rachel stopped by, and then I got another visit from your doe friend."

Josh raised his eyebrow like he did when he was confused. "What doe?"

"I've seen her several times. I love watching her. And those enormous brown eyes. She seems to look right through me. Wonder why she's hanging around your house?"

"I haven't seen any deer around here lately." Josh walked over to the bookcase beside the fireplace and pulled a book from a shelf. He flipped through it. "Ah ha. Here it is." He sat on the sofa and motioned for Enid to join him. "I thought I was right, but I wanted to check it out."

"What are you talking about?"

"You may have a spirit animal, my dear, no pun intended. It can come to you in your sleep or appear to you in waking hours, and sometimes no one sees it but you."

"Oh, come on. Really?"

Josh leaned over and kissed her lightly on the lips. "Yes. In Native American lore, the deer is a messenger, and an animal of power." He pointed to a passage in the book. "It's also associated with fertility. And it represents sensitivity, intuition, and gentleness." He looked up at Enid. "What's wrong? You look so sad all of a sudden."

"It's Hari."

Josh pulled back and looked at Enid. "Hari? What do you mean?"

"Everything you said describes her."

Josh shut the book and put it on the coffee table. "Are you saying Hari transformed herself into a deer?"

Enid stood up. "I don't know what I'm saying, but if you've never seen this deer, and it's my spirit animal, perhaps it's here to tell me something about Hari."

Josh laid his head back against the sofa. "Should I worry about you? Jack told me you get really involved in your stories."

"Well, I'm glad you two have got me all figured out. She took her empty wine glass to the kitchen. "I'm going to my room to work."

Josh joined her in the kitchen and put his arms around her. "I'm glad you're here."

CHAPTER 50

A noise woke Enid, and she looked at the clock beside the bed. It was 2 a.m. She pulled on her robe and went down the hall to Josh's room. The door was open, so she walked in and stood beside his bed.

"Josh, wake up," she whispered.

"What's wrong?" he asked, propping himself up on his elbow.

"I heard a noise outside my window."

"Josh pulled his trousers on and grabbed his gun from the nightstand. "Stay here."

Enid heard the front door open and saw a flashlight beam illuminating the woods outside the bedroom window. "It's probably that doe he thinks I imagined," she said aloud.

A few minutes later, Josh returned. "Nothing out there. I'm going to make some coffee. You go back to sleep."

"I'll make a cup of tea and join you."

A few minutes later, as they sat at the kitchen table, Enid asked, "Tell me about your wife."

Josh poured himself a second cup of coffee. "What do you want to know about her?"

"What was she like? How did she die?"

Josh took several sips of coffee before speaking. "She was an attorney and worked for one of the tribal councils in New Mexico. They provided her services to the tribal members who needed assistance. She handled mostly domestic abuse and family law cases. One day, she walked into a restaurant near the reservation, and the husband of one of her clients pulled out a shotgun and shot her."

Enid put her hand on Josh's arm. "I'm so sorry. That's terrible."

"She only wanted to help them because of me. She wasn't even Native American, but she loved the culture. Or at least what she thought was the culture. She hadn't grown up in it, so she didn't realize how much alcoholism, misogyny, and desperation they faced. She was naive and saw only a charming, romantic view of our people, at least in the beginning."

"That must have been horrible for you, to lose her like that, so senselessly."

"I should never have married her."

Enid sat her teacup in its saucer. "What do you mean? You loved her, didn't you?"

"Yes, but I fell in love with a beautiful woman who loved me so much that she wanted to help our people. My family warned me that she would never fit in. I laughed at them, because she was so charming. Surely everyone would love her as I did."

"Josh, that's not your fault. You couldn't have known what would happen."

"But I did. I had this feeling the morning she left the house that something bad was going to happen. I should have stopped her."

Enid reached over and put her arms around Josh. "It's not your fault. Loving someone doesn't make you guilty." Enid winced as she heard own words. "I know how guilt can tear you apart."

Josh took one of her hands and kissed it. "That's enough sad talk. Let's try to get some sleep."

"Just one more question. How did you end up here in Madden as the police chief?"

"Let's save that for another time. I'm tired."

"Will you at least tell me if her killer was caught and punished?"

Josh put his empty coffee cup in the sink. "You might say that."

CHAPTER 51

Rachel got in the car with Enid and fastened her seatbelt. "I'm so excited. I'm going to meet Tommy Two."

Enid frowned. "He's a hacker, not a rock star. And I still don't feel good about this. He may not even agree to talk to you. And even if he does, what can you hope to learn from him, that is, anything that's not illegal?"

"Not all hackers are criminals, you know. Don't worry. I just want to see how he works in case I decide to study cyber forensics." Rachel turned in her seat so she could face Enid. "I want a report on you and Josh."

Enid made a face at Rachel. "No. That's none of your business."

Rachel settled back into her seat. "I'm just curious. I do want you to be happy. For real."

Enid kept her focus on the road for the next ten miles, while Rachel texted. "He may not be there. It's not like he keeps bankers' hours," Enid said.

"I know. That's okay." Rachel kept her eyes on her cell phone screen.

Nothing further was said until they reached Columbia. Enid was grateful to see a parking space near the coffee shop. "Okay, we're here. Now remember what I said."

"I know, I know. Nothing illegal. No more visits. Got it."

As they walked up the dark stairway to the coffee shop, Rachel said, "This place is creepy. This is where he works?"

"Well, this is where he hangs out. Some of the time, anyway."

When they entered the coffee shop, it took a few seconds for Enid's eyesight to adjust to the low lighting. As she scanned the room, she was both relieved and disappointed when she saw Tommy sitting in his usual spot, his hands flying across the keyboard like a classical pianist. At least they wouldn't have to make another trip to find him. "You wait here," Enid said to Rachel.

Enid approached Tommy, who tried to ignore her. "Tommy, may I have a minute to talk with you?"

He stopped typing but continued to stare down at his fingers on the keyboard. "We don't have anything more to talk about."

"I appreciate the information you sent me. It was very helpful. But I have another favor to ask. A personal favor." Enid pointed to Rachel standing near the door. "That's Rachel, a good friend who is like family. She was studying to be a vet, but she's taking some time off to figure out what she wants to do. She's fascinated with cyber forensics and may want to study the field if she returns to school."

Tommy looked up and took a quick glance at Rachel.

"She wants to meet you and pick your brain, so to speak. I know it's a lot to ask, but would you be willing to talk to her for a few minutes? It would mean the world to her."

"What have you told her about me?" Tommy asked.

"Only what I know. That you're a computer geek who has been helping me locate a missing girl." Enid paused briefly. "Although, I also warned her to stay away from you. I don't want to romanticize what you do. Understand?"

Tommy stood up and looked toward Rachel. Enid turned and saw that Rachel was approaching them. "I asked you to wait," Enid said.

For the first time in their brief acquaintance, Tommy smiled slightly. "Hi," he said, as he pulled out a chair for Rachel to sit down. He looked at Enid. "I promise not to corrupt her." He didn't offer a seat to Enid.

"If you prefer, I'll sit at the bar."

Rachel and Tommy exchanged a brief glance. "I'll be fine," Rachel said to Enid.

Enid reluctantly left them and took a seat on one of the wooden bar stools. Through the big mirror in front of her, she could partially see the pair. They were both staring at Tommy's computer screen. Rachel was talking animatedly, while Tommy mostly typed. There was something totally different about the way he related to Rachel, something she had not seen in her previous conversations with him. Rachel was an attractive young woman, and she had a great personality, so it was no wonder Tommy reacted the way he did.

Enid now regretted this meeting. What if Rachel decided to experiment with hacking? What if she got caught and went to prison? Enid was staring down at her mug of hot tea, mulling over these questions when she got a tap on the shoulder.

"Okay, I'm ready to go now," Rachel said.

"Well, that didn't take long. Did you get what you needed?"

"Yeah, he's pretty cool. Thanks for the intro."

"Is that it? Or did you two plot on how to meet without a chaperone?"

Rachel folded her arms across her chest. "Don't you trust me?" She turned and walked toward the exit.

"Rachel, wait." Enid pulled a five-dollar bill from her wallet and put it on the counter. Chasing after Rachel, she said, "Yes, I do trust you, but I don't trust him. I don't know him."

"He's not like that, you know."

"Like what? He hacks into private accounts and steals information. What part of that is not criminal?" Enid had to walk fast to keep up with Rachel.

• • •

The ride back to Madden was mostly silent. Enid tried to make small talk a few times but finally gave up. As they pulled into the dirt driveway that led to Jack's house, Enid stopped the car and turned toward Rachel. "I'm not going to let you be mad at me. You know how much I love you, and I just want to protect you. There's so much danger out there, especially for young women. I'm sorry if I offended you."

Rachel took Enid's hand. "I know. I'm sorry I got mad. I love you, too. You're like my big sister. A bossy big sister," she said smiling. "Just give me some credit, okay? I'm not as naive as you think I am."

Enid nodded. "I know. You're much smarter than I was at your age. Did you learn what you wanted to from Tommy?"

"He showed me some coding that I would never have figured out on my own. I really enjoyed talking with him."

Enid started the car and drove up to Jack's house. She had intended to stop in and talk with Jack, but Josh's police car was in the driveway. "I'll see you later. I'm going to head on."

CHAPTER 52

As Enid drove to Josh's house, she turned the music up loud enough to drown out her thoughts. Later, when she turned onto Josh's property, she slammed on the brakes. Something was in the road. She opened her car door and got out to see what it was.

As she approached, she saw that it was the doe. She was still alive, but barely. A bullet had penetrated her side, and she was bleeding profusely. "Oh, God, no. You poor thing." Against all advice Enid had ever heard about not approaching a wounded animal, she dropped down to the ground and took the doe's head in her hands. The large brown eyes looked up at her and then closed, the doe's body shaking slightly. Enid gently laid the doe's head back on the ground and ran to the car, grabbing her cell phone. "Josh, someone shot my deer. Please hurry home."

But when Enid returned to the doe, all that remained was a puddle of blood and a trail leading to the nearby woods. Enid followed the blood until it ended, but the doe had vanished.

When Josh arrived, the three of them looked again but could not find the wounded animal. Based on the amount of blood, it was unlikely the doe would survive.

"Who would do such a thing? And why?" Enid asked.

Josh took Enid's hand and kissed it. "You look exhausted. Go on inside, and I'll be there shortly. I just need to do a few things first."

After Enid left, Josh took his gun and flashlight and went outside. He walked to the back of the house. Stooping down, he looked at the large boot prints in the dirt around the plants beneath his bedroom window. The toe was slightly pointed: cowboy boots, not hunting boots. He pulled out his cell phone and took a close-up photo. The soil was too loose to show any kind of identifying ridges or shapes that might help identify the type sole. He followed the footprints until they stopped just outside of the guest room's screened porch. Someone had been watching Enid's room.

Josh looked toward the woods. A gentle breeze stirred the slim pine trees. He loved the peace and tranquility of this place. Until now. Now it felt isolated and exposed. He looked around to satisfy himself that he had not missed any other signs of intruders.

When he went inside, Enid was lying across the guest bed, asleep. He kissed her cheek and shut the door quietly. He had work to do.

CHAPTER 53

Theo was making iced tea, the sweet kind most of the soup kitchen diners preferred, when the church secretary walked up to him. "Here, Theo, a letter for you," she said holding out an envelope.

"For me?" Theo reached out and took the envelope. Before he could examine it, one of the kitchen assistants ran up to him. "I sliced my finger. I can't stop the bleeding."

The church secretary grabbed a towel and wrapped it around the young woman's finger, while Theo went to get the first aid kit. During the rush of activities, Theo crammed the letter into his apron pocket and forgot about it.

By the end of the day, Theo was more tired than usual. It had been a busy day. He wiped the stainless steel prep table clean and pulled the apron over his head. He took it to the laundry area to drop it in the basket for tomorrow's wash when he noticed the envelope in the apron pocket. There was a bit of blood on it, from the incident earlier in the day. He looked at the handwritten address on the envelope. It was printed, not cursive, causing Theo to briefly bemoan the lost art of script. The return address was California. He didn't recall knowing anywhere there. Because he was so tired, he was tempted to wait until morning to read it, as it was likely a request for a donation. Or some kind of scam. But he opened it anyway, out of curiosity.

The envelope contained a single sheet of yellow paper, lined, with tiny perforations at the top where it had been torn from a legal pad. His hands began to shake as he read the note.

Dear Dad,
I hope you are well. Sorry I haven't been in touch. I just needed some time to get away and be on my own for a while. I'm in California working in a restaurant, one of those fancy places I love so much. Please don't try to find me. I'll come home before too long. Don't be angry.
Love, Hari

Theo sat on the cold concrete floor clutching the letter in his hands, sobbing. "Hari, oh, thank God, Hari. You're alive. I knew it." He cried until there was nothing left. While clutching the letter to his chest, he closed his eyes and saw Hari's face, as he often did. But she wasn't smiling. Something was wrong.

CHAPTER 54

Josh expected to see Enid still asleep, but she was sitting up in bed, working on her laptop. Her eyes were red and swollen from crying. "Hi, come on in," she said. "What's that? Am I getting room service?"

He put a tray on the bed beside her. "I thought you might like some tea."

"I could get spoiled here, you know." She motioned for him to come closer and then kissed him.

Josh sat at the end of the bed. "That's what I want to talk to you about."

"What? About spoiling me?"

Josh took her hands in his, his expression serious. "I don't know what I'd do if something happened to you."

Enid pulled away and sat up straight in bed. "What's going on? Is there something you aren't telling me?"

He didn't answer.

"It's about the doe, isn't it?"

Josh walked to the French doors and looked out into the back yard. "Maybe. I don't know. There were boot prints out here, near the back porch."

"The noise I heard sounded like someone on the gravel walkway in the garden. Who could have been here watching the house?"

"It might be someone I arrested, or anyone with a beef with law enforcement. I doubt it has anything to do with you, but I think you should go back to Jack's for a while. I've already talked to him. I hope you're alright with that."

Enid pushed the covers back and swung her legs off the bed. "I will not leave you. Not for that reason."

Josh laughed. "That's exactly how Jack said you would react. He knows you pretty well.

"I appreciate your concern, but aren't you jumping to conclusions? It could have been someone who just wandered by and got curious."

"I hope you're right, but I'm not taking that chance. Until we figure out who's snooping around, I don't want to worry about you constantly."

Enid sighed. "I admit I've learned a few lessons about being hardheaded, so we'll compromise. If it's okay with Jack, I'll stay with him a couple nights. Then we'll renegotiate."

Josh kissed Enid on the tip of the nose. "You drive a hard bargain." He got her suitcase from the closet. "Here, pack your things."

• • •

Enid declined dinner with Jack and Rachel. "I need some time alone. I hope you can understand." She hugged Jack. "Thanks for letting me come back. I hope it's not an inconvenience."

"You're kidding me, right? I'm happy to have you back here," he said grinning.

She unpacked her suitcase and was going to settle in for the night when her cell phone rang. It was Theo. As soon as she answered, he began talking rapidly. "I got a letter from her. She's alive. Thank God, she's okay."

"You got a letter from who? Wait. You mean, Hari?" All the alarms were going off in Enid's head. "Are you sure it's from her?"

"Yes, but the only thing is . . ."

"What?"

"She said she's working at a fancy restaurant in California." He paused. "I'm sure it's nothing."

"What do you mean?"

"It's just that we used to joke about this very thing. She once said to me, 'If you ever hear I'm in Los Angeles working in a yuppie restaurant, you'll know I've gone to the dark side.' I took her there one summer, and she hated those trendy places." He paused. "There's something else. How did she know I'm here in Columbia at the soup kitchen? As far as she knows, I'm still in Boston."

"What are you saying? Do you think she's trying to tell you something?"

Theo began sobbing. "I think she's in trouble. I want to believe what she said, but something is not right."

"What did Detective Pointer say?"

"She took the note and said she'd check it out. Hold on." He blew his nose and returned. "Sorry. I didn't mean to be so emotional. It's just that I want to believe she's alright."

"Of course you do. I'll talk to Detective Pointer and make sure she follows through and share your concerns with her. If you hear anything else, let me know."

Enid made a note of what Theo had told her, while trying to make sense of it.

CHAPTER 55

Josh called Pete from the Madden police station. "Hey, look, sorry to bother you after hours, but I need for you to get in as early as you can this morning. I want a full-court press on finding Rosanne Hermosa, you know, the woman that owns that farm." Josh told Pete about the injured doe and footprints near the house. "I don't know if any of this has any connection to our little visit to the airstrip, but I need to be sure."

Josh was doing some paperwork when his cell phone vibrated and jumped around on the metal desk. Enid's face appeared on the screen. "Hey, you. You feeling better?"

Enid filled him in on Theo's letter. "I'm going to call Detective Pointer now about this letter. I wish she'd show more urgency about Hari. And what about Kat? Any news?"

"No, nothing I'm afraid. Boogie, Sheriff Waters, has all his available men looking for her. They've alerted the surrounding areas."

"It's like she just vanished. Just like Hari. I'll talk to you later."

"Later." Josh laid his cell phone back on the desk. He made a pot of fresh coffee and put his feet up on the desk while he sipped. He long ago discovered that he did his best thinking that way: alone, with coffee, sitting in this very chair. And he had a lot to think about.

• • •

On the fourth ring, Detective Pointer answered the phone.

"Detective Pointer, this is—"

"Yes, Ms. Blackwell. What can I do for you."

"Did you get Hari's letter from Theo?"

"Are you actually following up with me to see if I do my job?" She paused. "Sorry. Bad day. Yes, we're doing what we can to validate it."

"Theo says it's her handwriting, but he thinks she's trying to tell him something is wrong."

"Yes, Ms. Blackwell. He told me all that, and as I said, we're checking on it." Another pause. "Look, I know you think we're not doing anything, but we are checking every lead and doing what we can."

"What about Kat, her roommate?"

"Her car was found outside our jurisdiction, so the bulk of that work is being done by Sheriff Waters and his deputies, and Police Chief Hart. We're assisting where we can, of course. I'm staying on top of it because she was a student here, as well as the possible connection to Hari. Now, is there anything else?"

"No, I—" Before Enid could say anything further, the call ended.

CHAPTER 56

One thing Enid loved about being at Jack's house was that meals were the way it should be: good company, unhurried, and delicious food. Breakfast today was no exception.

"I hate to leave you ladies," Jack said to Rachel and Enid, "but I need to get down to the paper."

"I'll clean the kitchen. You go on," Rachel said.

While Enid and Rachel were doing the dishes, Rachel's phone buzzed in her back pocket. Enid tried to tune out Rachel's conversation, but the mention of Josh's name caught her attention.

"You need to tell Chief Hart now," Rachel told the caller.

Enid dried the last plate and put it in the cabinet as Rachel ended the call. "Everyone okay?"

"Yeah, it's just, like, you remember my friend Lucy, the one who went missing for a while?"

"The girl I met at the Glitter Lake Inn party?" Enid's memory was suddenly flooded with images, but they were of being at Josh's house after the party, not of Lucy.

"Yes, that's her."

"Is anything wrong?"

"It's her boyfriend, Buddy. Actually, her ex."

"Is he bothering her? She could take out a restraining order. I'm sure Josh could help her."

"No, it's not that. It's just that he saw something that bothered him, and he told Lucy about it. Now she's worried about it. I told her she needs to tell somebody."

"What did he see?" Enid folded the dish towel and laid it on the drain in the sink.

"He saw a girl who might be in trouble."

Enid tensed. "I'd like to talk to Lucy. Would you be okay with that?"

Rachel clapped her hands silently in approval. "I told her she could talk to you."

"Why don't you ask her to come over here while Jack's out."

• • •

When Lucy walked into Jack's house, Enid was reminded of how stressed and pale Rachel had looked when she first met her more than a year ago—just like Lucy looks now. Something was definitely bothering Rachel's friend.

"Tell her what you told me," Rachel said to Lucy. "Go on. She'll tell us what to do."

Enid went over to the sofa and sat beside Lucy. "What's wrong? What did you see?"

Lucy had deep circles under her eyes and her nails were bitten to the quick. She shook her head. "I think Buddy is involved in something illegal."

Enid patted her arm. "Just take your time. Start at the beginning."

Lucy leaned her head back against the sofa and shut her eyes. "Buddy is not a bad person, but he doesn't think sometimes and gets himself into a mess. He's working for bad people, and he's afraid of them. He was worried about me, that's why he broke up, to protect me."

Enid tried to pull the pieces of Lucy's comments together. "Who does Buddy work for?"

"He's a mechanic, works on farm equipment and crop planes, stuff like that."

Enid's mind was racing. "Whose planes?"

Lucy shook her head. "He works for several different farms, you know, when they need him."

"You said he was afraid of them. Who are these people?"

"Buddy says it's a company that sells produce, but he thinks they're flying drugs, too."

Rachel jumped in, "Tell her about the girl."

"Buddy saw a girl they forced on the plane," Lucy said. "He said she looked drugged up. They had her hands tied up behind her with one of those plastic zip tie things."

"Why didn't he go to the police?"

Lucy stood up suddenly. "Look, this was a bad idea. Buddy will kill me if he finds out I talked to anyone. I'm sorry to bother you." She turned to Rachel. "I'll see you later." Lucy ran out the front door and drove away before they could stop her.

"She's clearly scared to death," Enid said.

"I know. She said Buddy was afraid they would come after her to make him keep quiet, so he broke up and made her promise never to contact him or tell anyone what happened."

"We've got to tell Josh."

"No, I can't go behind her back. She's my best friend. She trusts me."

Enid grabbed Rachel by the shoulders. "Listen, this is bigger than your friendship with Lucy. Do you understand? You, of all people, know the importance of coming forward when you know something."

"I know. You're right."

CHAPTER 57

Josh was sitting at his desk when Pete ran into his office. "Chief, I found her."

Josh looked up from the document he was reading. "That's great. Who did you find?"

"Rosanne Hermosa, the woman you wanted me to find. You know, the person who owns the landing strip. Well, actually, it's more than that. It's a big farm."

"That's good work. Where did you find her?"

"She's in California, right outside of Los Angeles."

"You got an address?"

Pete handed a piece of paper to Josh. "Here you go."

As soon as Pete left his office, Josh called Detective Pointer and filled her in on Hermosa. "She owns the property where the landing strip is located, which is also where we traced the website server your homicide victim was featured on. Do you want to follow up on her?" Josh asked.

"Sure, go ahead. Maybe the local police can make contact with her. Just keep me posted. And don't forget to include Sheriff Waters in your updates. I don't want to step all over his jurisdiction if this amounts to anything."

"Will do."

Josh briefly considered asking the Los Angeles PD to contact Hermosa, as Pointer suggested, but decided to first try it on his own. He called the number Pete had scribbled on the paper. It rang several times before a woman answered.

"Hello, I need to speak with Rosanne Hermosa, please."

"Who's calling?"

"I'm Josh Hart, the Madden, South Carolina, police chief. I'm calling about an airstrip on a farm located in our area. The tax records show you as the owner. Is that correct?"

"Is anything wrong?"

"I'm just doing a routine follow-up and need to ask you a few questions. Is the airstrip part of your farm or does it operate independently?"

"My ex-husband leases the farm from me. It's my understanding he subleases the airstrip. They do crop dusting and deliver produce for him in exchange."

"Seems like an expensive way to deliver tomatoes," Josh said.

"We haven't been in contact for years, so I don't know anything else. If you need more information, you'll need to talk with him."

"Do you have any family members, other than your ex, who live on the property?"

"My daughter used to live there, but no more."

Josh debated on how far he should push Hermosa. "To your knowledge, is your ex-husband involved in drugs or other illegal activities?"

She hesitated. "Do I need an attorney?"

"Not unless you're doing something illegal or covering for him. Are you?"

"That farm has been in my family for years, so I refused to sell it to him when we divorced. He leases it from me. That's all I know."

"I appreciate your time and cooperation, Ms. Hermosa, and I'll contact him. What's his first name?"

"I changed my name back to my family name when we divorced. His name is Malcolm James."

• • •

Josh called Sheriff Boogie Waters. "We need to talk," Josh said. "I want to fill you in and see what you know about a guy I'm checking on."

"I'm in the car headed in your direction now. I'll meet you at the diner."

Josh was on his second cup of coffee when Sheriff Waters walked in, striding like an old West cowboy entering a saloon. He stopped to flirt with the waitresses before joining Josh as his table. "Police Chief Hart, how are you today?"

"Right as rain, Boogie. What about you?"

"My leg's bothering me some. Danced until the wee hours last night." He stopped to order coffee and a piece of pie. "What's up?" he asked Josh.

Josh told him about his conversation with Hermosa.

"Marcus Xavier James, yes, I know him. He's one of the good guys, from what I can tell. Treats his workers well, pays them more than most, and donates a lot to the church."

"Sounds like a saint," Josh said. "Anything unusual about him?"

The waitress put a large chunk of apple pie on the table and refilled both coffee cups. "Let me know if you boys need anything else," she said.

Sheriff Waters was enjoying his pie when Josh asked again, "Anything unusual about Max?"

"Max, yes, sorry." He took another bite of pie. "Well, for one thing, his daughter went missing a few years ago. Poor guy was distraught. That girl, I can't remember her name right now, but she was the apple of his eye. He gave her anything she wanted."

"What happened to her?"

Waters shrugged. "Rumor was that she ran off, probably with one of the farm boys. She had begged one of them to take her away. Said her daddy was too strict and she felt like a prisoner." Waters wiped his mouth with a napkin. "Damn, that's good pie."

"Did you investigate?"

"I did, indeed. Never found any reason to suspect foul play. Her mother, in fact, I guess that's your Ms. Hermosa, she asked me to drop it. Said her daughter would show up again when she wanted to. As I recall, Mr. James was upset with me. Told me I wasn't doing my job. Now that I think about it again, it was all a bit strange."

Josh was busy taking notes. "Anything else? Anything recent?"

Waters shook his head and pushed the pie plate away and took a long drink of coffee. "Now let me get this straight. You're saying the airstrip is owned by Mr. James' ex-wife. Is that right?"

"She owns the whole farm. The airstrip is just part of it. She claims she doesn't know anything about the operations. Max leases it from her."

"Are you looking at him for some kind of illegal activity?" asked Waters.

"I don't know. It's a big place. Maybe he's not aware that some of his workers are hosting a website of girls for hire. And you said you had gotten some reports about drugs going through the airstrip. But if Max is as good a guy as you say, he wouldn't tolerate that."

"Want me to bring him in for questioning? Maybe we need to enlighten him about what's going on."

"No, not yet. I'll be in touch." Josh threw a $10 bill on the table. "Thanks. The pie's on me."

CHAPTER 58

Enid decided today was as good a day as any to confront her mother's former nurse. The whole thing had been gnawing at her for years, and she was ready to face whatever had happened the day her mother died. The agency where Rachel had tracked down the nurse specialized in hospice work. Enid tapped in the phone number, hesitating before hitting the call button. What would she say?

A female voice announced the agency's name. "May I help you?"

"I'm looking for Angelina Singer. Does she still work here?" Enid asked.

"Yes, would you like to leave a message?"

"Ask her to please call me. It's important that I speak with her. A friend has a message he wants me to deliver."

"What is your name and number?"

"This is, uh, Katy." Enid provided her cell number with the fake name.

Thinking she would likely never hear from Angelina, Enid was surprised when her cell phone rang a few minutes later.

"Thanks for returning my call," Enid said.

"What is the message you have for me? Who sent it?"

"Please don't hang up. You're not in any trouble. I just want to talk to you," Enid said. "My real name is Enid Blackwell. You were my mother's nurse."

After a brief pause, Angelina spoke in a soft voice. "She was a good woman."

Enid chose her next words carefully. "As I said, you're not in any trouble, but I need to know more about the day my mother died."

Angelina was silent.

"Are you there?"

Still no reply.

"I know my mother included you in her will, and I have no problems with that. She loved you, and you took good care of her."

"I didn't want her money. I told her to give it to you instead, but she insisted. She told me to go see my kids with it." Angelina paused. "Ms. Blackwell, what is it you want to know?"

"What did she talk about, you know, before she passed?"

Angelina sighed. "She mostly worried about you and wanted you to be happy. She was upset that you spent all your money and time taking care of her."

"But, I wanted to."

"She said you deserved a better life than taking care of a sick old woman."

Enid could contain her tears no longer. "I have to know, Angelina. Did my mother ask you to help her . . ." She couldn't bring herself to say the words. "She looked so happy and energetic when I left her that day."

"She was happy that day, at peace." Another pause. "Your mother was a wise woman. You should have a good life. That's what she wanted. Goodbye, Ms. Blackwell." Angelina hung up.

Enid held the phone in her hand for several minutes, just staring at the blank screen. What had she expected Angelina to say? *"I helped your mother end her life."* Enid went to the bathroom and splashed cold water on her face. Angelina was right. It was time to move on. Whatever Enid had hoped to gain from talking with her was replaced with resignation, or maybe it was just acceptance. After thinking about talking with her mother's nurse for years, it now seemed anticlimactic. At best, her mother might have lived another couple of months before the cancer totally consumed her. She was in pain and wasting away. Her mother had been happy that day, and that's all that mattered now. Enid could finally say it without pain. Her mother had wanted to set Enid free, wanted her to be happy. Enid owed it to her mother to grant her last wish.

"I will be happy, Mom," Enid said as she stared at her own reflection in the bathroom mirror. "I wish you hadn't done it, but I understand why you did. I love you."

CHAPTER 59

Rachel hated sneaking around and not telling Jack or Enid where she was going. Secrets had caused her so much pain in her life, and she had sworn to herself that she would never be deceptive again. But here she was, sneaking off to meet Tommy Two. Not only was she lying to the people she loved most, Enid had warned her that Tommy might be a criminal. All Rachel knew was that for the first time, she had met a boy that "got" her. They had been texting since they met, and she felt like she knew him, even though she knew she really didn't.

Rachel pulled into the parking lot of the small mom-and-pop restaurant on the outskirts of Columbia and looked around to be sure no one was watching or following her. That was another thing she hated about deception—it made you think everyone else was doing something wrong too. She shook off her regrets and walked inside. Tommy was in the back of the restaurant sitting in one of the vinyl-covered booths. As usual, he was slumped over his laptop, his hands moving so fast they appeared to be floating over the keyboard.

"Hey." Rachel said as she sat down across from him.

Tommy's face lit up with a smile. "Hi." He closed his laptop and stashed it away in the green canvas backpack beside him on the seat.

"Look, Tommy—"

Before she could finish, Tommy interrupted her. "I don't feel good about you sneaking around."

"I agree." Rachel put her hands on top of his. "I don't know much about you, and Enid says you could be a criminal. Are you?"

He caressed the side of her hand with his thumb. "I'm not proud of some of the things I do, but it's not what you think. And the last thing I want is for you to be afraid of me. That's why I wanted to meet here, in a public place, in broad daylight."

"I think you should talk to Enid and Jack. Once they get to know you, they'll like you."

"I can't."

"But why?" asked Rachel.

"It's complicated." Tommy pulled his hands away from hers. "Let's order something. I'm hungry." Tommy motioned for the waitress to come over, and they ordered a meat-and-three plate. Tommy ordered baked chicken, which, for some reason, surprised Rachel. Perhaps because she was going to order the same thing. That made her feel good, like they had even more things in common.

During the meal, they talked about geek topics, like the new AMD Ryzen 7 processor and whether the Russians actually hacked into voter files.

"Why did you become a hacker?" Rachel asked.

"I've always been into tech. I began building computers when I was ten. Went to college but got bored, so I dropped out and went to work for a data and software company. Part of the company was totally legit, but there was another side to it that wasn't. I got recruited for a 'promotion' and ended up hacking for them."

"Did you get arrested?"

Tommy nodded. "The company got busted by the FBI for corporate espionage."

"Did you go to jail?" She whispered across the table.

"Got probation after agreeing to testify and help the feds."

"Doing what?" she asked.

"I can't talk about it, but let's just say it's not much different than what I was doing for my former employer."

Rachel leaned back in her seat. "This is a lot to take in."

Tommy munched on a French fry. "I know, and you should probably stay away from me."

Rachel frowned. "Is that what you want?"

Tommy didn't answer the question. "Did the reporter find that missing girl yet?"

"No, and now her roommate is missing."

“I heard about Kat.” Tommy brushed salt from his hands. "I didn’t know her well, but she seemed okay. I tried to tell her and that other girl there's a lot of bad shit on the dark web. Sometimes it makes me sick to see it."

"I'd like to help the police find missing girls. You know, looking for them online."

"A friend of mine works for a group, some kind of center." Tommy laughed. "Weird thing is, everyone there uses the same name. Myra something. You should check them out. I'll send you something on them."

"Cool. Maybe we could look for that girl and her roommate. You know, work together."

Tommy pushed his plate off to the side. "Whoa, let's not get carried away. I can't get you involved in anything I do. And you sure as hell don't need to be tromping around in the dark web by yourself."

Rachel tucked her hair behind her ears. "I do know a thing or two about protecting my identity online. Can I tell Enid and Jack about your past? It would make them feel better."

"They probably know already. Someone has been checking up on me. I found tracks on my records."

CHAPTER 60

Josh was sorting through pink telephone message slips, trying to prioritize them. Which was more urgent? A stolen pickup or a cow shot with a BB gun by pranksters? The next note in the stack caught his attention. It was from Rachel.

"Pete," he called out to the desk officer. "When did this message come in?" Pete had an annoying habit of forgetting to note the time of incoming calls.

"Not too long ago," Pete yelled back to him.

Josh picked up the phone to call Rachel but then grabbed his hat and jacket instead. "I'm going out a bit," he said to Pete. "I'll take care of these calls on my way back." He stuffed the messages in his pocket.

When Josh drove up the driveway to Jack's house, he was happy to see Enid's car. Jack must be at the newspaper office or over at the inn. Rachel's old Ford pickup was there, too. When she bought it a few months ago, she had announced she was painting it purple. Right now, it was still a combination of faded red paint on the sides and bed, and primer on the two front fenders. Jack wanted to get her a new model car, but she insisted on that truck.

Before Josh could ring the doorbell, Enid unlocked the screen door and opened it. "Well, this is a nice surprise." They kissed, and Josh squeezed her hand.

"It's good to see you, too. I miss having you at the house." He followed Enid to the kitchen.

"Jack made coffee before he left. There's still some here." She reached for a mug in the cabinet and poured a cup for Josh. "If you're here to check on Madden's citizens, that's mighty nice community work, Chief."

Josh tapped her on the nose. "Very funny. I'm actually here to see Rachel. She in?"

"Rachel? Did she call you about Lucy?"

"Actually, I don't know. I just had a message to get in touch with her."

Enid took a plate of blueberry muffins from the counter and set them in front of Josh. "Here. Have one. I'll go get her."

Josh took a big bite of muffin, anticipating one of Ruth's delectable treats, but it was dry and a bit tasteless. He got some preserves from the refrigerator and slathered a spoonful on the muffin, which helped it go down.

As he was taking the last bite, Enid and Rachel came in the kitchen. "Hey, Josh," Rachel said. "You didn't have to come out here to return my call."

Enid and Josh exchanged glances. "Well, unless you need me here, I'm going to my room to do some work," Enid said.

Josh appreciated Enid's ability to read a situation. He should have respected Rachel's privacy. Truth was, he just wanted to see Enid again. "I'll talk to you later."

Rachel got a Sprite from the refrigerator and sat down at the table with Josh. She looked at the plate of muffins. "Did you actually eat one of those?"

Josh smiled. "Yeah, but it was pretty bad."

"Enid is trying to learn to cook. For you, I guess."

Josh shifted in his seat. "I doubt that. Pete said you wanted to talk to me."

Rachel took several gulps of soda, so Josh waited until she was ready to talk. "My friend Lucy, she's got, or had, a boyfriend who saw something. I tried to get her to talk to you, but she doesn't want to get anybody in trouble." She turned the soda can upside down to get the last of the contents. "Enid said I needed to talk to you. Will you keep this to yourself? Lucy doesn't know I'm talking to you."

"If you know something about illegal activity, I can't promise that. But I'll do my best to keep you out of it."

Josh took notes for the next ten minutes while Rachel told him about the girl in captivity. "So Lucy's boyfriend saw this girl being put in a plane, and she was in restraints?"

Rachel nodded. "Please don't tell Lucy I told you."

"I'll check it out. In the meantime, you stay away from that place." Josh stood up to leave.

"Wait." Rachel put her hand on Josh's arm. "There's something else."

Josh sat down again. "What's that?"

"I've met Enid's hacker. His name is Tommy, and he's not a criminal." Rachel told Josh about her conversation with Tommy. "And he says someone has been checking on him."

"It wasn't me. But even if I did, it would be official police business, and I couldn't comment on it." He looked directly at Rachel. "You're hanging out with some questionable folks. You need to stay away from Tommy. I'm sure that's what Enid told you too."

"I think he's working for the FBI."

"All the more reason to stay away. If he's working undercover, he could put you in danger." Josh spoke from experience.

Rachel stood up and unexpectedly kissed Josh on the cheek. "Thanks for worrying about me and Enid. But I'm not in any danger with Tommy."

Josh watched Rachel leave the room. He wanted to warn Enid about Tommy and Rachel, but that would be stepping over the line. Rachel had few people she could trust, and he was glad she felt comfortable enough to confide in him.

Josh looked for Detective Pointer's number in his cell phone but waited until he was in the car before calling. She needed to know about the girl Buddy had seen at the airstrip.

CHAPTER 61

Hari could hear thunder in the distance. Though the small barred windows were caked with decades of grime, she could see lightning flashes periodically. Theo had once told her that thunder was God speaking and that she should be quiet and listen. God might be talking, but He wasn't listening to her. She had begged Him for help. Most days, she was optimistic that people were looking for her and she would be found. But by now, they had probably given up hope that she would ever return. Soon, she would be a painful memory but nothing more. She would never finish school, fall in love, or have children.

Her thoughts drifted to Kat. Had she been buried? Or had Kat been dumped somewhere? She cringed at the thought. Hari walked around the small shed several times to stay limber. She tried to exercise at least once a day, but she was losing interest. What was the point?

She was being fed well, but her appetite was gone. Since being held captive, she had lost weight. Even the new clothes Max had brought were now hanging on her slim frame. One day, he fed her some corn chowder. He said he had made it from the corn on his farm, but it tasted just like her father's recipe. She was consumed with sadness.

The storm was close now. She could hear the wind howling and the window rattling in its frame. Hard rain pelted against the glass. She had an idea. If she broke one of the window panes and was able to hold onto a piece of it, she could end her misery. The fact that she could even think that way made her more depressed. She pushed the thought away—for now, at least. Theo used to say that soup was like life—it's always better the next day.

The small ceiling light, actually only a bare light bulb, flickered in the spring storm, and then she was sitting in total darkness.

• • •

Josh sat in his pickup with Gabby, one of Pete's friends who belonged to a volunteer group of amateur drone operators. When Josh said they needed a better idea of what was going on at the farm, Pete quickly found an eager volunteer. Typically, the only requests the drone group got were to help find wayward animals. Occasionally they searched for a missing person, usually a child or elderly person who had wandered off. The group's members were just hobbyists, but their equipment was top notch. Pete said many of the members had invested thousands of dollars in their drones and cameras. Such technology was beyond Madden's small-town budget, but Josh was fascinated by it.

Josh and Gabby waited for the storm to pass so they could take a look at the Hermosa farm. They were about a half-mile away from the private airstrip where he and Enid had visited earlier.

Gabby played with the controls like she was playing a video game. The telescopic camera showed details that could only be seen from above. She explained that she would fly high enough to avoid detection.

Josh pointed to the screen on her laptop. "There, can you zoom in on those two guys?" He watched as the faces became more visible. "Get a still shot of those faces, if you can, without alerting them."

For the next few minutes, they watched the two men at the airstrip load produce crates on the plane. Nothing suspicious or out-of-the-ordinary.

"Let's look around the farm a bit," Josh said.

The operator navigated the drone away from the airstrip. "There's a house and some small buildings ahead. Want to see those?"

"Sure."

A large farmhouse at the end of a long driveway came into focus. Behind the house were three small buildings, all with bars on the windows. "That's odd," Josh said. "Why would you have bars on farm outbuildings?"

"Maybe he keeps farm equipment in them and doesn't want anyone to break in."

"I guess that's possible," Josh said. "I don't see anyone around. Let's go in closer and get a look."

"Our group has guidelines about how low we can go, but we'll still get a good look." She maneuvered the drone controls so they had a good look at the buildings.

"Wait. Hold up here," Josh said. "Did you see something move in that window?"

The operator looked at the screen. "It's hard to tell." She moved the drone in a bit closer. "There. I see it. Definitely looks like some kind of movement."

"Take some still shots and look around some more," Josh said. The drone passed over the farm fields where workers were crating produce. One of the men had a pistol in holster on his hip. He pointed up toward the drone.

"Uh, oh. We've been spotted." The operator took the drone to a higher altitude. "At least we know it's a working farm."

Josh nodded. "But what else are they selling?"

CHAPTER 62

Enid packed the last of the picnic items into the big wicker basket Ruth had filled with lunch. "That was the best chicken salad I've ever had. I wish I had Ruth's cooking skills."

Josh leaned over and kissed her. "You have other talents."

"Can I talk to you about Hari's case before you go back to work?" she asked.

"There's not much to tell. I'm still trying to find out more about the Hermosa farm."

"What about Max? Have you found out anything about him?"

"He seems to be a farmer. Plain and simple."

"But what about that airstrip?"

Josh brushed bread crumbs from his trousers. "Why didn't you tell me about Lucy's boyfriend?"

"I offered to, but it was better that Rachel talked to you."

"Protecting your source. I guess that's an occupational pitfall when dealing with you reporters."

"Ouch. That was a bit harsh." Enid took his hand in hers. "I didn't mean to withhold anything. It's just a bit complicated with Rachel. Other than me and Jack, she doesn't have anyone on her side." She kissed the back of his hand. "Can you understand that?"

Josh pulled her into him and hugged her. "I guess I have to if I want to keep you."

Enid eased away. "Do you? Want to keep me, I mean?"

He kissed her and ran his hand through her hair. "Yes, I do."

Josh's radio crackled with static. "Chief, you there?" It was Pete's voice. "When will you be back?"

Josh rolled his eyes. "So much for a leisurely lunch," he said to Enid. He pressed the button on the two-way radio. "I'll be there shortly. Over and out."

As Enid watched Josh walk up the hill toward the inn, she tried to imagine life with him, but this time she thought of her life as a reporter being married to a cop. He wouldn't answer her question about the airstrip. On the other hand, she didn't tell him about her conversation with Rachel and Lucy. Was this how their life would be? Withholding information and skirting around sensitive questions?

She gathered the picnic basket and returned to the inn. Ruth was in the library with a guest, so Enid put the basket in the kitchen and scribbled a brief thank-you note for the delicious lunch.

As she headed back to Jack's, she impulsively decided to drive down the road by Hermosa's farm. Following the route she and Josh had taken, she found the road near the airstrip. She followed the narrow road for about a mile until she saw a farmhouse in the distance. The house was sitting in the midst of acres of well-tended farmland. Irrigation equipment was spraying the crops. There were no cars at the farmhouse, and no garage that she could see. The other buildings around the house appeared to be storage buildings.

For a moment, she considered driving up to the house but then decided it was too risky. If confronted, what excuse did she have for being there? She drove past the entrance to the farmhouse. After a short distance, the paved road ended, and she was on a narrow dirt road. The trees were denser in this area, and the road was covered with a green canopy. She slowed to avoid the potholes. A dusty cloud formed behind her car. After a slight turn in the road, she was blocked by a metal gate, chained shut with a padlock. All she could see beyond the gate was that the road continued beyond it.

She turned off the ignition and looked around as she got out of the car. She left the car unlocked in case she had to leave quickly. There was no way out other than to back out the way she had come in. For a moment, she considered calling Josh and telling him where she was, but he would be furious with her for meddling, so she decided against it.

The air was warm and fragrant with the smell of earth and flowering trees near the road. The gated area was fenced with two strands of barbed wire. She put her foot on the bottom strand and held up the top one, giving her just enough space to get through. There were no signs warning against trespassing, but that would not be a decent defense if she got caught. Nervously, she glanced back at her car to be sure no one had followed her.

A small bee hovered around her face. She swatted it away and kept walking. The road eventually narrowed to a footpath. She could see tracks in the dirt, probably from an ATV. She followed the tire tracks until she saw a building ahead. It was one story, made of concrete blocks and painted green and brown, like camouflage. Two ATVs were parked beside the building. She looked around and saw no one.

At the back of the building, the entrance door had a glass panel at the top that was pushed up so that only a screen covered the top half of it. She looked around again and eased her way to the door. A red and white checkered curtain blew gently inside the door's screen opening. Enid tiptoed up the two wooden steps and looked in the back door.

A man's voice came from inside the building. "You, get over here," he said. "Now."

Enid crouched below the door window and then slowly eased up again. The screen was black with grime and rusty in places, making it hard to see inside. She made out the shape of a small female. The young girl couldn't have been more than a teenager. She moved slowly, as though she were sleepwalking. The only clothing she had on was a pair of panties and a cropped top that exposed her bare midriff. A large man sitting on a cot grabbed her by the waist and pulled her toward him, then fondled her breasts under her top. Enid's stomach churned.

The sound of a motorized vehicle approaching made Enid jump. Apparently, it was an ATV based on the tracks she saw on the path. She crouched lower and slipped around to the other side of the building, out of sight. She kneeled down and peeped around the corner. Two men got off a four-seater ATV. Both men carried guns on their hip. One headed to the front of the building, but the other one walked toward the back where she had been standing. She looked at the woods around her and decided the only way she could get away was through the thicket of trees and bushes surrounding the building. She was glad she had on sensible shoes, as Josh had called them.

As the man's footsteps got closer, she slipped into the woods, moving quietly. No time to consider how many snakes and bugs were waiting for her in the dense undergrowth. A few feet to her right was a narrow path. It had signs of being used recently. A few footprints were still visible. She took the path, walking quickly while trying to figure out how to get back to her car.

The path widened a bit, so she broke into a slow jog. Suddenly the path split. The wider side was to her right, which would take her even further from her car. She chose the left side of the path, which was narrow but still passable.

She patted her cell phone in her pocket to make sure it was still there. If she couldn't find a way back to her car soon, she would have to swallow her pride and call Josh. She didn't want to think about what his reaction would be.

Ahead of her the path veered left again, so she jogged a little faster. She should be able to see her car soon. Sunlight streamed through the trees ahead as she approached a clearing. Enid slowed to a walk and looked around before leaving the cover of the woods. Her car was barely visible on the road.

Movement to her right caught her eye. Several buzzards hovered around their meal. Probably a small dead animal. She kept walking straight toward her car. The large birds ignored her and kept pulling away bits of whatever they were dining on.

Enid's hand was shaking as she started her car. This was no time for a panic attack, so she forced herself to breathe deeply as she glanced in the rearview mirror. Backing up as fast she could, Enid soon got back to the paved road and turned around and headed back to the main road.

CHAPTER 63

Josh glanced at his cell screen, where Sheriff Boogie Waters' name appeared. "Hey, Boogie. What's up?"

"Got a body here, thought you might want to know about it."

Josh felt uneasy. "Why is that? Anybody I know?"

"The tattoo matches that girl you're looking for. You know, the missing student whose car you found. You want to see her before we take her to the county morgue?"

"Give me the coordinates. I'm on my way."

Josh told Pete about the call as he rushed out the door. "I'll be back when I can."

About thirty minutes later, Josh found the wooded area Boogie had described. The Ford SUV with the sheriff's name on the door was parked beside the coroner's van.

"Thanks for waiting for me," Josh told the coroner.

"Not my decision." He wasn't smiling. "I need to get this one checked in. Don't be long." He motioned for Josh to follow him. Inside the van was a black body bag. "You might want to stand back. Doesn't smell too good." He unzipped it.

Even though Josh had smelled death many times, it was worse each time—something you never got used to. He put his arm across his nose and mouth. "Good grief."

Boogie peered in the van. "She's been here a couple days, maybe more, maybe less. In this heat, you can't tell until they examine her." He pointed to her upper torso. "Turn her so he can see her back," he said to the coroner.

The coroner pulled up what was left of the deceased's left shoulder. She had decomposed considerably, so he had to move her gently. He pointed to the tattoos.

Josh had to look closely to see what was left of the outline. "That's Kat's ink, there," he said pointing.

"I'll put a call in for Detective Pointer, to let her know."

Josh turned to the coroner. "I know it's probably too early to ask, but can you tell how she died?"

"Violently, I imagine." The coroner zipped the bag. "Can I go now?" he asked Boogie. "My wife is expecting me for dinner. Wouldn't want to upset her by being late."

Boogie and Josh watched as the coroner loaded his equipment and drove off. "Damn shame," Boogie said. "The world's a dangerous place for young girls."

Josh nodded, but his mind was on Enid. He wanted to tell her about Kat before she heard it from someone else.

• • •

Between the dust, bug bites, and sordid scene she had witnessed, Enid needed a hot bath by the time she got back to Jack's house. As the warm water ran over her hair and down her body, questions were forming. What was going on in that place? Did Max know about it? Who was the girl? And how would she tell Josh she had been there without making him mad?

At least, she was glad Jack and Rachel were gone. She needed to be alone with her thoughts, to sort through it all.

After putting on fresh jeans and a t-shirt, she was getting ready to dry her hair when she heard Josh's voice.

"Hello, anybody home?"

Enid let Josh in. "I just got out the shower. If you can wait a minute, I'll make myself a bit more presentable."

"Are you kidding me? I love that au naturel look. You're gorgeous."

Enid blushed. "Are you looking for Jack? No one is here but me."

Josh sat on the sofa and patted the seat beside him, motioning for her to sit down. "I need to talk to you, actually."

Enid noticed the change in Josh's expression. "Has anything happened? You look concerned."

"There's no easy way to say this. They found Kat's body."

Enid put her hands to her face. "Oh, no. What happened to her?"

"Looks like foul play but too early to tell. She's decomposed but you can still see the tats on her shoulder. Hair matches too, from what I could tell. You could see some purple streaks in it."

Enid buried her face in her hands. As much as she hated hearing about Kat, it was Hari that was on her mind. "Where did they find her?"

"A man had his hunting dogs out in the woods training them, when one of them zeroed in on something. The sheriff said she had been partially buried. The guy who found her started poking around and realized it was a human body." Josh put his arm around Enid.

"Was Kat found near the Hermosa Farm?"

Josh pulled away to look at Enid. "Yes, as a matter of fact. How did you know that?"

"I need to tell you something too." Enid proceeded to tell Josh about what she had seen in the building near the farm.

Josh stood up and paced the floor a couple of times. "What kind of crazy are you, trespassing onto someone else's place, especially since you know something is going on there?"

"Actually, I don't know that, other than what you said, because you haven't told me anything about Max or the airstrip."

Josh sat down again beside Enid and turned to face her. "You are a reporter. I am a police chief. Don't you see how that's a problem with me sharing everything with you?"

Enid didn't want to tell Josh just how much she had thought about their dilemma. "I guess we'll have to figure that out. But will you check out that building?"

"I'll talk to Sheriff Waters. I can't go busting in there without a warrant." Josh paused briefly. "Can we agree that you won't use anything I say without my permission?"

Enid nodded. "Of course."

Josh told Enid about the drone Pete's friend Gabby has used to surveil the farm. "But we didn't find anything unusual, so there was nothing we could do." Josh caressed Enid's face. "Promise me you won't do anything stupid again. I'll see if Sheriff Waters can get a warrant based on what you saw. That gives us a solid connection between the farm and illegal activity. It's time we find out what's going on at Max's farm and how much he knows about it."

CHAPTER 64

Max paced the floor in his living room. "How could they have found her? I thought you buried her away from here."

"It was way out in the woods," said one of Max's men. "No one ever goes there. I figured it was safe."

Max slapped the man with the back of his hand so hard the man almost fell backwards. "No, you didn't think, you imbecile."

The man rubbed his face.

"It won't be long before the sheriff shows up here, once they find out that she was on my land. You need to wrap up your operation and get out of here. Now. If they get a warrant, we're screwed." Max glared at the man. "You got that?" Max poked the man's chest with his finger. "Got it?" he repeated.

The man nodded. "What you want me to do with the girls?"

"You're making the money, you figure it out. But do it quick. Now get out of here."

The man turned to leave, shoulders slumped. Before he walked out the door, he turned back to Max. "Want me to take her too?" He motioned toward the building where Hari was held.

"I'll take care of her," Max said. "You should have handled that nosy reporter like I told you to. She and her police chief boyfriend are behind all this."

• • •

Max poured himself a couple jiggers of Kentucky bourbon and paced again. When he had emptied the glass, he got the keys to the shed and walked outside. He looked around to satisfy himself that no one was watching before he unbolted the big padlock on the shed door.

Hari was crouched in a corner. He wished she had learned to trust him. After all, he had taken good care of her, bought her new clothes just like she wanted, and had even let her write to Theo so he'd stop worrying about her. It bothered him that she behaved just like Belle had before she left. He had hoped this one would be different.

"Get up," he told Hari.

She stood up but stayed in the corner.

"Get all your things together. Here." Max threw a big drawstring canvas bag at her feet.

Hari began gathering her few belongings. "Where are we going?"

"Time to move. Hurry up."

When Hari put the last item in the bag, she pulled on the drawstring to close it. "I'm ready."

Max grabbed her small arm, his long fingers encircling it. He worried that she had gotten so skinny. "You try anything cute and you'll be sorry. Understand?" He tried to sound tough, but his heart was breaking. What should he do with her? Briefly, he considered letting the men take her away. She had not worked out the way he wanted, so maybe he needed to let her go with them. But the thought of them pawing over her made him sick to his stomach. Besides, she was not like those other girls. She was special.

Max pulled Hari outside, practically dragging her. No one had showed up yet, but they would soon.

CHAPTER 65

Rachel sat on the bed in her room at Jack's house, looking at the text messages on her phone. She had texted Tommy Two frequently but got no replies. Something was wrong. In their brief relationship, he had never failed to respond. She went to Enid's room and knocked on her door. "It's me. Can I come in?"

Enid opened the door for Rachel.

"Have you talked with Tommy lately?" Rachel asked.

"No, I haven't, but then I don't have a way of contacting him or any reason to do so."

Rachel looked down, avoiding Enid's gaze.

"And neither do you," Enid added. "I thought we agreed you weren't going to have contact with him."

"I know and I'm sorry. But that's not fair. He's not like you think. Something is wrong. I'm going to the coffee shop to see if I can find him."

"I'd ask you not to, but you obviously wouldn't listen. And you're an adult, free to do what you want to." Enid sighed. "I'll go with you."

"No, I need to go alone." Rachel put her hands in the back pockets of her jeans.

Enid put her hands on Rachel's shoulders. "Look, I trust you completely, and I know you're a smart young woman who can take care of herself. But when we care for people we're sometimes blind to who they really are. You share a lot of common interests with Tommy, but you don't know anything about him." She hugged Rachel. "Just be careful, and text me when you leave the coffee shop, so I can stop worrying."

Rachel returned the hug and then pulled away. "Just don't tell Jack. Okay? I don't want him worrying too." She blew a kiss to Enid as she left the room. "I'll be fine, really."

• • •

Rachel looked at the table where Tommy normally sat in the coffee shop. A young woman was sitting there, drawing frogs on a large sketch pad. Rachel then walked to the coffee bar. "Excuse me," she asked the barista, "have you seen Tommy today?" You know, Tommy Two?"

"Caffè Macchiato for Kevin," he called out. The man standing next to Rachel reached for the steaming cup. The barista turned to her. "Wait a minute." He pulled an envelope from behind the counter and read the name scribbled on it. "Are you Rachel?"

"Yes. Is that for me?" Rachel felt the knot tightening in her stomach.

He barista handed the envelope to her and immediately returned to his work. "Chai Latte for Jennifer."

Rachel waited until she was back in her car before opening the envelope. She broke the seal and pulled out the single-page note.

Rachel,

I had a feeling you'd come here looking for me. Don't worry I'm fine. If you've been trying to reach me, that cell number is no longer good. Don't try to call or text. You are a smart girl, and if you decide to go into cyber forensics, I feel sorry for the bad guys. You've got a knack for this stuff.

Just stay on the right side of the line. I like you a lot, but I couldn't let myself fall for you. Be safe.

T.T.

Rachel blinked back the tears. How could he just leave like that? She knew there was no way to find him. He was too careful to leave tracks.

. . .

When Rachel returned to Madden, she didn't go home. Instead, she went straight to the Madden Police Department. She breathed a sigh of relief when she saw that Josh wasn't in his office. She was also happy to see Pete at the front desk. "Hey, how's it going?"

Pete looked up and smiled when he recognized her. "Are you looking for the chief?"

"No, I was actually hoping to talk to you if you're not too busy," she said.

Pete leaned back in his chair back a bit. "Sure, what do you need?"

"Criminal convictions are public information, right?"

Pete nodded. "Correct."

"Can you tell me how to check on somebody? I can probably figure it out, but you could save me a bunch of time."

Pete hesitated before responding. "Okay, but are you going to tell me what this is all about?"

"I just need to see if someone has a criminal record."

Pete pulled his chair back up to the desk so he could reach the keyboard. "What's his or her name?"

"Well, you see, I don't exactly know the last name, but he goes by Tommy Two, so I'm guessing he's a junior. Could you search by the kind of crime?"

"I can't look that up for you."

"Could you just try? Maybe we'll get lucky."

"You need to talk to Josh. I can't say any more. Sorry."

Rachel thanked Pete and left the station with a heavy heart.

CHAPTER 66

Sheriff Boogie Waters pounded on the door of Max's farmhouse. "This is Sheriff Waters. Open up." Waters motioned for his deputies to cover the back in case someone tried to get away. Waters knocked a few more times before the door opened slightly. A dark-haired, middle-aged woman peered out at him.

"Yes?" she asked.

"You live here?"

"I'm looking after the place. Mr. James is not home."

"Open the door. We have a warrant to search the premises and outbuildings."

The woman opened the door and stepped aside, motioning with her arm for them to come in. Josh was behind Waters and followed him inside.

"I'll be in the kitchen if you need me," she said.

When she was out of earshot, Josh said to Boogie. "She didn't seem too surprised."

"Yeah, I thought the same thing." Boogie gave instructions to the deputies to look around the house. "Hey, ma'am," he called out to the woman.

She emerged from the back of the house.

“You got keys to the outbuildings?"

The woman handed him a ring of keys. "Here."

"Come on," Waters said to Josh. "You're with me."

They went outside and after checking to be sure no one was lurking about, Waters pointed to the nearest building. "Let's check this one first." Waters tried several keys on the ring until he found one that fit the large padlock.

Josh had one hand resting on the gun in his holster. With the other hand, he held an LED flashlight that illuminated the interior. It was empty, with the exception of a few wooden produce crates and cobwebs, which appeared to be undisturbed. "Doesn't look like anything is in here."

"Nope. Let's try another one."

They went next to the small building directly behind the house and opened the padlock. "Looks better than my first apartment," Josh said as he looked around.

Waters ran his hand across the small table. "Somebody's been keeping it clean."

They looked around but found nothing. They were ready to go to the next building, when Josh spotted something. He leaned over and inspected a small piece of pink yarn that was wedged in a crack in the wooden table leg. He carefully put it in an evidence bag. "You think Max has taken to wearing pink?" he asked. "Here, help me turn this table over."

Waters grabbed the table on one end and helped Josh turn it over. "What you looking for?"

Josh shined his light beam on the underside of the tabletop. "This," he said pointing to something written with what looked like red lipstick. "What does that say?"

Waters pulled his reading glasses from his shirt pocket. "I used to see without these damn things." He peered at the crudely written message. "Help me Hari."

"Holy mother of Jesus," said Josh. "That's the other missing girl. She was here."

Waters yelled into his two-way radio. "Call Detective Pointer at CPD. Tell her to get her forensics team out here, stat!"

CHAPTER 67

When the phone message appeared on Enid's phone, she didn't recognize the number. Lately, she had been getting more robocalls than ever. Yet, junk callers typically didn't leave messages, so she pressed the play button on her phone.

"Hi, this is Myra Nicholas. We've got a package to hand deliver to you, so you'll have to pick it up here."

Enid looked at the time. It was late afternoon and the traffic would be brutal on the interstate this time of day. She knocked on Jack's open office door. "Hi, I've got to go to Columbia to pick up a package. I'll be back later."

"Wish I could go with you, but I've got to work on the next edition. Loved your last article." He rummaged through some papers on his desk. "In fact, we've gotten good feedback from our readers. They want more on Theo and Hari."

"I don't know how much more I can write until something turns up. I'll try to see him while I'm in Columbia."

Enid was about to leave when Jack's phone rang. He motioned for Enid to come back as he listened to the caller. "Thanks, buddy. I owe you one."

"Who was that?" Enid asked.

"One of my police contacts. CPD was called out to our area. Come on. Let's go." Jack grabbed his messenger-style bag and brushed past Enid. "Well, are you coming?"

Enid wanted to pick up her package, but Jack was waiting at the door to lock it behind her.

• • •

"Are you headed to the Hermosa Farm?" Enid asked when she recognized the area.

"Yeah. Do you know the place?"

Enid shrugged. "I'm familiar with it."

As they approached the farmhouse, Enid could see several police vehicles in the driveway. She recognized Josh's truck as one of them.

Jack parked his pickup off to the side. "Let me do the talking. They're not going to be happy to see us."

Enid followed slightly behind Jack as he approached Josh, who was standing beside the farmhouse. A large spotlight on a stand illuminated the area.

Josh nodded toward them. "Enid, and Jack. Surprised to see you here."

"What's going on?" Jack asked.

Josh and Enid exchanged glances. "Forensics is checking something we found in one of the sheds. Boogie called CPD in to collect any evidence." He pointed to Jack and then to Enid. "Not a word of this yet, you two. Understand?"

"Sure," Jack said. "Can we ask you a few questions?"

"Not now," Josh said. "Stay out of the way. I've got to go back over there." He motioned to the shed. "Remember, not a word." As he walked away, he turned back to Enid. "Please stay out of the way. We don't know who or what we're dealing with."

As Josh disappeared into the shed, Jack said to Enid, "What was that all about? He didn't look too happy."

"It's a long story."

"Well, we've got a long night. Let's go back to the car. I grabbed a couple bottles of water on the way out."

Enid laid her head back against the seat's neck support and closed her eyes. "I don't have a good feeling about this."

"It can't be too easy for you and Josh these days. I guess you two will have to figure out the boundaries."

"I've already pushed past those." Enid rubbed her eyes and proceeded to tell Jack about what she had seen on the farm. "They're here because I told Josh about the girl in the building."

Jack turned in his seat to face her. "Wow. You really are like a moth drawn to fire. I told you that more than a year ago."

"Are you fussing at me, too?" she asked. "I'm tired, so please don't."

"No, just concerned, that's all." Jack flashed his familiar grin. "On the other hand, what a scoop! I doubt we'll get much here tonight. They'll be here for hours. Let's go back and see what we can find on Max James."

• • •

Enid pushed back from the conference room table at the *Madden Gazette* office. "I'm beginning to think Max James is too good to be true. There's nothing about him other than the wonderful things he does for the community. Why can't we find more?"

Jack pushed his glasses up and rubbed his eyes. "I think you're right," he said, yawning. "I need some sleep. You ready to get out of here? We'll look some more in the morning."

Enid slapped her forehead with the palm of her night. "Oh, crap! I forgot about the package I was going to pick up on Columbia. If it's okay with you, I'll go get it in the morning. I have no idea what it is, but I'm intrigued."

CHAPTER 68

The next morning, Enid drove to Columbia to the Myra Nicholas center. When she walked in, there were two girls in the small waiting area. One had bruises down her legs and on her arms. When she looked up at Enid, the girl stared with a blank expression, devoid of any emotion. The other girl was picking at a ragged cuticle on her finger and never looked up.

Enid walked past the girls to the desk and rang the bell. Immediately, one of the volunteers came out to greet her. "I'm here to pick up a package," Enid said. "Someone left me a message."

The girl walked to the back and returned with a manuscript-sized box. The address label simply had "Enid Blackwell" written on it, with her phone number beneath the name.

"Do you know who left it?" Enid asked.

"Sorry, I have no idea."

"Okay. Thanks."

As much as Enid wanted to return to her apartment and examine the contents of the box, she needed to talk with Theo while she was in Columbia. She checked her phone messages and texts. Nothing from Josh or Jack on last night's search of the farm.

• • •

"So good to see you," Enid said as she embraced Theo. He was gaunt, with dark circles beneath his eyes.

"Hello, Enid, my dear. How are you?" he whispered. "Come, sit with me. Can I get you some tea?"

"No, thanks. I just wanted to talk a minute if you have time."

"I hope you can tell me what's going on. Detective Pointer said they had some leads they were following up on. She called me early this morning."

On the drive from Madden, Enid had debated on what to say to Theo. "What do you know about Marcus James?"

"You mean Max? Why do you ask?"

"Just curious."

"He's a good man, from what I can tell. He gives to the church and found me a place to stay."

Enid hesitated before proceeding. "Precious said he was unusually upset about Hari's disappearance. Why do you think that's so?"

"He cares about her. I assumed nothing more." More alert now, he asked, "Please tell me why you are asking. I don't have the energy for guessing games."

"The police have reason to believe someone on Max's farm is transporting drugs." Enid paused. "And maybe girls, too."

Theo's hands flew up to cover his face. "What are you saying to me?" He lowered his hands and shook his head. "Are you telling me he has something to do with Hari? I can't bear it."

Enid took his hands and held them. "I don't know, but there's something strange going on there. Maybe Max doesn't know about it. I understand it's a big place and that he subleases part of it."

"Take me there. Now. Please." Theo's eyes were filled with tears.

"I can't do that. You've got to let the police do their job. They searched his place last night. I'll see what I can find out." Enid squeezed Theo's hands gently. "If they had found anything . . ." Her voice trailed off. "I'll be in touch soon. In the meantime, if you hear from Max, don't say anything out of the ordinary to him, but let the police know. Promise?"

Theo nodded. "Please let me know what they found. I can't bear this burden much longer."

CHAPTER 69

On the drive back to Madden, Enid switched radio channels restlessly, trying to find something to take her mind off Theo's agony. She pulled off the road beside a roadside vegetable market near Madden to call Josh.

"I'm sorry I haven't called you," he said. "It was a long night, just got in."

"Anything on Hari?"

"Are we off the record?"

Enid hid her irritation. "Yes, of course. I just left Theo. He looks so weak and tired."

"You don't need to get further involved in all this."

"I'm already involved. I can't turn my back on Theo. He's got no one else to turn to." She took a deep breath. "Sorry, I'm tired, too. Jack and I worked late last night doing some research. Please tell me what you found."

"Max is gone, and I imagine he's out of the area by now. He didn't take his pickup, and he hired a house sitter to watch the place. She claims she doesn't know what vehicle he was driving. She says she doesn't own a car, and we didn't find one registered to her. None of the rental agencies nearby show him renting a vehicle. So, we can't put out an APB for him."

"Did you find anything that would help you find Hari?"

"No, but we found something that leads us to believe she was there at some point." He told her about the pink yarn and the message under the table.

"Is there a chance she's still alive?" After the research she had done on human trafficking, she wasn't sure death was Hari's worst fate.

"I have no idea. Remember, you can't use any of this. Not yet. I've got to run. I'll try to see you later today."

Before she could reply, the line was dead.

• • •

Less than an hour later, Enid was in the conference room at the *Madden Gazette.* She opened the package, looking for a note or some indication as to who had sent it. Inside the box, she found a stack of screen prints. After spreading them out and examining each one, it was evident all the information related to Marcus Xavier James, aka Max. Someone had accessed his finances, real estate holdings, and business records. There was also a copy of a police report, charging him with abuse. Those charges were later dropped.

She was so intent on studying the documents that she didn't notice Jack come in.

"Hey, what have you got there?" he asked.

She pointed to the papers spread across the table. "Someone sent me this information about Max."

"Anonymously? Wonder who sent it?"

"I don't know but one person who could have gotten his information." She didn't want to consider that Rachel might be practicing her new skills. "Look at this." Enid picked up one of the documents and handed it to Jack. "His daughter filed abuse charges against him through a guardian ad litem. She claims he treated her like a prisoner, held her against her will. But the charges were later dropped."

"Any allegations of sexual assault?"

"I don't see any here," she said.

"Did you put this star here?" Jack pointed to one of the papers showing the real estate holdings.

Enid studied the screen print. "No, I didn't, but that's on the other side of Madden."

Jack put on his reading glasses and looked more closely. "If I'm not mistaken, that's actually in the town limits. As I recall, Madden annexed that area about fifteen years ago. I didn't think there was anything out there but woods, though. Awhile back, the turpentine industry grew pine trees to harvest the sap. When the industry shut down in the 1940s, a lot of that land just remained pine forests. You can still see where the pines were planted in rows, so it looks different from natural growth. The town of Madden annexed it to put a big water tower on the land. Looks like Max owned all of that area. As I recall, nobody fought the annexation because Madden town taxes are low, and I think the owner was given about ten years before the town taxes kicked in. Madden just wanted the land to erect the water tower on it."

Enid looked at some of the financial records. "It doesn't look like he's got a business or anything operating there. No income is associated with that address, but it looks like it's owned through a holding company. That's probably why Josh didn't find it."

"Don't you need to share this information with him?"

"There's nothing to tell Josh at this point. That star beside that property could be meaningless."

"So what do we do with all this?" Jack swept his arm across the papers spread out on the table.

"Everybody thinks Max has left the area. What if he's right here?" She pointed to the "X" on the map.

"I don't like that look on your face. I've seen it before, and it's usually trouble," Jack said.

"We'll just have a quick look around and call Josh if we see anything unusual."

Jack sighed. "If I say no, you'll just go without me. He pointed his finger at Enid. "For the record, I think this is a bad idea."

CHAPTER 70

When they reached the edge of Madden, it was just as Jack had described the area. It was heavily wooded, and the pine trees were all lined up, like skinny soldiers waiting for a command. A tall silver water tower with "Madden" on it stood guard over the forest. The road they were on was narrow, but at least it was paved. For the next few miles, all they could see was more pines.

"Is this it?" Enid asked when Jack stopped the car.

"I told you it's an abandoned turpentine farm." Jack motioned with this hand. "See, nothing here. Can we go back now?"

"Then why would Max hold onto this land?"

"Well, the taxes can't be too high. Why not keep it? Might be worth something later. Maybe Walmart will put a distribution area here one day." Jack looked at the surroundings. "I need to find a place to turn around. I'll drive a bit further." They drove about a half-mile. "Ah, here's a place." Jack turned left onto a narrow dirt road.

"Wait. Where does this road go?"

Jack looked ahead. "I don't know, but this is private property. We can't just go driving in and snoop around."

"Then park here, and I'll walk a little way down." Enid opened the car door.

Jack grabbed her arm. "If, and that's a big if, Max is somehow involved in Hari's disappearance, he's not going to like you or anyone else waltzing up to his door. What are you going to say? 'Hi, is Hari here?'"

"Then walk with me." Enid made a face at Jack. "I wasn't planning on waltzing in—just getting a closer look." She eased her arm from Jack's grip. "Well, are you coming?"

"Oh, for Pete's sake. I'll pull the truck up there in that little clearing so we're not blocking the road. But if anyone comes in this way, they'll see the car."

Jack checked his cell phone. "We have no signal out here, so let's hope we don't have to call 911."

"Stop being melodramatic and start walking," Enid called out to him as she took long strides ahead.

After they walked a short distance, Enid pointed ahead to a small cabin sitting on the bank of a pond. "Look."

"Well, I'll be. There is actually something here." Jack pointed to the right. "Stay by those trees over there, and I'll check it out." Enid reluctantly followed Jack's orders, while he walked slowly toward the cabin and then disappeared from sight.

• • •

Jack eased his way around the cabin to the front, which faced the pond. A wooden dock protruded from shore to about twenty feet over the water, where a small jon boat was tethered to it. A bevy of mourning doves sat near the dock, pecking at the ground. It appeared someone had recently tossed seed on the ground for them. When he walked closer, the doves took off suddenly, generating a burst of cooing sounds as they flew toward the woods. Near the spot where the doves had been feeding, large shoe prints marked the damp, sandy soil.

Nervously, Jack looked around. If the birds had not alerted anyone, then he must be alone. The cabin had a door and small window on each side. Both were boarded shut, and a large padlock secured the door. He cautiously walked up to one of the windows and tried to pry one of the boards off, but the multiple nails held tight. He knocked on the door a few times before walking away. There was nothing to indicate anything unusual. That is, until he walked to the opposite side of the cabin. The same large footprints were accompanied by smaller prints that looked more like drag marks at times. Jack took some photos with his iPhone before heading back to the road where Enid was waiting.

• • •

Hari's head was throbbing, and everything sounded like it was underwater. What was that tapping noise at the door? She tried to stand up, but her head was spinning. After deciding it was her imagination, she curled up in a fetal position on the small cot and drifted off again.

Some time later, she awoke again. This time when she tried to get up, her head hurt but at least the room wasn't spinning. This was not a familiar place, and she didn't like it. It felt damp and smelled like a smoldering campfire. A rusted potbelly stove sat in the corner, and a battery-operated lantern on the floor by her cot cast shadows on the walls and ceiling.

Hari picked up the lantern and examined her surroundings. On one side of the room, child-like drawings were stapled to the bare wood walls. The paper was yellowed with age. She pushed aside the curtain that served as a closet door. Inside the small area, a bucket and a roll of toilet paper occupied one side, while an old metal storage trunk took up the rest of the space. At least she'd have a little privacy using the toilet.

On a small folding card table, a few snacks had been laid out: several bottles of water, a pack of Oreos, a box of Cheez Its, and a small plastic bag of beef jerky. Just looking at the food made her stomach roil, and she felt faint.

Hari made her way back to the cot and lay down. She closed her eyes and tried to pretend she was a child, a time when she was safe and loved.

CHAPTER 71

Josh looked across his desk at Jack and Enid, while rubbing his temples. "Please tell me you didn't go chasing after Max on your own." He looked at Jack, who looked down at his shoes, and then at Enid, who stared at him defiantly. "Never mind. I should know better than to ask." He picked up the screen prints she had shared with him. "Are these from your hacker friend?"

"I don't know who left the package for me."

"Can't we just focus on what I found at the cabin? Isn't that what's important?" Jack asked.

Josh rubbed the back of his neck. "Sorry, you're right. It's just that I worry about both of you playing amateur detectives. That picture you showed me of the shoe prints is pretty convincing. The good news is it's my jurisdiction, so I can check it out without involving anyone else. Although, I do need to keep Detective Pointer in the loop. Boogie, too. But I may not be able to get a search warrant using anonymous information."

"You mean you can't do anything?" Enid asked.

"I didn't say that." Josh called out, "Pete, come in here please. It's urgent."

The desk deputy quickly responded by showing up with his pad and pen. "What do you need, Chief?"

Josh handed him the documents. "I need to know whatever you can find out about this property and the company that owns it."

Pete studied the papers. "Anything else?"

"Just see if you can verify this information."

Pete nodded and returned to his desk.

"I'm going out there to the cabin to see what I can find," Josh said. "You two go back to the newspaper office where you belong."

• • •

On the drive to the cabin, Josh's thoughts were on Enid. The things he admired about her were also the things that worried him. How could they survive as a couple if she didn't understand boundaries? When he first met her, she was in a shell, afraid to live. He couldn't blame her for withdrawing after what she had been through. Now, she had returned to her roots as an investigative reporter. He doubted Jack would be able to restrict her to community articles for the *Madden Gazette*. Reporting was in her blood, just like it was in Jack's. In fact, Josh wasn't sure Enid would ever be content with small-town life. At least her reporter's instincts had given them a new lead to finding Hari.

CHAPTER 72

Rachel's vibrating cell phone bounced around on the table where she had left it. No name or phone number showed on the text message on her screen. "girl 4sale in the dark. use tor." It was followed by a link. Rachel sent the link to her laptop. Using her Tor browser, she accessed the link on the dark web, the way Tommy had shown her. When she clicked on the site, she was sent to a page that contained several photos on the right side of the screen. But in the center, filling up most of the screen, was a picture of a young, blonde girl. Except for her lifeless eyes, the girl was beautiful. Bidding for the "luscious young virgin" would begin in half an hour. The description also included, "This prize will be the last sale for us for a while, as we're relocating. Free delivery anywhere."

Rachel copied the image and forwarded it to Enid:

"Is this your missing girl?"

In less than a minute Enid replied:

"Where did u get this?"

Rachel:

"IDK. Link sent to me. No name or number."

Enid:

"Forward to me. I will send to Josh."

• • •

Enid tried to call and also sent several texts to Josh, but no reply. She jumped in her car and drove to the Madden police station, breaking all the speed limits along the way. At least she knew who to call if she got a ticket.

She also tried to call Jack. No answer, so she sent him a text to call immediately.

When she drove up to the Madden police station and didn't see Josh's car, her heart sank. She ran inside. Pete was on the phone, so she waited until he hung up. "Where's Josh?"

"He went to look at the cabin you and Mr. Johnson found. Can I help you?"

Enid showed the picture to Pete. "They're going to sell her. Can you get in touch with Josh immediately?"

"Sell who?"

"Hari, the missing girl," Enid said.

Pete pulled at his sleeve as though it needed to be longer—something he often did when uncomfortable. "I'm not sure if I can reach Chief Hart. He's likely on radio silence, you know, to keep quiet."

"Tell him I've gone to the airstrip. Keep trying and make sure he gets the message."

As Enid raced out the door, Pete called after her. "I don't think the chief will like you going there."

• • •

Josh parked on the side of the road, a short distance from the cabin Jack described. Although the place was not far from Madden's town center, it seemed remote. The dense, towering pines provided cover, and unless one knew there was a cabin nearby, it would have been impossible to see it from the road.

Getting through the trees was difficult at times due to the underbrush. If anyone actually used the cabin, there had to be another way in, other than tromping through the woods on foot. As Josh stepped across a fallen tree, a king snake slithered across one end of the dead wood. Involuntarily, Josh shivered. Even though rattlers and other snakes were common near his previous home in the Southwest, they always gave him the creeps, even the non-poisonous kind, like this one.

Anxious to get as far away from the snake as possible, Josh picked up his pace, walking as fast as he could without tripping. He reached a small clearing, and there it was, the cabin by the lake Jack had described. Josh instinctively put his hand on his holster.

The place seemed empty. A small chimney protruded from the roof, but no smoke was visible. He walked around to the front of the cabin and knocked on the weathered wooden door. "Anybody here? This is Chief Joshua Hart of the Madden Police. I just have a few questions for the owner." He stepped to the side in case of a shotgun blast through the door. He knocked again, but the only noise was the sound of the lake water gently lapping the shore.

He looked around the ground outside the cabin. Two sets of footprints led away from it to the dock: one set of large footprints and also smaller ones. Josh looked out across the water and then at the rope tied to the dock. At least that explained how they got to and from the cabin. Travel by water would be much easier than the way he had come in.

He turned his radio on and then his cell phone. Several messages had come in during the time his phone was off. He'd check them later. First, he had to talk to Pete.

"Hey, it's me," Josh said. "Did you get me a warrant?"

"You need to get back here right away," Pete said. "Actually, you need to go to the airstrip on that farm."

"The airstrip? Why? What's going on?" Josh listened as Pete relayed his earlier encounter with Enid.

"I told her you wouldn't be happy," Pete said.

Josh hung up without replying. "Dammit, Enid!" he said, hurling his words into the silence surrounding the cabin. He began walking back toward his car and never saw the man behind him.

CHAPTER 73

This wasn't the way Max planned it. It was supposed to be simple. He was going to work with Hari until she understood her role. Then he could live again, be the father he was meant to be. Hari was his second chance. He was a good father, he knew he was, which made it all the harder to understand why Belle had left and why Hari had failed to live up to his expectations.

Thinking of Belle always made him sad. He tried to ignore her flirting with the farm hands, and when she rebelled against Max's strict rules, he tried harder to make her understand. Why had she not obeyed him?

And now, he was losing another one. That reporter had ruined it all, asking all those questions and prying into his business. She was the real reason his plan had not worked, and he would handle her later.

As hard as he had tried to help Hari understand, she wasn't Belle. Never would be, even though the first time he had laid eyes on her at the soup kitchen, he was convinced she was the one. She would make him forget Belle. But it hadn't worked out, and he would have to look again for the perfect replacement.

The smart thing to do was to kill Hari and dump her in the lake outside. But that would be like throwing good money away. She would fetch a good price.

He had never harmed her, had bought her everything she asked for, which wasn't much, and tried to help her understand her destiny. But like Belle, she had resisted. Now Max had to live with the fact that Hari would belong to someone else soon. So be it. He would keep looking.

Max had mostly stayed out of the trafficking business, leaving it to the man who leased the airstrip from him. It all seemed a bit sordid to him. Even so, he called the man and made arrangements to list Hari and to deliver her, when sold, to the lucky buyer.

When the man in the truck arrived, Max pulled back the tarp covering Hari on the floor of the old fishing cabin. She was so thin now that he hardly recognized her. Dark circles under her eyes made her look older than her young years. He gently brushed her long blonde hair from her face and wiped away the tears with the back of his hand. So lovely. So disappointing.

"I gotta take off soon," the man said. "Weather moving in." The man picked up Hari to move her to the airstrip.

"Let me wash her face first," Max said. "I'll get a wet rag inside." He headed back into the cabin, while the man rolled his eyes.

"Old fool," the man muttered. "Gonna throw me off schedule." He yelled after Max. "Come on, man, I gotta go. Gonna make somebody happy tonight," he said, grinning.

CHAPTER 74

Hari had a sense of being moved again, but the drugs had dulled her senses. The man's familiar voice sounded like it was underwater. Her nose itched, but when she tried to scratch it, she realized her hands had been bound with tape. With the little strength she had, she tried to break loose, but her binding was strong. Her father had once told her that you could hold or fix most anything with a roll of duct tape.

As the man grabbed her arm and pulled her along, she tried to walk, but her legs felt rubbery. Maybe they were releasing her. When they moved her from the farm to the lake cabin, there had been no attempt to make her feel comfortable or to provide even the hint of permanence. It had only been a holding place. Wherever they were taking her now would be the final destination. She was sure of it.

She was torn between despair and hope, and worn out from the stress of captivity and the emotional drain of fear and longing. The man loosened his grip slightly, and she fell to her knees, scraping one on a sharp rock. She could feel the warm flow of blood on her shin. At least Max had been gentler than this man.

Suddenly, she felt herself being picked up. The man threw her over his shoulder and carried her like a sack of potatoes. She was helpless to resist. The sudden movement made her nauseous, and she prayed she wouldn't throw up on him. No telling what he might do to her if she did.

He threw her into the back of a pickup truck and then threw a heavy, foul-smelling tarp over her. The air under the cover was putrid and stifling. Hari gagged and bile filled her throat. The truck engine roared to life and they started to move. If they were taking her somewhere to kill her and dump her body, then she was ready. Tears filled her eyes and trickled down her nose, landing on the metal floor of the truck bed. Her father would likely never find her body or know what had happened to her. After reading the letter she had sent him, he would search all over Los Angeles, depleting his savings to find her. Hari prayed hard, not for herself, but for Theo.

CHAPTER 75

Enid hated guns, especially after what happened last year. But now, the feel of the gun gave her comfort. She was not going to let Hari get away from her. Once they took her to who-knows-where, she would be gone forever. There would be no more opportunities to save her.

When she drove past Max's farm, she glanced over at it but saw no activity, no cars or trucks at the house. When she reached the point where she had to turn off the main road, she hit a pothole that caused her to hit her head on the door and almost lose control of her car. Her tote slid off the seat, its contents flying all over the floorboard on the passenger side. No time to stop now.

As she got closer to the airstrip, she slowed down and pulled off to the side of the road, trying to get as far as she could into the mangle of weeds and growth. She undid her seatbelt and began gathering the contents from the tote. The gun must have slid under the seat. She reached her hand underneath it until she felt metal.

A loud noise caught her by surprise. She crouched as low as she could behind the wheel. Ahead, she saw a small plane descending toward the airstrip. Enid grabbed the gun and pushed the car door open. As she ran toward the runway, she put the gun in her jeans pocket so she wouldn't drop it. The closer she got to the cabin, the faster her heart beat.

She heard a man's voice. "Yeah, I can take her there. No problem. We'll leave now." He wasn't in view yet, but from the sound of his voice, he wasn't too far away, so she stayed near the edge of the woods. Enid carefully made her way to the back of the cabin, to the same spot where she had watched the man and young girl on her previous visit.

Enid peered inside the open window. Without warning, a dark shadow appeared in the cabin, right in front of her face. Max! And he had seen her.

With heart pounding, she tried to turn and run, but her ankle twisted on an exposed tree root. A searing flash of pain traveled up her leg like liquid fire. She tried to put her weight on the injured leg but fell to the ground.

"Well, well, if it isn't our little miss reporter lady," Max said as he grabbed Enid by the arm. "I might have known you'd show up."

Enid tried to pull away from him. "Let me go. The police chief is on his way and will be here any minute."

Max laughed, his demeanor much different from the kind man who supported the soup kitchen. "I don't think so. One of my men caught him snooping around the lake cabin. By the time he wakes up, you'll be long gone." He threw back his head and laughed again. "You ready to travel?"

"Why are you doing this? Was all of this just about making money selling girls?" She softened her voice. "I know you have a good heart. You helped Theo and you support the soup kitchen to feed the homeless. How could you have taken his daughter?"

For a moment, Enid saw Max's face transform again.

"That's none of your business," he said, regaining his composure. "I gave her a chance and she blew it. You should be thankful we're sparing her."

"Do you have any idea what kind of life she'll have? If you cared anything about her, or about Theo, you'd let her go. Please."

One of Max's men joined them. "Here, take her," Max said as he pushed Enid toward him.

"What do you want me to do with her?" the man asked.

"She'll make good domestic help, if nothing else."

The past year flashed through Enid's mind. Why had she not stuck to her plan of writing about community events—a safe career? Had she not learned anything from the past? Now, she would end up in another state, or worse yet, in some developing country with no one to help her. What life could she have had with Josh? Or perhaps even with Jack and Rachel? Her heart was racing with fear.

Because she was having problems walking, the man pulled her alongside him so roughly she was afraid her shoulder would be dislocated. They were approaching the small plane. Enid was about ten feet from a life of unimaginable misery. And there was nothing she could do about it.

In the shock of all that had happened, she had briefly forgotten about sticking the gun in her pocket. Thankfully, her loose top covered the slight bulge. The small .380 semiautomatic was a gift from her ex-husband, Cade. He had encouraged her to carry it at all times. At close range, she might be able to stop one of the men, or at least slow him down. Even though she was fairly proficient in target practice at the shooting range, this was different. The odds for hitting her target and escaping were not good. If she shot and missed, there would be no second chances. And, there were at least two men here with Max. Besides, if she tried to escape now, even if she was lucky enough to get away, they would still have Hari. Enid had never had to consider sacrificing herself to save someone else, but she might soon have to make that choice.

The man pushed her up the metal steps into the four-passenger plane. As he stepped aside, a young woman with long blonde hair appeared with the second man. Enid immediately recognized her from Theo's photos. Hari looked startled, since she didn't know who Enid was. With her eyes, Enid tried to convey a message: *I am here to help you.* Although at the moment, there wasn't much she could do to help herself, much less anyone else.

Hari sat beside her on the back seat of the plane. When the two men walked a short distance away from them, Enid twisted slightly and tried to get the small pistol out of her jeans pocket. Had she been standing, it might have been easier, but it was deep in her pocket and there was no room to stand or straighten her leg. She twisted in her seat to face Hari.

"My name is Enid," she whispered. "I'm a friend of your father. I'm trying to get this gun out of my pocket."

Hari looked back toward the two men and shook her head. "No, they'll kill us," she whispered.

"Trust me, that's the least of your worries right now."

After what seemed like an eternity, Enid managed to free the gun and pull it out of her pocket. She watched over

Hari's shoulder to keep an eye on the men. One of them was coming back toward the plane.

"Lean back and keep your eyes shut," Enid whispered. She prayed the second man would walk away. If she shot this man, the other one would surely come after them. But if she waited, they would be in the air and would crash if she shot the pilot. In a split-second decision, Enid released the safety on the pistol and racked the slide. One of the men heard it and looked up, but Enid kept the gun between her legs and looked away from them. She would get just one chance to save Hari and herself.

Enid looked at the young woman beside her, who was staring wild eyed at Enid. "Close your eyes. Now!" Enid whispered as loud as she could. This time, Hari obeyed. In the following few seconds, Enid's life passed before her, just like she had always heard it would. The good times with her mother, and then the bad years of her mother's illness played like a movie. Her marriage to Cade. The tragedies of last year. Rachel and Jack. She would miss being part of their lives. And Josh.

The man leaned into the plane and checked the binding on Hari's hands. "You ready for a new life?" he asked Hari. He then looked at Enid. "Cleaning toilets might not be so bad," he said, laughing.

As he reached over to pull Enid's hands from between her legs to check her bindings, she aimed at his chest and fired. In the small plane, the noise was deafening. Hari screamed, just as the second man ran to the plane and raised his gun.

Enid pulled the trigger again and the second man stumbled backward. As a dark stain spread on his chest, he hit the ground.

CHAPTER 76

For a few seconds, Enid and Hari were silent. And then, Enid reached over and took Hari's hand. She remained silent but squeezed Enid's hand tightly.

"Stay here." Enid got out of the plane and looked at the two men. She could tell one was still alive. She reached down and pulled the gun from his hand and put it on the floor of the plane, near Hari's feet. The other one, the second one she shot, wasn't moving at all or making any noise. She wasn't about to get close enough to check his pulse.

Suddenly, she realized Max was standing a few feet away. She pointed the gun at him, her hands shaking. "Don't come any closer."

Max held up his hands. "I'm not going to hurt you. I'm not even armed."

"Sit on the ground with your hands on your head." For once, watching TV shows paid off.

Max did so. "I need to talk to her."

"No. Shut up and stay there." Enid glanced over her shoulder to be sure Hari was still in the plane.

Since Enid's hands were still bound, she backed up closer to Hari and asked her to reach into her back jeans pocket to get her cell phone and call Josh's number. Enid kept the gun aimed at Max. Despite what Max had said about Josh being attacked, she called his number first, hoping Max had been bluffing. If Josh didn't answer, she'd call 911.

After two rings, Enid was ready to hang up, but someone answered. "Josh, is that you? Are you okay?"

"I've got a bitch'n headache, but, yeah, I'm fine. Where are you? You alright?"

"I'm at the airstrip. I'm fine. And so is Hari."

"You found her?"

"Just get here as quick as you can. And get Pete to send an ambulance." Enid hung up before Josh could start asking questions. While keeping an eye on Max, she asked Hari, "You holding up okay?"

Hari nodded and smiled for the first time. Enid wished she could get the bindings off Hari's wrists, as she wanted nothing more than to give the young woman her freedom. But she would have to wait a little longer.

"Stay here in the plane until the police arrive."

• • •

After Josh tore through the woods to the airstrip and saw Enid and Hari, he breathed a sigh of relief. Enid was standing near the front of the building, gun pointed toward Max. Even though she looked disheveled, she had never been more beautiful. The sunlight through the trees illuminated her copper hair and her face seemed to glow. Maybe it was just because he was grateful she was alive. He took the handcuffs from his belt and put them on Max.

"You can stop pointing that gun now," Josh said to Enid. "He's not going anywhere."

Enid slowly lowered the gun, and Josh cut the tape from her wrists with his pocket knife. Her hands were shaking even more, as the adrenalin wore off. "I need to sit down." She walked back to the plane and sat on the metal step.

Josh walked over to the two men on the ground. Since they were lying close together, the area was a pool of blood, and he could hear the hum of the flies swarming over them. He didn't want to disturb the crime scene, but he needed to check to see if either had survived. He took one step into the pool of blood and reached down, checking each man's neck for a pulse.

"He's alive," he called out to Enid, after checking the first one.

After he checked the second man's pulse, he looked at Enid and shook his head. He walked over to where she was sitting. That's when he saw the blonde girl inside the plane. "Hi, I'm Police Chief Hart. You must be Harriet Linard."

"Yes, I am." Hari extended both hands, still bound together. "Pleased to meet you."

Under the circumstances, Josh was amused at her polite manners. He cut the tape from her wrists. "Same here. Do you need medical attention?"

"No, sir," Hari said.

Josh put his arm around Enid. "Remind me not to get into an argument with you."

Enid threw her arms around Josh and cried. "I love you," she said softly.

Josh pushed her hair from her face and looked into her eyes. "I love you, too."

CHAPTER 77

Within a few minutes, the county fire department EMT arrived. They quickly assessed the two men and focused their attention on the one still alive. Enid watched as the two medical technicians lifted him onto a stretcher and rushed him back down the path to the ambulance. They left the other one for the coroner. As soon as the EMTs disappeared into the woods, a robust man in uniform arrived with another man dressed in khaki slacks and a golf shirt.

Josh nodded toward the big man. "Boogie, glad you're here."

"Hey, man. What you doing trashing up my county like this?" He motioned toward the other man. "I think you know the county coroner, Alex. He was in my office when I got your call."

Josh filled him in on what happened.

"You're damn lucky they didn't kill you." Sheriff Boogie Waters nodded toward Enid. "That your woman?"

Enid stood up slowly to steady herself before she walked over to Boogie and extended her hand. "I'm Enid Blackwell." She pointed toward the plane. "Harriet Linard, the missing girl, is in the plane. She seems to be okay but needs to be checked."

Boogie looked down at the dead man on the ground. "You do all this?"

Josh jumped in. "Enid, if you want to speak to an attorney first, just say so."

"Now don't go getting bug-eyed crazy on me," Boogie said to Josh. "I know it was self-defense." He looked back at the man and then at Enid, chuckling. "Damn, girl."

"Have you notified Detective Pointer?" Josh asked.

"Yep, called her just before we left. She'll be here any minute."

• • •

It was almost an hour later when Detective Pointer arrived at the scene. "Sorry, everyone. We had a botched bank robbery in town. Some fool wearing a Halloween mask walked in waving a gun and declaring that he was going to give the money to the poor people and make America great again."

Boogie and Josh filled Pointer in on what had transpired at the airstrip. "I'll need a full statement from Ms. Blackwell," Pointer said.

"Of course," Enid said.

Josh started to speak but Enid held up her hand. "Let me handle this." Despite her bravado, Enid was scared. Maybe she should have aimed for something less deadly on the man, like his leg. On the other hand, she would likely have missed altogether, or the small caliper wouldn't have stopped him. And then she would be the one lying on the ground dead, and Hari would be in the air, headed to the highest bidder.

She had once seen a quote by Vince Lombardi on the wall of a car dealership waiting area when she was getting her oil changed: "Fatigue makes cowards of us all." She was tired. Mentally and physically washed out. She wanted to curl up and sleep, to forget about everything that had happened. Knowing the day was going to get even longer, she forced herself to focus on Hari by imagining her reunion with Theo and how happy he would be.

CHAPTER 78

It was nearly 9 p.m. by the time Enid finished giving her statement to Pointer. The shooting had occurred in Sheriff Boogie Waters' jurisdiction and Josh was involved, but both men agreed to let Pointer take the lead, as it was her case. However, Josh insisted that they do it at either Boogie's or his police station, so Enid wouldn't have to go into Columbia. Pointer reluctantly agreed to go to Madden, and Boogie was happy to take a back seat. He had a fishing date with an old college buddy early tomorrow morning and was anxious to wrap all this up.

Against Josh's recommendation, Enid waived her rights to an attorney. She would be as truthful as possible, and since she had a concealed weapon permit, she had a right to carry a gun. As much as Enid hated violence, that little gun Cade had given her saved their lives. Guns were a necessary evil in a scary world, especially for a woman.

Enid could see the strain on Josh's face, as he looked through the half-glass wall at her and Pointer. Because of his relationship with Enid, they all agreed he needed to stay out of it as much as possible.

When Pointer opened the door to the office to leave, Josh rushed in. "You finished here?" he asked Pointer.

"We may have some follow-up questions later, but we're good for now." She extended her hand to Enid. "Off the record, I'm proud of you. You brought Mr. Linard's daughter back."

Enid was uncomfortable with the praise. She had killed one man and seriously hurt another. That was nothing to be proud of. "Where's Hari? Has anyone told Theo?"

"She's in Columbia at the police station. One of our men is picking up Theo now to bring him in. I asked him not to say anything. I thought you might want to tell him yourself—a small reward for what you went through. But I suggest you call him now. He'll be at the station by the time I get there." She scribbled a number on a piece of paper and handed it to Enid. "Call this number and they'll patch you through to him in the patrol car. I gave them a heads-up to expect your call."

"Thank you," was all Enid could say. Her mind was racing ahead to Theo and Hari's reunion.

As Pointer walked past Josh, she whispered to him. "That's one tough lady you got there. Don't let her get away." In a normal voice, she added, "We'll pick up Max in the morning."

"I'm going to step out while you call Theo, so you can gather your thoughts and be alone," Josh said to Enid. "This is your moment. As bad as I know you're feeling about the shootings, you saved a life. Don't forget that." Josh walked out of his office and shut the door behind him.

Enid nervously called the number Pointer had given her and asked to speak to the officer transporting Theo to the police station. Then she heard a woman say, "Officer Hardy here."

"I understand you have Theo Linard with you. May I speak with him?"

The line crackled so loudly she thought they had been cut off. "Yes?" a male voice said.

"Theo? Is that you?"

"Yes. Ms. Blackwell, what's going on? Why are they taking me to the police station? Is Hari . . .?" His voice trailed off.

"Hari is at the police station. She's safe." Enid could no longer contain her emotions. The roller coaster events of today overwhelmed her. "Hari is waiting for you," Enid said through the tears. The line crackled again. "Theo, are you there?"

"How? What happened? Where has she been?" A brief silence, and then, "That's not important. Thank you. Thank you. Praise God."

"We can catch up later when I write the end of this story. We'll talk soon. Goodbye, Theo."

Enid opened the door and motioned for Josh to come in. "Now I need a *big* hug." They embraced and held each other. Words were unnecessary.

Finally, Josh pulled away. "Pete's coming here to stay with Max tonight. As soon as he gets here, I'll leave. Jack's on the way here now to get you." He kissed her gently. "You need to sleep."

CHAPTER 79

Not long after Enid left with Jack, Josh heard someone ring the bell on the locked door of the police station. The old school bell had been the topic of discussion in the town for decades. It had been used in Miss Inez's kindergarten until she died and the place was torn down. Some wanted to get rid of the old antique that was rung by pulling a rope and to replace it with a modern doorbell. The old bell had stayed in the storage room of the police station for years before one of Josh's predecessors decided to mount it outside the station door. Some in town considered the bell a relic of the town's history and wanted it to stay; others wanted it removed. Josh tried to stay out of the argument.

Josh assumed the ringing bell was Pete, who had likely forgotten to bring his office key ring. But instead of Pete, a young woman in her early twenties stood before him when he opened the door. For a brief second, he thought it was Hari. They could pass for twins, although this young woman looked a few years older.

"May I help you?" Josh asked.

"I believe you have my father here. I'm Juliana James, Max James' daughter."

Taken aback, Josh stammered a bit. "Sure, come on in. We can talk in my office." He motioned for her to sit across from his desk. "Please, have a seat."

Juliana sat upright in the chair, rigid as a steel pole. "Thank you. I'm sure you're surprised to see me."

"I hear you've been gone from around here for a while. Mind if I ask where you've been?"

"Here and there. Is my father in trouble?"

Josh rubbed the back of his neck. All he wanted was a hot shower and a meal. His head was throbbing where he had been hit earlier. "Yes, I'm afraid so. He'll be taken to the Columbia Police Department tomorrow morning." He paused briefly. "May I ask how you knew your father was here?"

She smiled. "I'm sure you know by now that news travels fast in a small town, especially bad news." She leaned forward. "May I see him, just for a few minutes? I have a lot of apologizing to do for the way I behaved when I was younger. I don't want him to go to jail thinking I don't love him." She paused and looked down at the floor. "You see, all of this is my fault."

"I'm sure you can see him after he's processed at CPD."

Juliana reached forward and put her hand on Josh's. "Pretty please. I just want to tell him I love him. Five minutes. That's all I ask."

Josh pulled his hand back. "Five minutes. That's it. You'll have to leave your purse here, and I'll have to run the metal detector over you."

"Of course. I would expect you to follow proper procedures. I'll just put my purse on the floor over here by the door." She dropped the large purse outside of the office, which Josh thought was a bit odd. "And you are welcome to scan me." She held her arms out parallel to the floor.

Josh went to Pete's desk and got the metal detector wand from a cabinet beside his desk. He scanned her from head to toe. "Follow me."

Juliana followed Josh and waited as he unlocked the steel door that separated the office from the two cells in the back of the police station. "Wait here. I need to make sure he wants visitors."

Max was sitting on the edge of his cot with his face in his hands. He looked up when he heard Josh's voice.

"Max, there's a young lady here, Juliana, who says she's your daughter. She wants to see you."

Max's eyes widened. "My Belle? She's here? Yes, please let me see my baby."

"She'll have to stay outside the cell. Five minutes is all you've got."

Max stood up and grabbed hold of the cell bars. "Thank you."

“Back away from the bars and stay there.” Josh opened the door and asked Juliana to step inside. "Is this your daughter?"

Max's face went from shock into a broad grin. "Yes, Juliana is my Belle." He looked at Juliana. "I can't believe you're here, Belle."

"I'll be right outside," Josh said. "Remember, stand away from the cell while you talk. I'll be back in five minutes."

• • •

"Belle, is it really you?" Max asked.

"I'd appreciate it if you'd call me Juliana. That's the name Mother gave me." She paused. "I heard you had been arrested because of your little enterprise on the farm."

Max's shoulders slumped. "I really wasn't involved. I just leased part of the land. You know, the part with that little airstrip on it."

"Is it true that you were holding one of the girls for yourself?"

Max buried his face in his hands. "I'm so sorry. Please forgive me. It's just that she looked so much like you."

"So you thought you could just take someone and replace me? You're a sick bastard."

Max shook his head slowly. "I'm sorry if I hurt you. I missed you."

Juliana leaned forward slightly and lowered her voice. "We only have a few minutes. I know you did it because you love me. Just like you've always loved me. Come here and let me hug you through the bars. No one is watching us."

Max smiled and stepped forward, getting as close as he could. "My Belle, my sweet Belle."

In one carefully planned and swift action, Juliana held onto Max through the bars with one hand. With the other, she reached into the back of her jeans and pulled out a plastic knife, sharpened like a razor to a fine edge. The man that sold it to her also showed her the best angle for maximum damage. She thrust the knife upward into Max's heart, the heart that had ached for Juliana, his Belle, for years.

Max's face changed from a smile to a mask of shock, and then to horror as he realized what had happened. His contorted face turned red, making the scar from Belle's previous attack on her father even more prominent.

Juliana grabbed Max's chin with her free hand, still holding onto the knife protruding from his chest with the other hand. "You held her prisoner, just like you held me. You're not God. You had no right to control me."

"Wh . . . why?" Max struggled to talk.

"Why am I killing you? Or why did it take me this long?" Juliana watched as Max sank to his knees.

She positioned herself behind the steel door, waiting for the police chief to return. She glanced briefly at her father lying on the concrete floor of the cell, his life draining away. She wanted to regret her actions, but all she felt was release. She was free at last.

CHAPTER 80

What should have been a simple reunion got bogged down in red tape. When the officer and Theo arrived at the police station, no one could find where Hari had been taken. Detective Pointer was tied up in another matter, and by the time she was available, an hour had passed while Theo waited alone in a small room for the long-awaited reunion with Hari. He kept pinching the skin on the top of his hand. If he could feel it, surely he wasn't dreaming. Hari was actually safe, and he was going to see her soon.

Finally, a female officer opened the door to the room. "Theo Linard?"

He jumped to his feet. "Yes, I'm Theo. Where is my daughter?"

"Follow me, sir," the officer said. They walked quickly, but Theo didn't mind. Each step brought him closer to Hari. Finally, the officer stopped at a door and opened it.

Theo's mind was racing. What if it wasn't really her? What if she had run away and didn't want to see him? But when the door opened, and he saw Hari's smile, all doubts and questions were erased.

"Daddy," cried Hari as she threw her arms around Theo's neck. "I love you."

All Theo could muster was a feeble response. "I love you, too." Tears streamed down his cheeks as he buried his face in her blonde mane.

"I'll leave you two alone," the officer said, quietly shutting the door.

When Theo pulled back to look at Hari, he saw a different person than the young girl he had last seen in Boston, months ago. The young woman in front of him was somehow more mature, and thinner. "You look wonderful. Are you okay?"

"I'm okay, but how are you? I know you must have been worried sick."

Theo smiled slightly. "You could say that."

"They got the man who took me. I'm safe now. You don't have to worry anymore."

Theo's worse fears were now reality. "Someone took you? Where? Why? Who did this to us?" He forced himself to calm down.

"That man from the soup kitchen, Max, he held me at his farm."

Theo wrung his hands. "Did he . . .?"

Hari held Theo again. "No, he never hurt me in any way. He wanted me to be his daughter, to replace her."

"I remember him talking about her."

"He was very sad all the time," Hari said.

But Theo felt no sympathy for Max.

The female officer knocked on the door and opened it. "Detective Pointer wants to take your statement now," she said to Hari. "Please come with me."

Theo gave Hari a hug, not wanting to let her out of his sight again. "I'll be waiting for you." Just as he had waited these past months.

CHAPTER 81

Josh glanced at the big clock on the wall in the police station. Juliana's time was up. Grabbing the big keyring on his desk, Josh headed toward the door to unlock it. He was tired and ready to go home as soon as Pete arrived. He wanted to hold Enid and tell her he would always be there for her.

As soon as he opened the door, he saw Max lying on the cell floor. Where was Juliana?

Caught off-guard, Josh was pushed from behind. His head hit one of the heavy iron cell bars, and he felt the room spin. He reached for his gun, but was pushed into the iron bars again. This time, he hit the floor.

CHAPTER 82

"Chief Hart, are you okay?" The voice sounded like it was underwater. "Chief, I've called Doc. He's coming now. Just hang on."

Josh struggled to move and tried to get off the floor.

"Don't move. Just lie still."

Josh ignored Pete and positioned himself into a sitting position with his back to the cell bars. "Quit fussing over me. I'm fine." And then he remembered Max. Josh slowly stood up, holding onto the bars for support. "Let's check him." Although from the look on Max's face, whatever he had once had, a soul, a spirit, a life-force, it was gone now. All that was left was the shell that housed a twisted and complex man.

"I already did," Pete said, shaking his head.

"Where's Juliana?" Josh asked.

"Who's that?"

"Max's daughter. She was visiting him."

"Did she do this?" Pete asked.

Josh reached down suddenly for the gun in his holster, to see if it was there. At least, she hadn't taken it. "Damn. That little voice inside told me not to let her see him, but she sounded so sincere . . . and harmless." Josh looked at the plastic knife protruding from Max's chest. "Put an APB out on her. I have no idea what she's driving. I don't even have a photo of her."

Josh wobbled unsteadily back to this desk. He looked for Juliana's purse, but it was gone. "I need to call Detective Pointer. This isn't going to go down good."

• • •

Doc, a retired obstetrician, was the only person in Madden with any medical training. And he had been forced to retire after one of his patients filed a lawsuit against him for telling her she was going to have a girl when it turned out to be a boy. No medical negligence was proven, but during the investigation, they found that Doc was in the early stages of Alzheimer's. He was declared unfit to practice and lost his license.

"You got hit in the head," Doc said. "I bet that hurts."

Josh refrained from the smart-ass retort that came to mind. "Yes, it hurts." Josh waved the old man away. "Quit fussing over me. I'll get checked later."

"That's a good idea. Why don't you go to the hospital?" Doc looked confused. "When are you going?"

Josh looked at Pete. "Please get him out of here." Then Josh said to Doc, "Thanks for checking on me. You go on home now."

Doc's sister had driven him to the station. She dutifully took him by the arm and led him out the door. "Bye now," she called out to everyone. "Call us if you need anything."

"Sure thing," Josh said. He then called Detective Pointer's number. Thankfully, she had not been asleep. Waking her up would have only added insult to an already bad situation. For the next ten minutes, Josh explained what had happened. As expected, she lectured him on letting his guard down for a pretty face. The truth is, it wasn't Juliana's looks that distracted him. He was bone tired, nursing a severe headache, and worried about Enid. But, he admitted to Detective Pointer, and to himself, that he had made a grave mistake. And now Max lay dead in his jail because of Josh's lapse in judgment.

When Josh ended the call, he turned to Pete. "The State Law Enforcement Division is going to investigate this incident. In the meantime, Pointer has notified the airports, rental car agencies, and the surrounding police chiefs and sheriffs to be on the lookout. CPD will pick up Max's body."

Josh made a pot of coffee. Fatigue had overcome him, and he dreaded the next few hours of being on the other side for a change, of being interrogated. But it was necessary. He wasn't the first officer of the law to make a fatal mistake, and he wouldn't be the last.

Before the state police arrived, he had one more thing to do. After taking a few sips of coffee, he called a familiar number.

"Hey, baby. I'm sorry to wake you, but I need to talk to you."

CHAPTER 83

After talking with Josh, Enid wanted more than anything else to run to him, to put her arms around him and tell him that everything would be okay. But, with SLED officers at the police station questioning Josh and Pete, she needed to stay out of the way.

Enid changed from her sleep shirt to jeans and a t-shirt before knocking on Jack's bedroom door. "Sorry to wake you, but Josh is in trouble."

Without asking questions, Jack nodded. "I'll dress and meet you in the kitchen. You'd better get Rachel, too. She'll wonder what's going on."

When the three of them gathered together, Jack made coffee for him and Rachel and put a kettle of water on the stove for Enid's tea. Oddly, they all remained silent until Enid finally spoke. She recounted the events, beginning with Rachel's text about Hari being sold. "I'm worried about Josh. He's had two head injuries today. They're taking him to the hospital to check him before he gives a statement."

Rachel was the first to react. She jumped up and put her arms around Enid. "You saved that girl. And Josh will be fine, I know it."

Jack put his coffee cup on the table. "I'm not sure what to say. You could have easily been killed." His voice choked as he took Enid's hand in his. "It will be one helluva story though. Good for circulation," he said, smiling wanly.

"I expected no less from a newspaper guy like you." She squeezed Jack's hand. "I'll get right on it. But for now, I'm going to find where they have Josh and see him. He feels awful about what happened."

"You get dressed and go on. We'll be here when you get back." He kissed Enid's cheek. "Rachel and I will always be here for you."

CHAPTER 84

Less than two weeks after Juliana's escape, Josh was back at work, despite his neurologist's insistence that he rest a while longer. The post-concussion effects had left Josh depressed and out of sorts. His memory, however, was intact, and he had no trouble vividly recalling the night he let a young woman kill her father and then escape. Josh offered his resignation to the mayor of Madden, but she would hear nothing of it. SLED had completed their investigation and ruled that Chief Joshua Hart had not been negligent in his handling of the prisoner. They cited his earlier head injury as a contributing factor. But Josh knew he had failed.

After an extensive search across the state, Juliana had not been found. Although a nation-wide alert had been issued, she had seemingly vanished into the night. CPD had received a few tips and sightings, but none had panned out. Just as she had disappeared after running away years ago, there was no trace of her now. Juliana's mother, Rosanne Hermosa, claimed she had not heard anything from Juliana in years and had no idea where she could be. The local police had a tail on Hermosa, but she rarely left her house in California.

Enid and Josh discussed whether she should move back into his house, but they both agreed to wait. Their future together now seemed more like a fantasy. A year ago, it was Enid who was adrift in grief and guilt. And now, the man she loved was in emotional pain. His head injuries would heal in time, but his spirit might be damaged forever.

Enid joined Jack on his front porch, where he was sipping coffee. "Mind if I sit with you?" she asked.

"Please do. I was just thinking about you."

"How's that?" she asked, as she sat in the rocker beside him.

"Where are you going now? I mean, where will you live?"

"I told Madelyn I would be moving out. She's subsidized my rent long enough, so I'm going to get out of her beautiful garage apartment so she can finally get some decent rent for it."

"Madelyn doesn't need the money, and you know it. What's the real reason?"

"I don't know. I just don't want to go back there. I mean, Madelyn has been great. It's me. I'm feeling restless." Enid sighed. "Maybe I'm destined to be a wanderer, like Ruth."

Jack shifted in his rocker so he could face her. "Stay here. With me and Rachel."

"Jack, I ... I don't know what to say. I feel like I'd be in the way of you and Madelyn."

"Like I said before, we're good friends, and we have a hoot together. But neither of us has any illusions that it's more than that." He exhaled deeply and turned in his chair to lock eyes with Enid. "I can't imagine not having you around. And I know Rachel adores you. What about it?"

Enid stammered. "I don't know what to say. I can't focus on myself right now. Too much going on."

Jack took her hand in his. "If you'd rather, I'll be glad to help you find a place here in town until you and Josh can figure things out. I do have another offer, though. I'd like for you to be the managing editor of the *Madden Gazette*. With Helen retiring, I just don't have it in me anymore." He tapped her nose with his finger. "You, on the other hand, have a nose for a good story. And also for getting yourself in a jam, I might add."

Enid held her head in her hands. "This is too much for me to absorb right now."

"Just think about it," he said.

"I'm honored beyond words. Yes, I will consider it. And, if you're sure it's okay with you, I'd like to stay here with you and Rachel until I can find a place."

Jack raised an eyebrow and held up his crossed fingers. "Does that mean you're planning to stay in Madden?"

"For now. Let's take it slowly, okay? No promises, no long-term commitments. I just need a normal life for a while."

"Ha! Like that's going to happen." Jack stood up. "I've got to get to the newspaper office and finish tomorrow's edition. Oh, in all the excitement, I forgot to tell you Cade called. He wants to write a profile on you for the AP, you know, weekly newspaper reporter saves the day."

Tears filled Enid's eyes at the mention of Cade. Even though he had moved on without her, he still had her back. "I'll call him later."

After Jack left Enid alone on the porch, she closed her eyes and rocked rhythmically to a tune looping continuously in her head. It took her a moment to realize she was hearing the Platters' song played during her bride-and-groom's first dance with Cade at their wedding. *With this ring, I promise I'll always love you.*

CHAPTER 85

Theo stirred the big soup pot and smelled its aroma. Tonight, he was cooking a kale and sausage stew with a cream broth, a recipe he perfected in culinary school. He got a spoon and scooped up some broth, handing it to Hari. "What do you think? More salt?"

Hari blew on the spoon to cool the steaming broth before tasting it. "No, it's delicious." She put the spoon in the sink and then hugged Theo from behind as he was standing over the stove. "I love you so much, Daddy. I don't ever want us to be separated again."

"Me neither, baby. Me neither." He reached down for the bottom of his apron and wiped his eyes. "Now help me get the soup plates ready."

Even though Theo was cooking at the Glitter Lake Inn instead of his own familiar kitchen, he seemed to be at home: good food, good friends, and much to be thankful for. The sideboard had already been laid out with crusty French bread, salted butter, and a variety of meats, cheeses, and large black olives. The Chardonnay was chilled and the red wine ready to pour. He took off his apron and went to the living room where the guests were gathered. "My wonderful friends, dinner is served."

When everyone was seated, Theo proposed a toast. "Thank you for joining us tonight and sharing a bowl of soup with me and Hari. We can never repay you for what you've done. Each of you contributed to Hari's return." He stopped briefly to look at Hari, whose face was lit with a broad smile. Theo looked around the room where Enid, Jack, Rachel, Josh, Sheriff Boogie Waters, Detective Pointer, and Pete were gathered. Jack's sister Ruth was also present, although unaccustomed to being a guest in her own inn.

"When I went to culinary school, I insisted on becoming a soup chef," Theo continued. "'Why?' the master chef asked me. I will tell you what I told him, because it is fitting for this occasion. Soup is a magical dish. It's the only universal food, because every culture has its own version." Theo pointed toward the large soup tureen in the middle of the table. "But what makes soup magical is that every ingredient adds its own special contribution. When the ingredients meld, they become more than their individual worth." He smiled at Hari. "And it's always better the next day. That's what I kept telling myself. Tomorrow will bring hope. Tomorrow will be better. And so it was." Theo paused again to wipe his eyes with the back of his hand. "You, too, my friends, are magical. Each of you helped bring my Hari home. Each of you contributed in your own way. Together you did it." He raised his wineglass. "To you, my friends." He took Hari's hand, and may we all remember Kat, who lost her life trying to save my Hari."

Hari and Theo served the soup and for the next hour, the Glitter Lake Inn overflowed with food and love. When the meal was winding down, Jack stood and tapped his wineglass with his spoon. "I'd like to make a few comments before this party breaks up." He paused and looked around the table. "As you know, my sister Ruth is returning to

Chicago and will no longer manage this inn." He looked at her. "Thank you for stepping in when I needed your help. I'll never forget it."

Ruth raised her glass to Jack. "I will never forget this place or the people here. I'll miss you all."

"You can tell she's not from around here or she would have said 'y'all'." A ripple of laughter went around the table. "It's okay, Ruth, it took me a few years to adjust my vocabulary."

"What will happen to the inn? You're not closing it, are you?" Pete asked.

"Thanks for that segue, Pete. That what I wanted to tell you. Theo has agreed to stay on as manager, with the agreement that he can teach cooking classes at the inn anytime he wants to. First, he's got to train his replacement at the soup kitchen."

Rachel turned to Hari. "What are you going to do now?"

Hari and Theo exchanged glances. "I've got a few options, but I haven't decided yet." Her voice trembled. "There's not much I can add to what my father said earlier, but I also want to thank you. I literally owe my life to all of you." She looked at Enid. "Especially to you. You risked your life to save me, so I want to do something special with this gift I've been given." Hari held her glass toward the ceiling. "Here's to you, Kat. Thank you. I promise your death won't be in vain."

CHAPTER 86

After the dishes were cleared, some of the guests went out onto the large front porch. The night air was cool and refreshing. Rachel saw Pete standing alone by one of the columns and went over to him. "Hi," she said.

Pete looked nervous. "Uh, hi, Rachel."

"I hear you're a computer geek. By the way, that thing your group did with the drone was amazing. Jack told me about it."

"You like technology?"

"Sure. I mean, I'm just learning some things, but I think it's an important field."

Pete smiled shyly. "If you want to, maybe we can get together sometime and compare notes. You know, talk about technology and stuff. Maybe I can help you with a few things."

"That would be cool. I'd like that."

As Pete and Rachel were talking, Enid watched from the other end of the porch. She was glad Rachel had moved on past Tommy Two. Even if he had stayed in town, there was no future for them. He was hiding something about his past, and Rachel needed stability and normalcy. In her young life, she had already been through more than others had in a lifetime. Pete, with his goofy but endearing demeanor, would be a good friend for Rachel.

Josh had left right after dinner. Since his head injuries, he had frequent headaches. The only thing that helped was to lie still and rest. Suddenly, a need to be with him washed through her, a wave of longing and loneliness.

After saying her goodbyes to everyone, Enid decided to drive to Josh's house. In case he was asleep, she didn't want to call him. She still had her key to his house.

• • •

All the lights were out at Josh's house when she arrived, other than a small light at the front entrance. As Enid walked up to the door, she doubted the wisdom of coming here, unannounced. If she used the key, he might get startled and shoot her. If she called him, he might not welcome the intrusion. She sat down on the top step.

Where was her life headed now? Once again, she had no idea what lay ahead of her.

A noise in the nearby woods caught her attention. Startled, she reached for the gun in her purse. And then she realized it had been taken as evidence after the shooting. As she was debating what to do, a doe appeared at the edge of the trees. Her large brown eyes looked at Enid without fear. The doe took a few steps forward, and then a few more, until she was less than ten feet away.

"Hello, girl." Enid spoke softly and remained motionless for fear of scaring the deer away.

The doe raised her head slightly and made a bleating sound that pierced the enveloping stillness of the night. She then stamped her hoof and called out again, this time louder.

"What is it? Are you trying to tell me something?"

The doe stamped her hoof again.

"What's going on?"

Enid jumped at the sound of Josh's voice behind her. "You nearly scared me to death!"

Josh pulled the front door shut and sat down beside Enid on the step. "How do you think I feel? I got up to get a glass of water and find a woman sitting on my porch."

"I thought the doe must have woken you. She was making a terrible fuss."

"What doe?" Josh looked around.

Enid pointed to where the deer had stood. "She was right there."

"If you say so. You want to come in or do you plan to sleep on my doorstep?" Josh put his arm around Enid.

She followed Josh but turned to look over her shoulder before she shut the door behind her. The doe was in Josh's front yard, slightly moving her head up and down, as if in approval.

Enid pulled the door shut and smiled.

EPILOGUE

Finally, the Myra Nicholas rehab center for trafficking victims was moving to a bigger location in a century-old home near campus. It was twice the size of their original space, which meant they could help more women who had experienced the horror of being abducted and forced into servitude.

Some of the women died of drug overdose before they could be rescued. Some were killed while trying to escape. Many were used up on the streets until they became worthless to their pimps and were tossed aside. In addition, human trafficking often claimed collateral damage victims, like Kat, who merely got in the way.

The lucky ones who managed to get out needed help. They were scarred for life, and the best hope they had was to pretend to have a normal life again. Thankfully, the center was in a better position than ever to help them after receiving a very generous, anonymous donation. Such gifts from unnamed strangers were not unusual, but the size of the donation still had everyone at the center talking.

It might be moving day, but there was still work to be done. Volunteers scurried around, unpacking files and putting them in the new file cabinets lining the wall. With all the activity, no one noticed the young blonde in oversized sunglasses who had slipped in the back door. She glanced around until she spotted another blonde girl sitting on the floor, sorting paperwork.

"Hello, Hari, you ready to grab a quick lunch? Then I need to get on the road."

"Oh, hi. I didn't see you come in. Just give me a minute." The phone sitting on the floor next to Hari rang. "Let me get this call and we can go. There's a great new cafe around the corner." Hari answered the call, "Hello. Yes, this is Myra Nicholas. Do you need help?"

While waiting for Hari, the woman slipped into the restroom and pulled a crocheted beret from the large canvas bag slung across her chest. She tucked her blonde tresses under the floppy hat, adjusted her sunglasses, and surveyed her image in the mirror.

"I'm ready when you are," Hari called out as she knocked on the bathroom door. "I got someone to handle that intake call for me."

When the woman emerged, Hari linked her arm through her friend's and held her tight. "I'm going to miss you. Promise you'll stay in touch. Oh, and Rachel said to tell you not to worry about Escape. You know how much she loves horses. She'll take good care of him."

"I'll miss you too, but maybe I'll be back one day. No matter what, we'll always be connected." The two young women locked their fingers together. "Pinkie promise."

♀

A NOTE FROM THE AUTHOR

While this book is completely fictional, the story was inspired by the real-life disappearance of a young woman in Columbia more than twenty-five years ago. She simply vanished. This book is my way of bringing closure where there was none.

When I started *The Last Sale*, the second in the Enid Blackwell series, I had high hopes the writing would be easier the second time around. In a way, it was, as I finished this manuscript much quicker. However, the subject matter was far more difficult to write about. I wanted to provide enough information and details so that the reader could imagine the horror of the situation, but without getting too graphic or salacious. I hope I achieved that for you.

Thank you for reading *The Last Sale*. If you enjoyed it, please post a review on www.Goodreads.com or wherever you purchased the book. Reader reviews help sell books and encourage authors to continue writing.

You can also send me feedback through my website: http://RaeganTeller.com

Thank you!

Raegan

ACKNOWLEDGMENTS

Writing is a solitary process, but no book is written alone. My books would not be possible without my family and friends who support me. Without my wonderful husband, we would have nothing to eat, and the house would be in a perpetual state of disarray. He makes it possible for me to retreat into my office to write for hours on end. When I get stuck on a plot point, he is always there to listen, encourage, and help me find a better way to tell the story. He's also my number one fan. I cannot thank him enough. My sister, poet Jane Marie, bolsters my confidence and reminds me of what's important and what's not. My family and friends nurture my soul.

I also want to thank my beta readers, Irene Stern, Martha Anderson, Jane Cook, and William Craig for their time and feedback. Others who contributed to this book include my developmental editor, Ramona DeFelice Long; my cover designer, Teresa Spreckelmeyer of The Midnight Muse; and my proofreader, Marcia Merrill. Each made this book far better than I could on my own.

Finally, I want to thank you, my readers, for your continued support and loyalty. You are the reason I write.

ABOUT THE AUTHOR

Raegan Teller is an award-winning mystery author in Columbia, South Carolina, where she lives with her husband and two cats. Her debut novel, *Murder in Madden*, received Honorable Mention in the 2017 Writer's Digest Self-Published Book Awards. The judge stated, "It's one of the best I've read this year . . . good plot line . . . engaging characters . . . made me want to read more." *The Last Sale* is the second novel in the Enid Blackwell series. Both books were inspired by real-life cold cases in her hometown.

Before writing fiction, Raegan was a business writer and copy editor, a communications consultant, executive coach, and insurance manager—among other things. While working her way through school, she even sold burial vaults at a cemetery. How apropos is that for a mystery writer!

Visit Raegan at http://RaeganTeller.com

Made in the USA
Middletown, DE
23 September 2023